DESTINED BLOOD

NEPHILIM'S DESTINY: BOOK 2

TESSA COLE

Gryphon's Gate Publishing

Destined Blood

Copyright © 2018 Tessa Cole

Cover Design by Melody Simmons

Gryphon's Gate Publishing

550 King St. N.

PO Box 42088 Conestoga

Waterloo, ON

N2L 6K5

ebook ISBN 978-1-988115-68-9

Print ISBN 978-1-988115-67-2

CHAPTER 1

I COULD HEAR THE COUPLE YELLING AT EACH OTHER THE moment I got out of the cruiser even though I was outside on the residential street and they were, from the muffled sound of it, still inside their apartment building. I could also hear the traffic on the busy street five blocks over, the buzz from the streetlight fifty feet away, and, if I concentrated, the calm steady breathing of Hank, my partner, who stood on the other side of the car from me.

The woman screamed something incomprehensible, but my partner's expression didn't change, which meant he couldn't hear it, proving that my senses had in fact been enhanced.

I hadn't been sure of it when Amiah—the head of the medical team at the Joined Parliament Operations Building—had released me from her mini hospital. Of course, it had been hard to think past anything with my painful, grating buzz clawing under my skin, but even after I'd managed to medicate that down to a manageable level—now requiring two nicotine patches at the same time—I hadn't been sure.

Yeah, there'd been moments when I'd suspected, but nothing quite as definitive as this. With its surprisingly subtle   only-seeming-to-appear-when-I-concentrated manifestation, it had been easy to keep myself distracted and to pretend that life as I knew it hadn't completely changed two weeks ago.

In a way, it hadn't. I was back in my apartment—and the skylight and hole in the wall had been fixed—and I was back to my job in the Union City Police Department. And yet...

I couldn't deny that, core deep, everything had changed. And that scared me.

Yes, I'd survived having an unnatural angelic mating brand forced upon me by an archnephilim—a monster that was part archangel and part demonic wraith—and having his power tear through me as he'd tried to rip out wings I was sure... well, pretty sure I didn't have. But I hadn't gotten through that unscathed. My buzz was stronger than before, feeling more like I was in constant contact with a medium-voltage electric fence and not just a low-level one. Not to mention my eyes still glowed from blasting a massive amount of divine light into myself to stop him.

And it was my eyes that worried me the most. I couldn't pretend to just be a human if my eyes were glowing. I'd purchased enspelled contacts from a shady witch who'd promised discretion, and they were supposed to hide the glow until the divine light left my body.

But even after a week and a half the light hadn't

faded, and I feared it was still around because I was a nephilim and blasting all that magic into me had somehow awakened the angelic part of my DNA. To make it worse, I was sure my essence—readable by those supernatural beings who could sense magical essences—still said I was human, which made the angelic glowy eye thing look really suspicious.

Add to that my enhanced hearing... oh, and the ability to see in the dark... and my goal to live as a nothing-to-see-here human just serving and protecting my city had become nearly impossible.

It was only a matter of time before someone started asking questions, and those questions could get me imprisoned, experimented on, or killed. Probably all of the above.

At least I could attribute my enhanced senses to Jacob's vampire claim on me. The claim, at least, would go away... eventually... I hoped. But I wasn't sure how long the effects would last, and I wasn't sure I wanted to ask.

At least none of the guys had tried to contact me in the week and a half I'd been gone from Operations, so the risk of being revealed wasn't as great. I hadn't expected Marcus to. He'd been adamant in respecting my wishes to have nothing to do with the supernatural world, and had been gone before I'd even woken in Amiah's hospital. Jacob and Kol hadn't contacted me either, and much to my surprise, neither had Gideon, even with his angelic mating brand on my arm permanently bonding us together.

And I was going to ignore the empty ache in my chest

over him— over all the guys. It had been growing within me from the moment I'd returned home.

It would go away.

Just like the effects of Jacob's vampiric claim.

Really.

"Dispatch said the call came in for unit one-o-seven," Hank said, adjusting his duty belt at his slightly paunchy waist as we headed for the apartment building's front door. "That must be at the back or maybe they've resolved their differences and have stopped yelling."

Glass shattered and the woman screeched something else, her voice still too muffled with the building between us for me to make out her words even with my enhanced hearing. Hank still didn't react, but I was sure as soon as we got inside, he'd be able to hear them as well.

The building was a tired six-story structure that had been built in the 60s or 70s. Its utilitarian construction hadn't aged well and the owner had done little upkeep. Through the filthy glass front door, the vinyl tiled floor was scuffed with at least a quarter of the tiles missing. Holes and graffiti scarred the walls and paint peeled from the ceiling.

Three homemade missing person flyers were taped to the window beside the door, two for guys who looked like they were teenagers or in their early twenties, and the other for a middle-aged woman. The number of missing persons—all over town, with the exception of the precinct in the downtown core—had spiked in the last month and a half, and no one in the department had a clue as to why. Although I suspected it was probably one of the many after-effects of the war. Michael's slaughter to exterminate all humans and supernatural beings had only ended twenty-three years ago and most of the world's population was still coming to terms with what had happened. Some people dealt with that by running away.

Hank opened the door, not bothering to buzz the superintendent to unlock it. Every few months or so we'd get a call to this building, and, for as long as I'd been with this precinct—just over five years, which was as long as I'd been a cop—the building's door had been broken.

A man's angry voice roared around me as we entered. If I hadn't known I had enhanced hearing, I would have sworn the guy was standing in the hall with us.

"Hunh, guess they're still at it," Hank said, and he headed down the hall, his walk quick but his body language calm. Thankfully, not much bothered the middle-aged cop, or he was able to keep his emotions in check, which was good given how my next-to-useless weird empathic magic reacted to strong feelings. He had almost nine years of experience on me, and while he hadn't been happy to be partnered with the rookie who'd gotten another cop seriously injured, he hadn't tried to make my life difficult.

Of course, he hadn't tried to become friends, either. Four and a half years together and our partnership was still awkward. Which, given that I was trying to stay under everyone's radar, was better than a partner who wanted to know everything about me and stick his nose in my business—like why I didn't have a social or dating life.

My nerves, however, thrummed with adrenaline and

fear. This wasn't my first domestic call and it wouldn't be my last, but even with experience, I couldn't help but worry about how dangerous the situation could get.

The temperature rose as we drew closer to apartment 107, turning the early summer evening that was already unusually warm and muggy even warmer... at least it did for me because my empathic magic manifested as temperature changes and not something useful like being able to actually sense emotions.

Another glass something shattered, sounding like it had been thrown against the wall, and the man yelled obscenities at the woman. The woman screamed back.

Hank reached up to knock on the door, when a gunshot exploded inside the apartment.

My pulse leaped into a fast tattoo, and Hank's eyes flashed wide.

We drew our sidearms, and our gazes met for a split second, confirming we were good to go.

"Police," Hank yelled, and he kicked in the door.

Inside lay a living room filled with garbage—empty pizza boxes and beer bottles, food wrappers, and crumpled clothes—along with old, chipped, dented, and even broken furniture. We stood at the far end of the unit, which ran parallel to the hall, and while from my position I could see fully into the room, if both of us wanted a clear view of the entire room—and more importantly a clear shot—someone was going to have to enter.

I gritted my teeth and hurried inside. This situation was all human. There wasn't a super in sight. I had nothing to worry about.

At the back, near the closed patio door, stood a brawny man with swarthy skin in his twenties, wearing a black wife-beater and navy cotton-knit shorts with frayed ends. He pointed a Ruger 9mm at a short curvy woman, also in her twenties, with bleach-blond hair and a dingy yellow sundress. The guy had fingernail marks on his cheeks and arms—nothing supernatural looking about them—and the woman had a black eye and a fresh bruise in the shape of a handprint on her left biceps. She didn't look like she'd been shot, but both had ashen complexions and wild eyes.

They stared at us for a tense second and their expressions twisted with rage.

The room's temperature shot up another ten degrees, and sweat instantly slicked my body, making my uniform stick to my skin.

On the floor between them lay a spilled bag of little purple pills, and I inwardly groaned. Zip. Again? Jeez, this was twice in just over two weeks that I'd had to deal with someone high on zip. Except given their expressions, I was pretty sure they weren't high. They were starting to come down. And that meant aggressive mania and violent hallucinations enhanced by magic.

Just great. I pointed my Glock at the guy. "Police. Drop the weapon."

The guy snarled.

"Drop the weapon," Hank repeated.

The woman screamed and lunged at the guy. He fired two shots as she slipped on a half-empty pizza box and crashed to the floor. I dropped to the floor as well. The guy's rounds slammed into the wall above me, and my pulse jumped with the knowledge that I'd almost taken two in the vest.

"Drop the weapon," Hank yelled, not taking a shot because the woman was climbing to her feet and in the way.

The guy snarled and lunged toward the patio door. He wrenched it off its hinges with a burst of zip-enhanced strength and bolted outside, gun still in hand.

"Shit." I scrambled to my feet and gave chase. Hank followed close at my heels and called the change of situation in to dispatch on his radio.

The guy raced across the building's uneven parking lot and onto the street. This neighborhood had been old and tired before the war and had yet to see any revitalization money. Only half of the streetlights worked, making footing on the crumbling sidewalk dangerous, and the farther we went down the street, the fewer buildings had lighted vestibules or front doors that weren't boarded up.

I pumped my arms, trying to keep up with the guy. He ran with bursts of wild speed that came and went, making him jerk and stumble, but not enough to let me catch him.

Hank's footsteps pounded behind me, getting farther away. He was starting to trail, but I knew he wouldn't give up. He might not have the physique of any of the guys on Gideon's JP team, but he wasn't completely out of shape, either.

The guy stumbled, his arms windmilling to keep his balance, and he skidded into the narrow alley beside a seven-story building with a boarded front entrance.

My nerves thrummed stronger, more fear than adrenaline. The last time I'd run blindly into an alley, I'd gotten the shit beaten out of me and been branded by a serial killing archnephilim.

I gritted my teeth and pushed on. I couldn't let this guy get away. He'd already tried to kill his girlfriend, still had his weapon, and was in the middle of coming down from a magically induced high. He was a danger to others and himself, and I was pretty sure the violence-inducing hallucinations hadn't started yet.

The alley was narrow, not even wide enough for two people to walk side by side, and smelled of stale urine. A flashlight beam hit my shoulder and spilled against the alley walls on either side of me. If Hank had brought his light out, the alley was too dark for him to see properly, which meant it was supposed to be too dark for me.

Shit. I was supposed to be hiding my enhanced abilities. I could only pray that with the heat of the fight and the crazy zip addict with a gun, Hank wouldn't think much about my running down the alley without light.

Hank's light rose a little higher and caught the back of the guy we were chasing. The guy reached the end of the alley, crossed the street, and ran to a boarded-up entrance. With a roar, he ripped off one of the boards and darted inside.

I barreled out of the alley. Ahead of me stood a three-story partially-standing condemned school. The guy's footsteps pounded inside, drawing farther away. If he thought enough to slow down and hide, he might be able to slip past us while we searched the school.

I pulled out my flashlight, even though I didn't need it, waited a beat for Hank to get closer, and rushed inside.

This had been a side entrance to the building and it opened into a gymnasium, the space vast and empty, smelling of mold, dust, and decay as if an animal, or more than one animal, had died there. The sound of the guy's footsteps headed straight away from me but didn't echo, so he was already through the door and into the hall across from me.

Then his steps changed to the rapid patter of going down a set of stairs.

"He's in the basement," I told Hank, and put on a burst of speed.

I ran into a hall lined with metal lockers, their doors a mix of closed, opened, and missing, all tagged with graffiti on top of graffiti, while electrical and lighting boxes hung precariously from the walls and ceiling, their wiring scavenged for reuse. The smell of dead animal had thickened and a heavy layer of dust, marked with dozens of different footprints, coated the floor.

I hurried down the stairs into a dark corridor running right and left and stopped, nearly choking on the reek, the smell of death clinging to my nose and the back of my throat. More footprints trailed in both directions, and I couldn't tell if any of them were fresh.

Crap.

I really didn't want to lose this guy.

Hank reached the top of the stairs and clattered down, but I ignored him and drew a steadying breath. If the guy was still running I should be able to hear him.

Nothing.

Hank stepped close, his nose crinkled in disgust, his

sidearm raised, and his flashlight sweeping into the hall behind me.

"Did you see which way he went?" he asked.

"No idea." I squeezed my eyes shut, focusing on slowing my pounding heart and hearing past the rush of blood in my ears. Hank's breath came fast, and I could hear the faint thu-thump of his pulse.

Protocol said in a situation like this we had to stick together, even if that meant losing the perp. If the guy had been normal— or rather, if he'd *seemed* normal, we could have made a judgment call and separated, but no Union City officer faced anyone or anything magical alone. Ever. That was a policy only the dumbest or most desperate cops broke. And I was neither dumb nor desperate... not any more.

"Dispatch, two Charlie eleven in pursuit at Washington Park High School on Glendower," Hank said into his radio, his voice soft. "Requesting backup."

The radio crackled and clicked. "Ten-four two Charlie eleven, backup is on its way."

"Do we honestly think backup will arrive in time to trap him in the school?" I asked, still straining to hear the guy's footsteps.

"No, but at least there'll be more of us in the area to answer a call when he loses it on someone." Hank glanced the other way down the hall, his expression grim. "So which way?"

"It's fifty-fifty. How about—"

The temperature plunged and a scream ripped through the air. My pulse, not even back to normal, shot back into a rapid beat.

"Left," Hank said, passing me to take point.

We hurried down the hall. The guy screamed again, a desperate, wild sound that made the hair on the back of my neck stand up.

A door jerked open, and I could see the guy racing to get back out into the hall. But something yanked him back, pulling the door partially closed after him. Cold stung my hands and cheeks, the guy's fear a sudden, deep-winter freeze.

Oh, shit. This is bad. The memory of running into the alley and finding the archnephilim flashed through my mind's eye. *Please let it be a hallucination making him terrified of whoever is in that room.*

"Second door down," I said. "Someone else is in there."

"I see it." Hank hurried to the entrance, but the crack wasn't big enough to see inside.

The guy screamed again, followed by a low growl, crunching, and the sound of something wet.

Shit shit shit. That really didn't sound human.

I opened my mouth to warn Hank, but he shoved the door open and rushed inside to make way for me in the doorway.

I jerked into the opening to cover him and my thoughts stuttered. Time froze and all I could do was stare at the horror in front of me and wish to God I couldn't see in the dark.

The room was large, with no windows, and filled with massive pieces of equipment. Large pipes ran along the low ceiling and up the walls, snaking deeper into the room and beyond my ability to see in the gloom even with my enhanced vision.

The temperature had snapped back to normal, and I knew our perp was dead or awfully damn close to it. Hank's flashlight shone on him, his throat ripped out, his body limp and held in the arms of a pale, almost translucent-skinned woman. Blood covered her face around her mouth and her lips were drawn back in a feral sneer, revealing vampire fangs. Her eyes were all black, but didn't hold any of the intensity I'd come to recognize as pure vampire. All I could see was animalistic fervor and hunger. Desperate, consuming hunger.

Behind them, piled in the corner between two big pieces of machinery, were more bodies. All were mangled in some way, missing limbs, throats ripped out, faces smashed, and all in various stages of decomposition, the worst at the bottom of the pile. So many bodies. I could count at least two dozen, but with the size of the pile there had to be a lot more.

Bile burned my throat and I couldn't make my mind fully accept the horror. Vampire dens like this, with piles of discarded bodies, only existed in horror movies. They weren't real. Even before supernatural beings had come out of hiding to save themselves from Michael's war, vampires had had laws governing their behavior. Sure, some disobeyed those laws, but vampire society had been swift in controlling them. They were swifter now since humans knew about them, and there were enough interested in becoming blood bunnies that they didn't have to kill anyone to keep their secret.

But this was more than just killing to keep a secret.

This was primal, feral, inhuman in ways not even vampires or demons were inhuman.

The temperature plunged, this time with Hank's fear. Blood spurted from our perp's neck with his heart's last desperate beats to keep him alive. The viscous liquid oozed over the woman's arms and splattered to the concrete floor.

She hissed at us, her fangs extended and eyes filled with a wild hunger, and leaped at Hank.

CHAPTER 2

I FIRED TWO SHOTS AT THE VAMPIRE AND THE BULLETS slammed into her chest. Hank dropped his flashlight, drew his Taser, and shot from his hip. The barbs hit her square in the chest, the LEDs on them turning red, indicating Hank had pulled the trigger past the first and second catch to the device's highest voltage, intended to drop the average super.

She screamed but kept going, something I'd never seen before. Even without bullets enspelled to hurt supers, two shots to the chest and that much electricity should have made her at least stumble.

Hank scrambled back, but she grabbed his arm and tossed him deeper into the room. His Taser clattered to the concrete, and he slid across the blood-slicked floor into the pile of rotting bodies. Somehow he'd managed to keep hold of his gun, but without his light, he couldn't clearly see the woman leaping toward him as he scrambled to his feet.

My breath misted, Hank's fear growing stronger. I

fired again at the woman, and hit. She wasn't using enhanced vampire speed, but I didn't know if that meant she wasn't using it or if she was too young to have it.

The shot made her jerk around and hiss at me, giving Hank a second to eject the magazine from his Glock and grab the magazine of enspelled ammunition. But a hand reached out from the pile of bodies, seized Hank's ankle, and yanked, toppling him to his hands and knees.

Oh, shit.

The magazine slipped from his fingers and skidded across the floor into the band of light from his discarded flashlight.

Frost swept over the back of my hands and across my cheeks, making my teeth chatter. I aimed to shoot at the hand, but the woman lunged for me, yanking my attention back to her, and my shots hit her, point blank in the chest. She staggered—bully for that, she only had to be shot six times—but kept moving forward. Which meant I had to change my ammunition, because regular bullets sure as hell weren't doing anything.

She slashed at my arm with her claws. They weren't nearly as big as a shifter's claws but I suspected they were just as sharp and I didn't want to find out if that was true.

I jerked back and hit the edge of the doorframe.

The woman seized my arm and yanked me close, her fangs headed for my neck.

I dropped my flashlight and shoved her with everything I had. I wasn't strong enough to get her to let go, but the push did put enough distance between us for me to rush through saying the combat spell and summon a divine light strike.

Light flickered from my palm. Weak and uneven. The power wasn't even close to what I'd been able to summon when fighting the archnephilim, and not even as strong as it had been before that whole mess had happened, but it was all I had.

The vampire jerked her fangs back toward my neck, and I slapped my palm against her face, releasing the light strike.

She hissed and wrenched back, letting me go, and I scrambled away. With fingers numb with cold, I ejected the magazine from my sidearm, letting it drop on the floor.

The vampire snarled at me. She had a handprint on her face that only looked as bad as a mild sunburn, not the first- or second-degree burn it should have been. My blast had barely done any damage.

Hank screamed, and the frost on my hands swept over my wrists and up my arms. The front of his vest was shredded and so too was the left shoulder of his uniform, revealing deep, bleeding gashes. He fought with a bulky man wearing tattered clothes and covered from head to toe in blood. The man's eyes were wild and filled with hunger like the woman's, and his fangs were fully extended. They were ten feet away from the pile of bodies, and farther away from Hank's magazine of enspelled ammunition. And Hank didn't have the ability to summon any divine light like I did.

I opened the pouch on my duty belt containing the enspelled ammunition. The woman slashed at me again, her claws slicing into my vest.

Shit. I scrambled back, grabbed the magazine, and a

blast of lightning screamed through my right forearm from Gideon's brand and blazed through me.

My muscles seized, contracting tight as if I'd just been hit with a Taser. Panic raced through me, and my thoughts jerked to one thing: Gideon.

Gideon was in trouble. Gideon was hurt. Dying.

Every fiber of my being knew it.

For a week and a half, I'd been pretending I wasn't permanently bonded with the angel. With my increased personal buzz, even with two nicotine patches muting it, I'd been able to pretend the electric hum radiating from Gideon's angelic mating brand wasn't there. Now it was the only thing I could feel, and my soul was screaming.

The white lighenting sliced through my buzz, my thoughts, everything. Even the burn of my empathically created frost was gone. There was only him. There'd only ever been him, and I couldn't lose him. I had to go to him, help him, protect him—

Hank screamed again. The male vampire had tackled him to the floor and straddled him. The sleeves of Hank's forearms were shredded, the skin beneath bloody as he fought to keep the vampire's claws from his face and neck. He bucked and twisted, but couldn't get the vampire off of him.

The woman snarled and grabbed the front of my vest with both hands. I fought to move an arm, a finger, anything to defend myself, but Gideon's electricity burned through every command my brain sent to my body, and I couldn't think past the desperate need to go to him. Now.

With a roar, the woman jerked me around and

slammed me into the wall with her enhanced vampiric strength. Air burst from my lungs and my head cracked against the cinderblock wall. Darkness swam over my vision, but still my panic was for Gideon, not for Hank or even myself.

Save him. Save him. I had to save him.

The voltage surging through me suddenly stopped and all my muscles went limp. My gun and the magazine with enspelled ammunition clattered to the floor, and my knees gave out.

A rush of exhaustion swept through me as Gideon's brand stole strength from me to save him, and the woman yanked me forward and shoved me to the floor.

Hank howled in pain as the vampire gnawed on his forearm and the woman sank her teeth into my neck. I screamed the spell to summon divine light, praying the force of my summoning would somehow make my blasts stronger.

Somehow, the light hit with enough force to shove her off me, her teeth tearing my skin, and I dove for my sidearm and magazine. I managed to grab and slam the magazine into place, but the woman seized my ankle and jerked me toward her.

I twisted to face her and fired three times—because the bullet in the chamber wasn't enspelled—point blank into her head.

Blue lightning crackled around her body. She roared in pain and collapsed on top of me. I turned my aim to Hank, who was thrashing and screaming. The vampire had pinned him with his body and was now latched to his neck, feeding.

I fired two more shots, hitting the vampire in the chest, not wanting to risk hitting Hank by going for its head. The shots sent blue lightning crackling around the vampire, but the spell didn't drop him. It did, however, make him jerk away from Hank and rush toward me.

Another shot in the knee made him fall, and a final shot in the head—now that he was only a few feet away —killed him.

Hank gurgled and grasped at his neck, blood oozing between his fingers. The frost had thickened to ice on the backs of my hands, and my nose and throat burned with every frozen breath I gasped.

I scrambled to his side. My neck hurt. It was bleeding, but I didn't think I was bleeding out—just being magically drained by the soul mate I didn't want.

I dropped to my knees beside Hank, found the enspelled pip at his collar, and activated the distress beacon. The spell was for life-threatening injuries only, since it was ridiculously expensive. It immediately alerted paramedics to an officer's location, wherever he was. No need to call dispatch and try to explain where in the school we were. The spell would lead the EMTs right to us.

Hank gasped a weak wet breath, his eyes rolled back, and his hands slid away from his throat.

My pulse raced, and I slapped my hands over the ragged gaping wound on his neck, fighting to keep the blood from seeping between my fingers.

"Hold on, Hank. Just hold on. Help is coming." *Please, hold on.*

I shook with fear and adrenaline and jagged spikes of

electricity from Gideon's brand. And my skin hurt from the cold, even though the ice on the back of my hands was now cracking and falling off because Hank was losing consciousness.

I searched the room for signs of any more vampires, but nothing moved. Our flashlights shone with small stark bands across the floor, Hank's into the pile of decomposing bodies, mine under a hulking piece of equipment.

Hank jerked and his eyes opened and focused on me, his gaze desperate and afraid. A blast of cold swept around me and my breath misted, but I didn't care if Hank saw it. All I cared about was that he lived. *Please live.*

And I would God damn not leave his side to help Gideon. No matter what every cell in my body was screaming.

"I've got you. Just hold on."

He gasped another wet breath. His heart pounded, ragged beats pumping his blood through my fingers. *God, why couldn't healing magic be contained in a spell?* But for whatever reason, it didn't work that way. Spells could be created that enhanced immune systems, like the drug Divifend, or sped up healing for pulled muscles or the common cold, but no matter how hard every spellcaster tried, the innate magical ability to heal a life-threatening injury couldn't be replicated with a spell.

His body jerked again and his ragged pulse started to slow.

I fought back a sob. Hank and I hadn't been friends, but he'd been a decent partner and didn't deserve this.

Finally I heard footsteps racing toward us and saw beams of light dancing in the hall.

"In here," I gasped out, and an EMT team rushed into the room.

They took over, and I staggered back to the wall beside the door and sat. Gideon's jagged electricity had eased off a bit, and I couldn't tell any more if the dizzy exhaustion that numbed me came from him siphoning strength from me, shock, or blood loss.

I stuck my hands under my armpits to get them to warm up, my teeth chattering, my shivering spiking agony through my neck. I could only pray the EMTs would mistake it for shock and not actual cold.

And perhaps it was both. I'd had another horrible encounter in the world of the supernatural and another partner had been seriously injured. While there wasn't any chance he'd become a vampire, not even the one-in-a-million chance like there was with lycanthropy—the vampire had to perform a ritual to sire another vampire, not just bite someone—that didn't mean Hank's life wasn't in danger. *God, please don't let him die.*

Logically I knew this time wasn't my fault. I hadn't run headlong into this situation because I was naive. But that didn't ease the guilt churning inside me.

Fellow officer Brant Keels and his rookie—I still hadn't learned the guy's name—arrived, took one look at the scene, and the rookie promptly threw up in the hall. They called in the detectives, something I should have done the moment the EMTs took over. But it felt like I was thinking in slow motion and under water, every thought dragging and churning. Which wasn't like me at all. It had to be an effect of Gideon's brand draining me.

Hank was rushed away and another set of EMTs arrived. The bulky woman with a buzz cut checked out the dead zip addict, while the man, just as bulky but with a less severe haircut, knelt beside me and checked out my neck.

"You should probably get stitches, and you're going to have a nasty scar, but you must have a horseshoe up your ass," he said, his voice soft, calm, doing nothing to clear my muddled thoughts. "That vamp just missed your artery." He pressed a wad of gauze to my neck. "Hold this."

I obeyed.

"Any other injuries?" He shone a penlight in my eyes, making me wince.

"I don't think so." The back of my head hurt, but I didn't think I'd hit it as hard as I had two weeks ago when facing off with the archnephilim... although now that I thought about it, the blow could be another reason for my muddled thoughts.

"We should get you to the hospital anyway, just to check you out."

"Can that wait until we talk with her?" a firm feminine voice asked.

A set of practical shoes and gray slacks stepped into sight. I followed the legs up to Detective Abby McLellan's narrow face. Her already pale complexion was white, making the freckles dusting her cheeks and nose stand out.

"Are you up for answering questions, Essie?" she

asked, crouching beside the EMT and brushing her strawberry blonde bangs across her forehead.

I glanced at the EMT. "Am I?"

"You're not emergent, so you should be fine," he said. "Get her to the hospital if anything changes, detective." He rummaged in his bag, pulled out a roll of thick medical tape, and taped the gauze to the side of my neck.

"Jeez, Shaw," Detective Tim Snyder, Abby's partner, said as he strode up to us. His rich complexion hadn't paled, but the hard line of his jaw said he was as shocked by the scene as Abby. "You have the shittiest luck."

"Funny. The EMT was pretty impressed with my luck," I said.

"Sure, you can survive some serious shit." He rolled his eyes at me. "But that shit keeps finding you. I'm glad I'm not your partner."

Abby shot him a dark look, and he shrugged and walked over to the pile of decomposing bodies.

"Do you want to give your statement now and then again when the agents of the Joined Parliament arrive, or wait and only have to do it once?" Abby asked.

And by agents of the Joined Parliament, she meant Gideon and his team, since they were the only agents stationed in Union City.

I leaned my head back against the cool cinderblock wall, agony slicing through my neck, and groaned. A part of me thrilled at the idea of seeing Marcus again... and Jacob... and Gideon... and jeez, Kol, too. The rest of me wanted to cry that no matter what I did, how good I was, fate just kept throwing me back into the supernatural world. Not to mention Marcus was going to read me the riot act—most likely yell it at me—about being in dangerous situations, and I wasn't sure I was up for the sweltering temperature that came with that.

Of course, if they showed up, then I could vent my frustration on Gideon for doing something equally stupid. Because he had to have done something stupid to get so seriously hurt. If it hadn't been for him, I might have gotten through the incident without a scratch and Hank might not have had his throat ripped open.

Regardless, I was going to have to face them, so I might as well wait for them to arrive to give my statement. No point in giving it to Abby and then again to the guys. That, and once Gideon and the team arrived, the case would no longer be Abby and Tim's.

Hank and I had been attacked by vampires and the pile of bodies strongly indicated we weren't their first victims. That meant this was a Joined Parliament case, and I was pretty sure both Abby and Tim would be happy to hand it over. This wasn't like the Feds coming in and taking over. Union City's cops weren't equipped to handle powerful supernatural criminals, and a major supernatural case was usually deadly for human officers. Case in point.

"I'll wait," I said, feeling even more exhausted at the thought. "They're going to take this mess off your hands anyway."

Abby glanced at the pile of bodies. "And I couldn't be happier about that."

I sat against the wall watching the detectives and officers come and go, my head still whirling and my neck throbbing in agony. No one came to tell me to move, and I didn't want to risk standing and passing out. I really didn't want to face the guys from a hospital bed this time, and if I collapsed, I was sure I'd be rushed away.

The jagged electricity in Gideon's brand eased completely, but the sense of bone-deep exhaustion dragging at my thoughts remained. At least that muted the stomach-churning temperature fluctuations coming from the strong mix of emotions and the increased number of people in the room.

Summer, the angel who handled forensics at the Joined Parliament Operations Building, arrived with another guy who looked familiar. I was pretty sure I'd seen him while I'd been at Operations, but I couldn't remember his name.

They started working the scene, looking at the zip addict and the two vampires first. A little while later, the Joined Parliament Medical Examiner showed up. I recognized both guys from the motel where the archnephilim had left me a message written in his victim's blood.

They waited until Summer released the bodies then worked on loading them into body bags and taking them away.

After a bit, the Medical Examiner guys returned, along with a contingent of officers to help deal with the pile of bodies.

The temperature fluctuations strengthened—because the number of people in my immediate vicinity had increased again—and I tried not to look like I was going to throw up like the rookie had.

The new officers stood across the room from me, waiting for Summer to say she was done taking pictures and samples and whatever else she needed from the pile as she worked it from the top down. I recognized all of them. It made sense that the extra hands would come from my precinct. And every one of them shot me dark looks.

Some hid it better than others, but once again I was the cop who'd endangered her partner. Even the cops who hadn't been part of the precinct when the incident with Marcus had happened and hadn't looked at me like that before looked at me like that now. The rumors had been confirmed. I was a deadly incident waiting to happen for anyone who worked with me. It didn't matter that Hank and I had worked together safely for four and a half years. This was my second strike and the captain was going to be hard pressed to find someone happy about being partnered with me.

Which left me with what?

Angry and sad at myself for ending up in situations like this again.

Sure, I'd been living just fine without a lot of close friends, but I hadn't been completely ostracized. I'd still been able to go out and have beers with the handful of officers who'd been warming up to me.

Yeah, that wasn't happening any more.

I hated to think it, but perhaps it was time I put in for a transfer. I wouldn't be able to leave town without drawing Gideon's attention, since the mating brand would make him aware of my location wherever I was, but maybe I wouldn't be a pariah at a different precinct.

The idea of giving up stung. But knowing when to retreat wasn't giving up. This was a fight I couldn't win no matter how much I wanted to keep fighting. Better to retreat and regroup than risk making the situation worse.

The gut-churning temperature fluctuations made bile burn the back of my throat, and I feared if I stayed in the room much longer I would throw up.

Using the wall to keep my balance, I struggled to stand. A wave of dizziness washed over me, hints of darkness creeping over the edges of my vision, and the throbbing in my neck turned to stabbing pain.

God damn Gideon and his brand.

I blinked the darkness back, and walked—trying not to look like I was staggering—to the door.

Abby noticed and hurried to my side as I stepped into the hall. "I'm sure the JP agents will be here soon."

Given how seriously Gideon must have been injured for the brand to pull so much strength from me, I wasn't so sure. And I wasn't at all sure how I felt about that. "I'm sure they will."

"Should I tell them to meet us at the hospital?"

"I just need some fresh air." And to get away from all those emotions.

I headed for the stairs, Abby at my side, her flashlight lighting the way. The temperature didn't even out until I was back in the gym. I didn't know if that was a testament to the strength of my empathy or the strength of all those emotions.

A flicker of electricity danced over Gideon's brand, making my heart lurch that he was in danger again, but this time strength didn't drain from me. Instead, a soft heat warmed my arm and seeped across my chest, muting everything, my empathy, my exhaustion, even my God damned buzz.

We stepped out the side door, and I leaned against the rough brick wall, unable to remain standing without help.

Abby stood beside me, her gaze on the sliver of moon peeking out from behind ominous clouds, her expression grim. "I don't like what that room is saying."

A hint of cold—her fear—shivered across my skin. "I don't either."

The soft heat in my arm grew and the ache in my chest, my yearning for a man— an angel I didn't really know, swelled fully, replacing my buzz that was always nipping under my skin.

"All those bodies?" Abby shivered and the temperature dropped a few degrees more. "The Joined Parliament claimed our vampire horror movies were pure fiction, but—"

"That was definitely a horror show." The yearning and heat increased, bleeding through Abby's fear.

Gideon was close and coming closer. A part of me thrilled at that, but the rest was pissed. And I needed to focus on pissed or I was going to lose my mind. Hank was fighting for his life because I'd been frozen by Gideon's brand.

Abby slid her gaze to mine, her brown eyes dark in the dim moonlight. "Do you think this is an anomaly or something the Joined Parliament has kept hidden from us?"

"Why don't you ask their agents?"

Abby frowned and a large gray SUV, the kind driven

by the JP team, came around the corner. It pulled onto the curb and parked, half on the sidewalk, behind a cruiser.

The front passenger door opened, and Gideon got out.

My pulse stalled. All of me stalled and zeroed in on him, his strong, clean-shaven jaw, short blond hair, muscular shoulders and chest, narrow waist, and pale eyes. God, those eyes. They glowed with light, giving away his angelic nature, and I knew they were blue. The perfect blue of a cloudless summer sky. His soul called to me, and his brand heated my skin. All of me hungered for him, and I hated myself for that.

His gaze rose and locked with mine and even with the distance between us, I was falling into those pale depths and didn't care.

CHAPTER 3

"Good Lord," Abby breathed. "An angel."

She mustn't have been on site at the archnephilim's attack two weeks ago when Gideon had shown up or she would have already known the head of Union City's JP team was an angel. And while Summer, who was already at the crime scene, was also an angel, she didn't have the same magnetic draw Gideon had.

"Wait until the incubus gets out," I said, not wanting to talk about Gideon.

Abby's eyebrows shot up. "There's an incubus, too?"

Marcus got out from the driver's seat and the yearning in my chest turned into a throbbing ache. He was just as stunning as Gideon, but where the angel was a perfect clean-cut poster boy, Marcus was dark and brooding with a swarthy complexion and perpetual five o'clock shadow that made him look wild and dangerous.

His gaze, the night stealing all the warmth from his green eyes, jumped to me as well, and the snap of sizzling attraction between us stole my breath.

It had always been like that, ever since the moment we'd first met in the squad room and I'd been assigned to be his partner.

I hadn't known until a few weeks ago just how combustible the desire between us was. And a few days after that, just like the first time we'd been partners, he'd left without saying goodbye, leaving me to return home to my normal human life empty and cold.

It had been for my own good.

Honestly.

I just needed to figure out how to believe that.

Except in the time since I'd left Operations, I hadn't been able to convince myself of that.

His expression hardened, and he said something. Gideon gave a tight nod, and Marcus stormed away, heading around the side of the school, making me ache with the knowledge that he didn't even want to talk to me. He hadn't even gotten close enough for me to pick up a hint of his emotions.

The rear passenger door opened, Jacob climbed out, and all thoughts of Marcus vanished. My attention snapped to the vampire, completely out of my control, and the compulsion of his claim made me shift forward. I needed to go to him, please him, have him command me. I wasn't complete until he commanded me to do something, anything.

Crap. I'd hoped with time and distance the need to have him tell me what to do would have faded.

I gritted my teeth and forced myself to stay put. Jacob's dark gaze—his was actually black—held me captive, and his frown made my soul weep. He wasn't happy. He needed to be happy. The intensity in his eyes that indicated he was a vampire—something I'd seen him hide better than what he was doing now—filled the air between us with an energy that was on the verge of physically manifesting.

Out of the corner of my eye, I saw Abby shift, icy fear flickering over me. Her hand dipped to the Glock at her hip then her posture suddenly relaxed, and Kol stepped into my line of sight.

My thoughts stuttered as he rushed up to me—I hadn't even seen him get out of the SUV.

"Essie, are you all right? You're covered in blood." Kol's body blocked Jacob from view, releasing me from the pull of the claim—at least it had weakened enough that him being partially out of sight freed me, and I didn't strain to see past Kol to find Jacob.

And really, it was easy to stay focused on the incubus. He was drop-dead gorgeous. All the guys were hot, but Kol always stole my breath when I looked at him—which I supposed was part and parcel for a demon who survived on sexual energy. His T-shirt was tight and left nothing to the imagination, revealing perfectly sculpted muscles, and he wore blue jeans ripped at one thigh that I didn't doubt showed off his amazing ass... if only he'd just stand up and turn around.

He gingerly took my blood-covered hands, sending heated desire sweeping up my arms as he examined them. His black hair veiled his eyes, and when he lifted his gaze to meet mine, a hint of hellfire simmering with sexual desire burned within their dark orbs. If it hadn't been for that, and the small horns poking out of hair that perpetually looked like he'd just woken from the most amazing sex, he'd have looked like a human. A heart-stopping twenty-something who exuded wicked sexual grace that made me think of hot nights and even hotter sex.

Abby stared at him with blatant desire, a blush bright against her pale cheeks, obvious even in the dim street-light. I couldn't blame her. Even having worked with him, he was still breathtaking.

"Your vest is ripped," Kol said. "How bad is the neck?"

"Officer Shaw is fine," Gideon said, his voice icy and hard.

"This time," I mumbled, the words slipping out.

Kol's eyes narrowed, close enough to hear me, but I shot a glance at Abby, hoping Kol would understand the look. I didn't want this to be discussed, not while she was near. I didn't want her to know I was permanently bound to Gideon or that I had other connections with the team. I didn't want anyone to know, because then I'd have to accept the truth of my situation: that no matter how much safer it was for me to have nothing to do with the supernatural, it had pulled me in again.

Jacob stepped up beside Gideon, almost a head taller than him and twice as wide with his massive, muscular chest. With his black calf-length duster, one hand resting on his hip and the other on the grip of his Beretta, he looked every bit the part of a Wild West gunslinger. Given that he was older than a hundred, he very well could have been a gunslinger. His frown had deepened and his expression was tight with worry... or strain? I wasn't quite sure which.

Abby's gaze flickered back to Jacob, her fear cold on my skin. More sensual heat radiated from Kol's hands and slid up my arms, making me ache with desire, but I got the sense his enthrallment wasn't intended for me.

And just as I thought that, Abby's fear warmed and her attention turned back to Kol.

"Abby McLellan," she said, holding out her hand to Kol, her voice breathy. "Detective."

Gideon took her hand instead and gave it a firm shake. "Your precinct called in a vampire attack."

She shuddered. "More like a horror show."

"And Officer Shaw's involvement?" Gideon didn't even glance at me, which stung more than I wanted it to.

"Do you have time for Officer Shaw's statement?" Abby asked, pulling a notebook from her pocket.

"The JP M.E. and forensics are already on site." Gideon now turned a frosty glare at me, not even a hint of warmth in his eyes. Yeah, he wanted to be permanently bound to me for the rest of his life as much as I did to him. Of course, I couldn't blame him. He was in love with someone else and had just buried her, or whatever it was angels did with their dead.

His emotions were completely locked down so I wasn't getting a sense of anything from him, but that was probably a good thing. It meant I wouldn't be swamped with uncomfortable temperature changes from him or surrounded by mist from his grief for Zella's passing.

"Go ahead," he said to me.

I opened my mouth to speak—

Except I didn't. The thought didn't reach my body, because the command hadn't come from Jacob.

Jeez. I tried to fight through the compulsion to say anything, even just make a sound, but nothing came out, and all I managed to do was set off more agony in my neck with my straining.

Gideon's eyes narrowed. "Well, officer?"

"Your statement," Jacob said, his voice a low rumble, and the compulsion released me. Relief and joy and need swelled through me. And I hated a part of myself for having that reaction.

I gave a detailed statement, which included my observation that the female vampire hadn't been using enhanced speed, that a Taser at its highest setting and regular ammunition hadn't even made her stumble. The only thing I left out were the affects of Gideon's brand. That didn't need to go in anyone's report. As much as I was pissed that the brand had endangered my life and Hank's—and I really wanted to yell at Gideon for that—I had to accept that he had no control over it. Just like I didn't. And I couldn't tell him to stop getting hurt. His job was more dangerous than mine. Getting hurt was an inevitability in his line of work. I just had no idea how I was going to handle it if his job kept endangering me.

Which was just great. So much for venting all my frustrations on him.

Although if he kept up the frozen shoulder and the brand kept making me feel like my soul was breaking every time he talked to me in that icy tone, I might just snap anyway.

Thankfully Jacob didn't ask me if that was everything, because then I would've had to mention getting shocked by Gideon's brand and being unable to stop the vampire from biting me.

Abby was back to looking too pale and the guys were grim.

"So it's your case, right?" Abby asked, her voice shaky, her fear again cold on my skin.

"Without a doubt." But Gideon didn't sound happy about that. Which I couldn't blame him for, either. A pile of bodies and two crazed vampires looked bad for the supernatural community.

"Good." Abby shoved her notebook back into her pocket. "If you're done with Officer Shaw, I need to take her to the hospital to get stitches."

The muscles in Gideon's jaw tightened. "I'm done with her," he said, his tone so cold it made my throat tight.

Another bit of my soul fractured, and I couldn't help but feel there was more to his words than just a dismissal from this conversation.

I'd been told Marcus had demanded Gideon release me, let me return to my normal human life with no further involvement with the supernatural world. Now I was sure Gideon would have done that without Marcus's demand. The angelic mating brand wasn't a beautiful destined thing when you were stuck with someone you didn't love, and I was just a reminder to Gideon that his real love was dead. Not to mention, as far as he knew, I was a mostly powerless human, a detriment to any partnership.

And if he ever learned the truth, it would be even worse.

Abby stepped toward the street, but I didn't follow, Jacob's claim keeping me where I was even though I wanted to get the hell away from there and Gideon.

"Essie?" Abby asked.

The light from Gideon's eyes billowed. "Jacob, get her out of here."

Jacob shifted toward me. "Essie—"

My pulse leaped, and my essence zeroed in on him. *Give me an order. Tell me to do something. Anything.*

Please.

Release me from your claim.

But a vampire's claim didn't work that way. If he didn't bite me again, eventually his essence would work its way out of mine, but until then I was his to command whether either of us wanted that or not.

A silver sedan pulled onto the sidewalk behind the JP SUV, drawing everyone's attention, and an average-looking man in all respects, height and weight, with brown hair and brown eyes got out. Chief of Police Ken Fields.

I'd only met him once before and that had been at my graduation from the academy, but given that this was the second serious super incident in just over two weeks, it wasn't a surprise that he'd come to the scene himself to put whatever pressure he could on the JP agents to deal with this quickly and quietly.

Not that Gideon didn't already know the serious nature of this situation. Relations between humans and supernatural beings were still tentative, and while most humans were happy to abide by the law and let the supers be, many of them did that because the supers stuck to their Quarter and didn't mix with the human population.

"Done with the scene already?" Chief Fields asked as he marched toward us.

Abby straightened as the chief approached and my insides squirmed, desperate for Jacob to finish his command since there was also a chance the chief would want to have words with me for being involved in both of the recent supernatural incidents.

"We just arrived," Gideon said.

"You were called over two hours ago." Fields crossed his arms. "There's more to this city than the Quarter."

"And there's more supernatural crime than whatever your officers stumble across." The chill in Gideon's expression deepened—I hadn't thought it was possible for it to get any colder—but a hint of heat, which had to be anger, also started to dance through the air around me.

"Some are questioning if you have the safety of the human population in mind," Fields said. "Your JP team doesn't have a human agent and therefore doesn't have a human perspective."

The heat from the anger—best guess it came from Gideon—increased. "We don't deal with human perps."

"But you do deal with human civilians."

"What are you getting at, Chief?" Jacob asked.

"The LA news just ran an exposé on JP teams and their lack of human consideration. That's not the kind of press I or the mayor want for Union City. You may have managed to keep most of the details quiet from the case two weeks ago, but details still slipped out." Fields met

Gideon's glare head on. "Namely the damage done to an apartment building and all the 911 calls that night when we received the report about a fight among supernatural beings."

"That couldn't be helped," Gideon said.

"I don't doubt that," Fields said. "But that's not the point. Policing isn't just about catching the bad guy any more. It's also about optics. Showing up to a crime scene two hours later doesn't look good. Destroying an apartment with civilian neighbors still in the other units isn't good, either. It looks like supers are taking over without any consideration to humans."

"I don't know how we could make it more obvious that we're protecting humans from supernatural perps," Gideon said.

"The mayor has told me to assign a human member to your team and I heartily agree."

Sweat trickled between my breasts and I tried not to squirm. *Come on, Jacob, just tell me to leave.* If Gideon and the chief wanted to go at it, fine, but I didn't have to be standing there, aching for Gideon and straining for Jacob, while they did.

"You can't just assign someone," Gideon said. "My team doesn't fall under your jurisdiction or the mayor's."

"The trial period for a human agent has already been approved by the Joined Parliament. I'm sure you'll receive notification soon," Fields said.

Gideon's eyes narrowed and the heat around me billowed, making my face flush as if I'd gone out running in August at noon. "Our work is dangerous, even for a super. I can't guarantee your officer's safety."

"I'm aware of that." Field's attention slid to me. "Officer Shaw has taken advanced combat training for supers."

My pulse stalled. Oh, shit. He was going to assign me to Gideon's team, immersing me in the supernatural world again, and worse, forcing me to spend time with Gideon.

"Sir, I—"

"And she has more experience with serious crimes by supers than any other officer," Field said, cutting me off.

I doubted I actually had more experience than the senior officers.

"I can't—" I could barely stand five minutes with the yearning from the mating brand and Gideon's icy demeanor. I couldn't work with him. Not even for one case.

"Congratulations on your new assignment." Fields turned to Gideon. "She's all yours, agent. Now, Detective McLellan, show me this scene."

"I won't accept Shaw on my team," Gideon said, his words stinging a part of me I desperately wanted to ignore.

I didn't want to be on his team, either. In fact, I was thrilled he was fighting to keep me off the team. His rejection shouldn't have bothered me.

"You don't have a choice. The mayor wants a human seen working in the field with your team, and I don't want to sacrifice any of my other officers."

Jeez, he wasn't even trying to keep his true intentions a secret.

Gideon's back straightened, and the temperature

turned sweltering. Light flared from his eyes, and Jacob cleared his throat.

The light snapped back to normal and so did the temperature, as if Gideon had been reminded to control himself, something I'd never thought an angel would ever need.

"Feel free to complain to the Joined Parliament. I'm sure training more human agents will be in the works soon." Fields headed to the doorway into the school. "Remember, the mayor wants her seen working in the field with you. Now, show me the crime scene, Detective McLellan."

Abby shot me a worried glance but hurried after the chief.

"Just great," Gideon growled and marched after them as well.

The ache for him swelled as he left and so too did the buzz in my body, nipping under my skin almost at pre-nicotine levels. At least the temperature dropped back to normal, but the sweat slicking me from Gideon's anger made me shiver even though it wasn't close to being cold out.

"Well, that's a development," Kol said, his eyes wide with surprise. "Not it. No way am I telling Marcus the news."

CHAPTER 4

I HUGGED MYSELF TO WARD OFF THE CHILL FROM MY SWEAT, not caring if it made me look weak. I didn't need to be strong in front of Kol or Jacob, just Gideon and Marcus. My mind whirled, but there wasn't a way out of this situation. At least not one that let me keep my job. If my new assignment had come from my captain, I might have been able to ask for a transfer, but the order had come from the chief. There wasn't anyone higher in the ranks to go to.

If I wanted out, I had to quit.

That thought stung. All I'd ever wanted to be was a cop. A life of running from an unjust danger had only strengthened my desire to help those who couldn't help themselves. If I wasn't a cop, then who was I? I had to be more than just a nephilim, more than the nightmare monster everyone believed nephilim to be. I—

I drew in a steadying breath and squared my shoulders. I needed to not make any rash decisions, not after the night I'd had and with Gideon's brand making me exhausted.

I glanced at my watch. 2:30 a.m. "My shift is almost done. Jacob, please tell me to go to the hospital to get stitches and check in on my partner— *former* partner." I fought to keep my gaze down and not meet his eyes. If I did, my request would change to something personal and desperate. *Take me. Command me. Let me ease the worry I see in your eyes.*

How the hell was I going to be a productive member of the team if I couldn't do anything without Jacob's say so? But then the chief didn't know about any of my supernatural *conditions* and that wasn't the point.

"I can take you to Amiah and then we can check in on your partner," Kol said.

The memory of the first time Amiah had healed me flashed through my mind. It had been painful, like an electric current scorching through me, because she knew I was responsible for turning Marcus into a werewolf and she had—still had?—a thing for Marcus. I didn't know if she'd forgiven me or if she'd be back to being angry at me because I was now stuck on the team, recklessly endangering the guys again.

"The regular human hospital will do." I'd already hit my quota of angelic searing agony for the day. I didn't want a repeat even if it meant I'd have a scar.

Come on. Let me go. Please. Don't fight me on this.

"All right," Jacob said, the rumble of his voice sliding over me, drawing my attention against my will back up to his face. The strain around his eyes twisted his claim tighter within me. "If this is what I think it is, we're working through the night—" He glanced at the moon, partially hidden behind the clouds. "Or rather morning. Kol, take her to get stitches, then cleaned up, and then to Operations. Make it quick. Gideon will want to get on this, fast."

My soul thrilled at the order. I needed to go now. It would make him happy. It would—

I clenched my jaw. "Can I check on my partner?" I asked between gritted teeth.

The strain around Jacob's eyes tightened. "Yes," he said, the word clipped, then he headed into the school, leaving me with Kol, the only member of the team I wasn't somehow bound to—and yes, what I had with Marcus was as strong— no, stronger than what I had with Gideon and Jacob.

"Is he all right?" I'd been given my orders so I couldn't follow him inside even if a part of me wanted to, but something wasn't right with Jacob. I couldn't put it into words. I just knew it with a knowing that was more certain than anything I sensed from Gideon through the brand.

"It's been a rough night." Kol pulled out his phone and sent a text. "Gideon was seriously injured tonight."

"I know."

"How—?" His gaze jumped to my right forearm, where Gideon's brand lay underneath the sleeve of my uniform. "The brand, of course." His eyes widened. "Oh, jeez. No wonder you look like shit. The brand probably used your strength to stabilize him."

"Wow, way to make a girl feel pretty."

The expression in his eyes turned to horror. "No, I didn't mean— I— You look... fine? Hurt but fine?"

I rolled my eyes at him and winced as I started to shake my head, sending pain slicing into my neck. "Aren't you supposed to be the slick charmer?"

"Women don't usually tease me. Well, not in *that* way." A hint of hellfire flickered in his eyes.

Yeah, I imagined the teasing was a lot less innocent.

His expression turned somber. "I know Gideon said you were fine, but you really don't look fine."

"I hurt and I ache and I want to scream at the fact that two weeks later I still need Jacob's permission to do anything short of breathing." And now I had to work with the source of most of that pain. Unless I left the force. Which was the worse choice ever. "And my boss thinks I'm expendable. How was your night?"

"We raided a zip lab that had more security than we initially saw when we scouted, and Gideon took two in the gut just under his vest and one in the leg, severing his femoral artery."

No wonder the brand had gone crazy. Even with his angelic healing—which was better than a human's but not nearly as good as a vampire's or an incubus's—he wouldn't have been able to heal that. "Well, then, looks like it was a shitty night all around."

"You sure I can't convince you to go to Amiah?"

The claim twisted in my chest. Even if I wanted to risk her anger, I couldn't. "Jacob said stitches."

Another chunky medium gray SUV drove onto the street and stopped on the road across from us, not bothering to pull over.

"Then let's get you some stitches," Kol said, heading to the SUV.

An angel I also recognized from my brief stay at Operations got out, leaving the vehicle running.

"That was fast," Kol said.

"Summer had called for another set of hands, so I was already on my way." The guy pulled out a packed duffle bag from the back seat. "I'll grab a ride back with Summer, so it's all yours."

Kol got in behind the wheel and I settled into the front passenger seat. The buzz was getting stronger, but it was also nearing the eight-hour mark, when I needed to replace my nicotine patches. At least the exhaustion from Gideon's brand wasn't getting any worse.

We drove to the hospital, and Kol parked in an emergency-only short-term parking spot and flipped down the front visor, showing the SUV's JP credentials. But he hesitated before getting out of the vehicle.

"You should probably go in first," he said. "By yourself. Even if I do everything I can to suppress my nature, I tend to be... distracting."

"You were there the last time I was brought into emergency." A shiver of desire tickled along my spine and heated into embarrassment. He'd been there when I'd been on the verge of unconsciousness, in writhing agony, and the doctors had stripped me of all my clothes. Every last piece.

"You were in serious condition then. That's enough to make any doctor or nurse ignore me." He flashed me a wicked smile that made my skin heat, even though I suspected the smile was supposed to be encouraging and not sexual. "You're in much better shape this time."

Thank God for that. And while I hoped there wouldn't be a next time, the only way to guarantee that would be to leave my job. Which was looking like the only way out of this situation.

I bit back a sigh. "Are you going to wait in the SUV?"

"No, I'll give you a few minutes then join you." He frowned and for a second he looked uncertain of himself, the expression strange on the face of someone who exuded such sexual confidence. "Unless you don't want the company."

"I'd rather have the company while a doctor repeatedly pokes my neck with a needle."

"I'm sure he'll numb your skin first."

Not the point. "It's been a shitty night. Keep me company, Kol." Help me forget how much my heart hurts.

His smile brightened, sending a flood of sensual warmth through me. "See you in a few, then."

I got out of the SUV and walked through the emergency department's sliding doors. A nurse took one look at the uniform, the big piece of gauze taped to my neck, and all the blood covering me—it caked my hands and sleeves almost to my elbows, my shoulder and over my chest from the neck wound, and my knees—and hurried me to a bed.

Kol soon followed, sliding in the chair beside the bed with a sensual boneless grace, and shortly after, a doctor arrived.

"I'm doctor Ing," he said, sliding the privacy curtain aside to enter with his attention on a tablet, probably with my history already pulled up. "Officer Shaw—?" His gaze lifted and landed on me and my bloody mess. "The paramedic report says it's just your neck."

"Only about a quarter of this is mine."

"That's still a lot." He set the tablet on a nearby trolley and pulled on a pair of latex gloves. He was handsome in a very human, very comforting way, with warm eyes and short black hair. I pegged him at about my age, maybe a little older into his mid-thirties, and while the blood had made him pause, it hadn't been in horror, more in a professional assessment. "Are you light headed?"

I was, but not enough that I was going to tell him and risk getting held in the hospital for observation.

Although that at least would buy me some time to figure out what the hell I was going to do about my new assignment to Gideon's team.

The claim twisted tight in my chest, and I fought to keep my expression the same.

Jacob had said stitches, cleaned up, and then go to Operations. Quickly. A stay in the hospital wasn't quick.

"I'm good," I lied. "Nothing some stitches and a good sleep won't fix."

Ing's gaze jumped to Kol and back to me. "So long as you actually sleep."

Kol rolled his eyes and pulled out his identification. "JP agent assigned to Officer Shaw's case. How about we focus on those stitches."

Ing didn't look like he fully believed Kol, and I wondered if the incubus got that a lot. Was he always being judged when he was with a woman? God, I couldn't imagine trying to go on an innocent date with someone and having to deal with those assuming looks.

Of course, did an incubus ever go on an innocent date? Did Kol? How did someone who survived on sexual energy manage a relationship that was more than just sex?

"Let's get your shoulder out of your uniform so I can get a proper look," Ing said.

I undid the first button of my uniform and Kol shifted, a hint of hellfire flickering in his eyes. "I should wait outside."

"I'd rather have your company," I said, not wanting to be alone with my thoughts. Gideon and Marcus and Jacob were all problems I'd eventually have to deal with, but I didn't know how, and that scared me. Not to mention I couldn't think of a way out of this situation without losing my job. Besides, it wasn't as if Kol hadn't already seen me naked and at most I was barely going to show my bra. "Please. Distract me."

The hellfire dimmed in his eyes, replaced with worry, as if he could sense the whirl of emotions within me. "What do you want to talk about?"

"Did you manage to shut down the zip lab?" I undid the next button and Kol turned his back to me.

"Only in the sense that I'm sure the moment we dragged Gideon back to Operations, they packed up and moved locations."

"Just great. I'm getting tired of dealing with zip addicts." I shrugged my shoulder out of my uniform, clenching my jaw against the movement's pain.

"Me, too," Ing said, peeling the gauze from my neck,

taking a quick peek, and pressing it back in place. "Lie down on your side."

I took off my duty belt and handed it to Kol, who took it without looking at me, then I eased back onto the bed. Ing grabbed a needle, a vial of something, and a suture kit from a drawer, set them on the trolley, and pulled it to my bedside.

"And it's not just the addicts we get in here. It's their victims, because the damn drug makes them violent and strong." Ing removed the gauze and numbed my neck.

"It's worse with supers," Kol said. "Zip can also enhance their strength and speed. Even with supers who have beyond-human abilities. Their reaction is almost always violent and the odds that they'll OD is higher."

"I wouldn't have thought supers would be interested in zip," I said.

Kol shrugged, his back still turned to me. "A high is a high."

Jeez, a human with enhanced abilities in the throes of a terrifying hallucination was hard enough to handle. I couldn't imagine trying to deal with a super thinking he was being attacked from all sides. Would I have to deal with that now that I was on Gideon's team?

Only if I stayed on the force.

Which if I was smart, I wouldn't.

My throat tightened at that thought. *Damn, think of something else. Anything else.*

But I couldn't make my mind think past it. "Will there be a lot of cases that are that dangerous?"

Kol shifted and glanced at me, the hellfire still burning, tiny pinpricks in his eyes. "Gideon made a promise.

He doesn't break his promises. He'll find a way to get you off the team back to your normal life."

Except he'd broken a promise before. He'd said he'd be able to protect me from the archnephilim, before he'd known we were up against an archnephilim and he'd realized he wouldn't be able to.

"And until then, we've all got your back." He flashed a smile and sensual heat warmed my chest.

"Did you have her back tonight?" Ing asked.

"If we'd been there tonight, you wouldn't be stitching her up," Kol said, his tone fiercely protective, reminding me of Marcus, and an intensity filled his eyes, changing the hint of hunger to something else, something I couldn't quite recognize. Then the intensity vanished and he flashed another heart-pounding smile before turning his gaze away from me. "Are you done?"

I heard the snip of scissors, and Ing taped a fresh piece of gauze to the side of my neck. "You're free to go. Get this filled at the pharmacy." He peeled off his latex gloves, scrawled a prescription for painkillers and antibiotics on his pad, and handed it to me. "Don't get your stitches wet for twenty-four hours and make an appointment with your GP to have them removed in about a week."

I sat up and rebuttoned my shirt.

"Your file says this is your second super attack in just over two weeks," Ing said as he typed something into the tablet. "I hope it's your last."

"Me, too." But with my luck, I doubted it. "Can you tell me where my partner, Officer Hank Dacosta, is?"

Ing tapped on the tablet a few times. "He's still in surgery."

"Do you want to wait?" Kol asked, his gaze once again averted.

"Yes." But as soon as I said it, Jacob's claim twisted. There'd been nothing in his instructions about sticking around to ensure Hank got through surgery, only that I could check on him. God damn it. "But I need to get to Operations."

"We can wait."

"The waiting area for surgery is on the second floor, straight down that hall," Ing said, opening the curtain and pointing down the hall before he headed in the opposite direction to the nurse's stations.

"I can't wait. Jacob's command won't let me." I slid off the bed, too tired to generate any real anger at that. "Let's just go."

"Sure." He handed me back my duty belt.

We filled the prescription, left the hospital, and drove to my apartment, which sat in the top corner of a four-story walkup on a street of four-story walkups. When I'd returned home after being unconscious at the Joined Parliament Operations Building for five days, I'd found my place as good as new. Better than new, actually. The hole in the wall between my tiny bedroom and my slightly larger living room had been patched and all the walls were covered in a fresh coat of paint. And the skylight in the ceiling above my living room had been replaced, and so too had the bedroom window, where the archnephilim had crashed through to attack. Any furniture that had been broken during the fight had also been replaced and this was the first time I'd ever had a couch, TV, or bed that wasn't secondhand.

Because of the stitches, I couldn't take a shower like I desperately wanted, but I could certainly get out of my clothes—now tacky, and in places crunchy, with dried blood—and wipe most of the gore off.

Kol hadn't said anything on the ride over, and I wasn't sure what he was thinking. I, on the other hand, hadn't wanted to be thinking, but, like it had been all night—or rather morning—I just couldn't avoid my thoughts.

Stay or leave. That was what it came down to.

I grabbed a change of clothes from my brand new dresser and headed into the bathroom. Kol flopped on my couch, making even that look sexy, found the remote, and turned on the TV.

Stay or leave.

God, it was a horrible choice. I didn't want to do either.

I shrugged out of my shirt, my reflection in the bathroom mirror catching my attention. At least this time I didn't look as stunned as I had the last time something had happened, and I stared into the mirror. I had thought things had been bad when I had just been branded with a wraith's unnatural angelic mating brand, and then everything had changed. The wraith hadn't been just a wraith, and Gideon's brand had seared into my skin.

I turned my arm and looked at my left biceps, where the archnephilim's angry red mating brand had been. The brand was still thick and slightly raised, but it was now silvery like an old scar, with a spiderweb of silver threads around it. I turned to my other arm, where

Gideon's brand marked my right forearm. If I didn't think about the sigil forever binding me to an angel, I could see its beauty. Gold threads wove a complex design from the middle of my forearm up to my elbow and shimmered with a hint of light. A gentle heat and a soft electric hum, both barely noticeable, pulsed around it and into my soul.

If I stayed, I'd be able to be with Gideon.

My heart squeezed. But not Marcus.

Jacob's claim gave a fierce twist. If I stayed, I'd be able to please Jacob.

Which wasn't at all what I wanted, God damn it.

If I quit the force, the chief would either have to accept that he couldn't have a human on Gideon's team or assign the next expendable officer.

That thought made my stomach churn. If a human officer was going to be an equal member of Gideon's team and not a dead man walking, he was going to need extensive training to deal with supers. Whoever was picked would be in just as much danger as I was, more so because they didn't have an angelic mating brand that could help save them. They'd also have a family, certainly they'd have friends. I didn't have either. I never knew my father, and my mother was dead. She had a sister somewhere in New Mexico, but I'd never met her and didn't know how to contact her.

Well, that just sucked.

If I quit, I'd put someone else in danger.

Which meant once again I didn't have a choice.

Well, I supposed I did. I could go against my every instinct and let someone else be seriously injured or killed. But then I wasn't sure how I'd be able to live with myself. I didn't purposefully hurt people. I protected them. To the expense of my well being.

I could only pray, like the last time I'd worked with the guys, that I'd be able to fly under the radar and protect my secret.

Except this time I also had to protect my heart.

CHAPTER 5

I POPPED THE ANTIBIOTICS AND PAINKILLERS AS PRESCRIBED, cleaned up as best I could without being able to shower, and stuck two new nicotine patches to my left side. Pain sliced through my neck as I tugged on a black T-shirt and it brushed the bandage, but I gritted my teeth and finished dressing into a pair of jeans. From everything I'd seen, the guys' work clothes were casual and easy to move in. I'd stand out if I wore my uniform or a suit, and while I was sure the chief and mayor would love it if I stood out, I wasn't going to make myself any larger a target than I already was. And with my essence telling supers who could sense essences that I was a human and therefore the weakest member of the team, I was a pretty big target.

I packed a bag with an extra set of clothes, my box of patches, and my new prescriptions. Even if Jacob hadn't implied that the situation with the vampires was bad, I would have known it was. Which meant the team was going to work this case at top speed. Best case scenario,

I'd find a few minutes here and there to return home and change, but I wasn't going to hold my breath on that.

After the clothes, I added the gear from my duty belt, then rummaged through my top dresser drawer to find the waistband holster for my off-duty sidearm that I never used, secured it to the waistband of my jeans, and holstered my service weapon—still loaded with the rounds of enspelled ammunition. My off-duty Glock, which was in my gun safe, could stay in my gun safe since I was still on duty.

Kol watched without saying a word and then held the door for me when it looked like I was ready to go.

"Got everything?" he asked, a hint of mirth in his eyes.

"Are you making fun of me?" I hadn't packed that much. The small duffle bag wasn't even bulging.

"Actually I was wondering if you packed enough. I didn't see any toiletries go into the bag."

"If I'm staying at Operations long enough to want my own toothbrush, things have gotten really bad."

The mirth vanished. "You want to avoid us that much."

A whisper of cold and mist breathed through the air around me. I'd hurt Kol's feelings.

"It's not that—" Well, actually it was. Except I wasn't trying to avoid Kol because of who he was but because he belonged in the supernatural world. "It's complicated."

I grabbed a fitted, stretchy—for free movement—jacket from the hook by the door, spiking more pain through my neck, and stepped into the hall.

"Marcus said you were afraid of supers." Kol closed my door and stepped back so I could lock it.

"He did, did he?" It wasn't a lie, but I wasn't thrilled at the idea of Marcus sharing personal details like that about me.

"Gideon wouldn't agree to his terms without an explanation, and I overheard them arguing."

Did that mean Gideon hadn't been happy when I left? No, his reaction had to have been because of the brand and not being able to control me. If I died, he'd die or go crazy. Except, since I was mostly human, my death might not affect him at all.

Kol shot me a wary look. "I know you had a... difficult experience with the archnephilim—"

I snorted and headed down the hall for the stairs. "Difficult is putting it mildly."

"But you're not afraid of us—the team, are you?" He fell into step beside me.

I was as much afraid of them as I'd been of the archnephilim.

But for entirely different reasons.

Nephilim were enemy number one, responsible for the slaughter of thousands upon thousands of humans and supers. Even though I'd been a child, not even seven during the war, according to angelkind a naturally born nephilim was impossible, which meant they'd think I was one of those monsters, and I didn't want to find out what they'd do with me. If they thought I was from the war, I'd be sentenced as a war criminal, imprisoned, or executed. If they believed I really was natural, I could be turned into a lab rat to find out why I existed.

And now I was going to work with the team and increase the risk of being discovered.

The chill and mist deepened as we headed down the stairs.

"You know I wouldn't hurt you," Kol said.

I'd been quiet too long, and now Kol feared I was actually afraid of him because of who he was and not what he represented.

"I know you wouldn't hurt me." Jacob wouldn't either, not until he learned the truth. But the jury was still out on Marcus and Gideon, regardless of whether they knew my secret or not.

I offered Kol the warmest smile I could muster given my thoughts, strode out my apartment building's front door, and headed to the SUV parked at the curb.

Kol unlocked the vehicle with the key fob and got into the driver's seat. "The rest of the guys wouldn't hurt you, either. You're officially part of the team now. Not that they'd have hurt you before."

"I'm the powerless human member on the team, and I just about had my throat ripped out by a crazed vampire tonight. I'm not sure any human belongs in the supernatural world." My throbbing neck was proof of that.

He started the SUV and pulled onto the street. "Lots of humans do just fine living in the Quarter."

"Lots of humans aren't part of a JP team. Are you trying to convince me to live in the Supers' Quarter?" I couldn't figure out his emotions or this train of conversation.

"Not live, just visit."

Hunh? "Okay, why are you trying to convince me to *just visit*?"

His grip on the steering wheel tightened and he

stared out the windshield. The temperature grew colder, forcing me to fight my shivers and spiking agony through my neck.

Not the reaction I'd expected. "Kol? You wanna share?"

The muscles in his jaw clenched and his attention remained locked on the road.

"Kol?"

"I like your energy," he said, the words rushing out.

"You what?" I wasn't sure what I'd expected him to say, maybe that Marcus and Gideon were difficult to work with now that I was gone or something, but 'I like your energy' wasn't even close. "I thought I was off limits because of Gideon's brand?" Kol had made that clear when I'd offered to kiss him to help him restore his magic. Of course that had been before I'd burned his face with divine light and used the sexual euphoria of Jacob's bite to save him. Maybe things had changed.

"Not *that* energy," he said, still not looking at me. "I need *that* to survive, but some incubi have heightened attunement to essences and we feel essences more acutely than just about any other super and are drawn or repelled by certain energies."

My pulse skipped a beat. How much could he actually feel about my essence? Did he know I was a nephilim? He wasn't acting like I was, and he'd said he *liked* my energy. Would he still like it if he thought I was a monster?

"My attunement," he said, the words still rushing out as if this wasn't something he liked to share, "is ironically for essences on the light end of the spectrum."

"So divine light." Shit. He had to know I was a nephilim.

"Not just divine light. That's at the top of the spectrum, but there are varying degrees."

I resisted expelling a relieved breath. So he didn't know. Except— "You're a demon and you're drawn to the light and not darkness? Is that even possible?"

"I know. It's completely messed up. I'm completely messed up. I'm a being of celestial darkness and I feel better hanging out with an angel than my own kind. It's why I gave in and joined Gideon's JP team." His gaze finally jumped to mine and the temperature dipped a bit more with fear. He was terrified about what my reaction would be, and I sensed that he'd never told anyone else about this.

He jerked his gaze back to the road. "I hadn't realized how easy it was to be around you until everything was over with the archnephilim. Being around you is like hanging out with an angel without the attitude."

Gee, I wonder why that is? I struggled to keep my expression even. Out of all the guys on the team, I hadn't expected Kol to be the one best able to figure out I was a nephilim.

And what did I say to him? I liked his company. He was funny and charming, and his emotions were usually steadier than this. But now he was the one on the team I needed to avoid the most. He wasn't dumb. He'd eventually figure out why my energy was different.

"Jeez, it's not like I'm asking you out. Even if I dated, I wouldn't ask you out. You're Gideon's." The mist vanished with a snap and the cold turned bitter. His attention locked back on the road and his grip on the steering wheel tightened again. His expression hardened, but with my empathy I could see the hurt tightening around his eyes. And was that fear?

It couldn't be of me. It had to be of Gideon. But that didn't make any sense.

But then his reaction to me once he'd learned I wore Gideon's brand flashed through my mind's eye. He'd been quick to refuse me, adamant to keep his distance. I'd assumed that was because he was Gideon's friend and not wanting to hit on his friend's girl, but maybe there was more to it than just that.

He'd said he owed Gideon and Jacob his life and had been summoned by Michael to control the women who were being used to create the nephilim army. It hadn't sounded like he'd been a willing party to that, and because he was someone drawn to the light, Michael must have been confusing as hell. The archangel had been vicious and cruel to everyone but those angels who'd joined his cause. Everyone else, humans and supers particularly, were a virus that needed to be eliminated.

"I'm just asking you to stay with the team. I'd rather have you than some human who grates on my senses." The muscles in Kol's jaw tightened and for a second his fear was crystal clear. Fear of Gideon, or rather what Gideon represented. Even if Gideon had saved him, beings with light in their essences had still hurt him, and he was asking for something that he believed belonged to Gideon. I could only imagine his horror at being manifested in the human realm with the pure energy of an archangel only to find that angel's soul was blacker than night. And while lots of demons were older than their appearance, Kol might not be much older than his twenty-something years suggested.

How old had he been twenty-three years ago, when Michael had held him captive using his magic against unwilling women? God, he could have been as young as sixteen, just when his ability to enthrall had strengthened enough to control multiple people at the same time. And while he'd said he'd joined Gideon's JP team, he'd also said he'd *given in* and joined. He *needed* to be around angels, but was still afraid of them. I was an opportunity to satisfy his need for light energy without reminding him of Michael.

And now I really had no idea what to say. I wanted to tell Kol it would be all right, he had every right to ask this of me and I wouldn't let Gideon hurt him because of his request. But that would be a lie. I didn't know if it would be all right, and if I had any sense of self-preservation, I'd keep my distance from him.

"Being part of the JP team is dangerous for me," I said.

"I get it," he replied, his voice flat, breaking my heart.

Shit.

"But right now I'm part of the JP team, which means I'm going to need someone to show me around the Supers' Quarter." Which was true, and I'd rather it be Kol than any of the other guys. Kol might have this deep emotional scar, but he hid it well enough that it usually didn't affect his emotions, and I wasn't bound to him like I was the others.

The freezing air warmed a bit. Was that hope? "I'm sure Marcus and Gideon would rather be the ones to show you."

Given my reception at the school, I doubted they would. "I asked you first."

"Then it's a date." The cold around me vanished, and he flashed me his breathtakingly wicked smile, the sultry incubus returning and hiding the fear and insecurity I'd just glimpsed.

I was still a little stunned by him as we drove through the park ringing the Supers' Quarter and reached the Joined Parliament Operations Building a few minutes later.

Kol hopped out of the driver's seat and checked his phone. "The guys are back from the crime scene and waiting for us in the cafeteria."

My stomach rumbled, reminding me I'd just gotten off a shift and needed to eat. Well, good thing the guys liked to meet in the cafeteria. At this hour, I suspected all I'd be able to find would be cold sandwiches and salads, but that was good enough. Given how the mess with the archnephilim had gone, eating when I could was a good idea.

We headed inside and down the long white institutional-looking hall with its pale gray floor and fluorescent lighting, and past the elevator sitting in the new five-story high rise section just past the edge of the original old two-story warehouse. It had only been a week and a half since the archnephilim had destroyed the cafeteria, killing Zella and nearly killing the guys, and the back section that had been a bank of glass windows and a door leading to the patio was cordoned off with large sheets of heavy plastic hanging from the ceiling.

The rock wall that the nephilim had pulled down, crushing Marcus and blocking the entrance, was standing again, creating a separation between the regular seating and a sunroom-style glassed-in section, but it was surrounded by scaffolding, the plants missing and the water not running.

Gideon, Marcus, and Jacob sat at a six-seater table in the center of the room, and everyone's gaze turned to me the moment I set foot on the first of the five shallow steps leading down into the room. Heat billowed around me, and I knew instantly it came from Marcus. The attraction between us zinged through me and my pulse sped up, but my gaze dragged past him to Jacob and his claim twisted in my chest.

I heaved my attention back to Marcus—

And I actually did this time. But it took everything I had to hold my gaze with his, and I was trembling by the time I'd gotten down the stairs, making the throbbing pain in my neck radiate into my chest and down my arm.

I let myself go back to Jacob. Fighting the claim right now just wasn't worth it. I needed to save my willpower for when it really mattered, and preferably when it wasn't going to cause me agony.

"So this is actually happening," Marcus growled.

CHAPTER 6

THE LOOK MARCUS GAVE ME WAS TIGHT WITH ANGER AND the temperature in the room sweltering, and even then I could see and feel the sizzling attraction between us in his eyes.

"This is God damn happening," he growled again.

"Unfortunately," Gideon said, his gaze stony and fixed on the bandage taped to my neck.

His tone stung. He really didn't want me there.

Well, I didn't want to be there, either. "I could just quit and let you have whatever yahoo the chief decides to send you next."

Kol stiffened and a flicker of cold snapped around me.

"That would be great," Marcus said, his heat bleeding through the cold.

Jacob gave a slight tilt of his head to the chair between him and Marcus, the order clear. *Sit.* "We at least know Essie can summon divine light," he said.

I set my bag on the table behind the indicated chair and sat. Kol slouched into the chair across from me beside Gideon, looking sexy as hell, but now that I knew what I was looking for, I could see the hurt in his eyes.

"And can you actually request to leave our team?" Jacob asked.

"I'd have to leave the force." Except now that I was there, as much as a part of me was screaming this was dangerous, I didn't want to leave. I wanted to stay beside Marcus, hell, be wrapped in his embrace and kissed breathless by him, but I also wanted to be near Jacob. Even Gideon called to me, the unwanted compulsion to draw closer to him oozing from his brand.

I gritted my teeth against all of that and focused on my throbbing neck. I'd get worse than that if they learned the truth. Why was that so hard to remember?

"So you'd lose your job," Kol said.

Marcus shifted beside me, his feral werewolf nature darkening his green eyes and sending a shiver of desire down my back.

And that was why it was so hard.

"The chief can't force this on you," he said.

"The chief can and has." Gideon glared at me, his summer-sky eyes filled with ice, but the chill didn't change the room's temperature. His emotions were back to being locked tight, only a fraction escaping through his gaze. "It is what it is. Are you staying, Officer Shaw?"

As much as I should say no, I'd already decided I couldn't risk another cop's life. "I'm staying."

The tension in Kol's body eased, but Marcus's and Gideon's tightened, and Marcus's heat burned hotter with his confusing ferocious fear. Jacob didn't move. It felt as if he was holding his breath, waiting for something or trying to come to a decision, but I couldn't figure out what that meant. All I could really tell about him was that he was tired and strained, the same sense I'd gotten about him back at the school.

"It'll be a while before the Medical Examiner has a report," Gideon said, his tone brusque, moving on to the business at hand, "but we all know that was a feral vampire nest, and we can't wait on a report to catch them."

I tightened my body, trying to suppress a shudder and spiking more pain through my neck. "How common is this? The JP assured humanity that vampires didn't do that sort of thing."

"The last time I saw one was about a hundred and fifty years ago," Jacob said. "I'd heard the previous one happened almost three hundred years before that."

"And what? The master vampires didn't say anything because you thought it would stop happening because humanity now knows about vampires?" Marcus asked.

Jacob sighed. "It's the same as when a shifter goes feral."

"Not really. Humanity knows we can go crazy." Marcus sat forward, his body drawing ever so slightly closer to me. "You assured us—" He cleared his throat. "You assured *humans* that horror movie vampire stuff was just fiction."

"So they lied," Kol said, matching Marcus's posture and drawing his attention. "That's not the point. The point is what we're going to do about it."

"We need to hunt down every last one of them, and fast. The longer this takes, the more people are going to die," Jacob said. "The sun will rise in a few hours and they'll go dormant, but as soon as the sun sets, they'll start hunting again."

"So we have about twelve hours before the body count rises," Marcus growled. "Jeez."

"And we need to figure out who's siring them," Gideon said. "This won't stop until the master vampire is arrested."

"Except—" Jacob pressed his palms to the table. His hands were wide, powerful, twice the size of mine, and yet I knew how tender he could be when he held me. "It doesn't have to be a master to create ferals."

"You mean any vampire can sire another vampire?" I hadn't thought that was possible. Everything I knew about vampires said only a master, someone who'd lived long enough to amass enough power in their essence, could make another vampire. And now there were laws about when and how a vampire could be created, laws the masters had helped create.

Jacob shook his head. "Not just any vampire, but more than just a master. I doubt a master would sire a feral in the first place. Ferals are hard to control and ruled by their hunger and base instincts, and not much else."

"So who are we looking for?" Marcus asked.

"A vampire who was a witch before he or she was turned," Jacob said, "or one who's claimed a witch."

"Well, that makes it easy," Marcus said, his tone dripping with sarcasm. "Any vampire who might be connected to a witch, and within twelve hours."

Gideon leveled a frosty glare at Marcus. "If it was easy, it wouldn't be our case."

"No shit," Marcus said.

"The nest looked fairly new, so this could be someone new to town." Gideon blew out a heavy breath. "Jacob and I will go to Rouge and talk with Victoria. She's the master in town. Even if the new vampire hasn't paid his or her respects, she's the only one who might be able to sense the newcomer."

"Are you sure it's worth the cost to see her?" Marcus asked. "It's always some kind of fucked up game with her. You probably won't even get a straight answer."

"We need to get on top of this before the ferals kill anyone else," Gideon said. "We don't have a lot of time and Victoria is the fastest way to our solution."

"What about the price?" Kol asked, his worried gaze jumping to Jacob. I couldn't blame him. The last time we'd encountered Victoria, she'd used her power over Jacob to fill him with agony and threatened to lock him up.

Gideon rubbed his face and for a second he looked exhausted, then his icy demeanor fell back into place. "If it's too high, we'll leave."

But I got the impression that if he were the one paying, no price would be too high to save lives.

"We need to move now and catch her before she retires for the day. Marcus, you go back to the school and see if you can pick up any more scents. See if you can figure out if these ferals have a second nest or a preferred hunting ground. Kol and Essie, go with him."

Marcus stiffened. "She shouldn't be in the field."

"Our orders are she has to be in the field." Gideon pushed his chair back and stood.

"I think she should come with us," Jacob said, shooting me an apologetic look.

The temperature in the room plummeted and my fear joined whoever was suddenly afraid. The last time I was in Rouge, I'd let Jacob claim me to stop Victoria from torturing him. I didn't want to go back and find out what other things the master vampire wanted from Jacob or me.

Except the part of me claimed by Jacob was doing a happy dance at the suggestion. He wanted me near, needed me. Jeez.

"We already know Victoria won't give something for nothing, not even information requested by the JP. Seeing Essie with my claim as strong as it is will... amuse her," Jacob said.

Marcus growled low in his throat. "I'd rather not amuse that sadistic bitch."

"Neither would I," Jacob said, his voice rumbling through me, making my essence vibrate and grate against the hum from Gideon's brand as well as my buzz. He wanted me to go with him. I had to go with him. "But I can guarantee that if I show up without Essie, she'll be furious."

"And it's less than fifty-fifty that she'll even talk to me without you present," Gideon said to Jacob. "Fine. Officer Shaw comes with us, but she's going to need to see Amiah. She can't walk into Rouge with a fresh vampire bite. Be in the garage in twenty." He stormed away, his emotions locked up so tightly the room's temperature didn't even shift.

Jacob stood as well. "Let's call Amiah down. We can meet her in triage."

Wonderful. For all the trouble I'd gone through to avoid Amiah, I was being ordered to let her heal me anyway—even if Gideon's argument did make perfect sense about walking into a vampire dance club with a fresh wound.

Jacob's compulsion took over, and I stood whether I wanted to or not.

"I'll take her," Marcus said, standing as well.

"But Jacob wants—" I snapped my mouth closed. I was not going to let the claim make me argue with Marcus. I couldn't even ask for a change in orders, could only think of Jacob's initial command. This was going to become a serious problem if it didn't ease up soon.

The words to agree with Jacob pressed against my lips. But Jacob said we could meet Amiah. *We.*

I clenched my jaw. God damn it. *We* could mean me, Jacob, *and* Marcus.

"I'll call Amiah." Jacob gave a tight nod. "You can take Essie to meet her," he said to Marcus.

Marcus cleared his throat and shot a glance at the fridge sitting near the cafeteria's metal serving counters. If its selection hadn't been changed when it'd been replaced after the fight with the archnephilim, it would have prepackaged sandwiches and salads.

Jacob pursed his lips, his expression strained. "Eat something, too," he said and hurried away.

I sagged back onto my chair, the pressure of Jacob's claim easing the farther away he got. I'd known working with the team was going to be hard, but this was a disaster.

"I'll—" Kol jerked his thumb to the stairs. "You know —" He shrugged, grabbed my bag from the table, and rushed after Jacob.

Marcus turned and towered over me, his eyes hard, his arms crossed. His heat—my best guess was that it was a mixture of fear and desire, because fear wasn't usually hot—turned humid.

"What the fuck are you doing here? Didn't you listen to anything I said?"

Jeez, really? I shoved to my feet so he wouldn't be glaring down at me. "It's not like I volunteered for this."

"Yeah, but I bet you tried *so* hard to avoid it or protest the reassignment," he said, his tone mocking.

"You don't know what I did because you weren't there." And that hurt more than his anger. The desire between us might be combustible, but that didn't mean anything good could come from it. I ached for him and he still avoided me. "You ran the moment you saw me."

"I was respecting your God damn wishes." He jerked closer, and his lips pulled back in a snarl.

The memory of those lips on mine, his kiss ferocious and commanding, sent a shudder through me. I'd fantasized about kissing him since I'd returned home, replaying the moment in the elevator over and over again where he'd brought me to climax.

Jeez, I was still fantasizing about him.

"You wanted your life back, wanted nothing to do with me and my world," he said, his gaze boring into mine, daring me to deny it. "That was your choice. You made it perfectly clear."

"And you just gave up. You didn't even try to fight for me." Which was what had really eaten at me in the week and a half since I'd woken up after the fight with the archnephilim. I'd thought he'd given me a gift— Hell, he'd probably thought he'd given me a gift when he made sure I could go back to my normal human life, but the more I thought about it, the more it hurt that he'd just left. Again. "You could have at least said goodbye."

"If I had, my wolf wouldn't have been able to let you leave," he growled. His gaze dipped to my lips and his pupils dilated.

My pulse picked up, and my ache for him swelled.

"You *had* to leave. And now you're back." His expression hardened and he stepped back from me. "You're a liability on the team, and worse, you're fucking up my life. I had a perfectly good life before you crashed back into it." He raked his hands through his dark locks. "Stop being a fucking idiot and leave the team before you get one of us killed."

"And you think some other human cop would be better?"

"I know he would." He waved at my neck. "You got bit tonight because you can't handle a fight with supers."

I got bit because of Gideon's brand, not because I couldn't handle a fight with supers.

"I took down an archnephilim that handed you your ass. Twice. I'm not a complete pushover." And that was something I had to remember. I'd had the grit to stand toe to toe with the archnephilim, which meant I had the grit to handle this. "Stop being an asshole, and be a partner in this. I don't want to do this without you."

"I don't want you to do it at all. Guess neither of us gets what we want." He stormed up the cafeteria steps.

Jacob's claim jerked in my chest, stealing my breath. Shit. "You have to take me to Amiah."

"Take yourself to Amiah. You don't need me. You can handle anything, right?" He left, taking his heat and humidity with him.

"You want to know what's wrong with me, Marcus Diaz?" I yelled after him. "You." *God damn you and my desire for you.*

And that hurt all the more because I knew exactly what he was doing, and I'd still taken the bait. He was pushing me away to protect me. That's what he'd done the last time. I'd just thought after everything that had happened with the archnephilim and in the elevator that he'd be different.

But everything he'd done had been to protect me and the life he'd thought I wanted, and now here I was back in the thick of the supernatural world, taking the world's most dangerous job for a human. He might still be trying to push me away to protect me, but it was clear by how hard he was pushing that he was also trying to protect himself.

And even knowing that, his words still hurt, adding to the ache of desire for him.

Jacob's claim twisted tighter in my chest, begging me to go after Marcus and fulfill Jacob's command.

I ground my teeth against it, grabbed a turkey club

sandwich from the fridge, and took my God damn self to the miniature triage room and Amiah.

The angel, who could have been Gideon's sister with her brilliant blue eyes and blonde hair, sat on the tan padded-leather couch in the waiting area side of triage. She wore pale green scrubs and had her hair pulled back in a ponytail. She looked nothing like the slick, put-together angel I'd met before, but then it was after four in the morning and she'd already used a great deal of energy that day to save Gideon's life.

Her eyes narrowed when she saw me.

Swell. Looked like healing my neck was going to be as excruciating as the energy that had seized me and got me bitten in the first place.

"I've barely gotten a few hours' sleep, so I'm not at full," she said, pointing to the floor in front of her.

"I know."

Her gaze slid to my right forearm and a hint of the hardness in her gaze melted. "Which is why, in part, you're not at full."

"Yeah." I sat at her feet, facing perpendicular to her and giving her the best access to the wound.

She peeled the gauze away and frowned. "This is nasty. I won't be able to heal it completely. You'll have to come back once I've had time to rest."

"Can you do enough so it's not completely obvious to a master vampire?" That was the whole point in doing this.

"I can, and eliminate any possible infection, but you'll probably have a nasty scar."

I cocked my eyebrow at her.

"Which, if you keep the stitches, you'll have anyway." She brushed her fingers along my neck, close, not touching the wound, but somehow still making it sting. "Your lack of vanity doesn't make me feel better about you now being on the team. I still think you're reckless."

"What happened with Marcus was because I was an inexperienced rookie."

"That doesn't make me feel any better." Electricity snapped from her fingers into my skin, making me jolt. It sliced pain through my neck and sent my buzz into a wild frenzy. "Your other partner is in the ICU."

"The ICU?" Oh, thank God. A pressure in my chest that I'd being doing my hardest to ignore released. Hank had made it out of surgery.

Amiah's power flared and I tensed against the pain, the agony searing into every cell in my body even though it was just my neck she was supposed to be healing. My buzz roared, no longer controlled by the nicotine patches, stinging under my skin as if I were being bitten by a million bugs.

Then the blazing agony of Amiah's magic vanished. It happened so fast that I was still vibrating with the memory of it surging through me. It felt like this healing had happened even faster than the first time. Of course, maybe it had. This was just a stitched-up bite on my neck, not the broken ribs and collarbone and concussion I'd had before.

The buzz, however, didn't return to normal. It eased off a bit, but only to pre-nicotine levels even though I'd just applied two new patches. Whatever Amiah had done, her magic must have negated the patches' effect.

Wonderful. Now I was going to have to figure out an excuse to find wherever Kol had taken my bag and replace my patches.

"That's the best I can do right now." Amiah sagged back into the couch, her breath a little too fast, as if she'd been physically as well as magically exerting herself. "Grab some tweezers from that trolley and pull out the stitches. They're just under your skin now."

I stood and crossed the small hall into the medical side of the triage area and found the tweezers on the indicated trolley. A small mirror hung on the wall over the sink, and I leaned in to get a better look. I hadn't seen the bite before so I didn't know how bad it had originally looked, but from the raised, dark pink, jagged scar, it looked as nasty as everyone had said it did.

The bite hadn't been clean or two simple punctures. It looked more like I'd been mauled by an animal than bitten by a vampire. And there was nothing I could do about it, especially since I didn't particularly want to go back to Amiah for another session to get rid of the scar.

I plucked the stitches free and was just about to go find my bag and replace my nicotine patches when the frosted-glass sliding door to the main hall opened and Gideon strode in.

CHAPTER 7

GIDEON'S ICY GAZE JUMPED TO ME AND MY PULSE TREMBLED with yearning. The buzz in my body softened and the hum from his brand warmed my forearm. The connection between us made me want to cry and scream at the injustice of being forever bound to an angel, and yet beg him to hold me at the same time and ease my fears.

I squared my shoulders and tried to steady the whirl of emotions. If I was going to be an equal member on this team—or as equal as a human could get on a team of supers—I was going to need to deal with my unwanted emotions, or I'd end up proving Marcus and Amiah right and someone was going to get hurt.

"Officer Shaw," he said, his tone as icy as his gaze.

"I was just on my way to the garage." So much for replacing my patches. Although it seemed that if Gideon was close, my buzz wouldn't be so bad and I'd be able to think straight. Which only made me more frustrated at my situation.

"Where's Jacob?" Gideon asked.

"I don't know."

Amiah shifted on the couch, her scrubs sighing against the leather, but Gideon didn't look away from me, keeping me captive with his gaze.

"He said he'd meet you in the garage," she said.

"Good." Gideon's gaze dipped to my hip. "Do you have enspelled ammunition in that sidearm?"

"About two-thirds of a clip."

"Only use the gun as a last resort," he said. "Stick to your light strike. Things will get complicated if we kill one of Victoria's offspring." He turned on his heel and strode back out the door.

My buzz flared, and I hurried to follow.

"Your sandwich," Amiah said, reminding me of Jacob's command to eat.

The claim twisted tight. Crap. I rushed back to the couch, grabbed the sandwich where I'd left it on the floor, and rushed after Gideon.

"And don't you dare get any of my guys killed," Amiah said as I stepped into the hall and the sliding door closed behind me.

"It's not the guys I'd be worried about," I said under my breath.

"What was that?" Jacob asked. He stood in the hall between me and the door to the garage. The claim squeezed but the compulsion to answer him wasn't overwhelming, so I didn't.

No matter how much my insides squirmed.

I could do it.

Really.

Jacob frowned, the strain in his expression deepening.

"Are you okay?" I headed toward him, keeping my gait even and not rushing to his side like the claim wanted.

See, I could fight it. Maybe it was weakening and if fate had only waited a few more days before shoving us back together, it wouldn't have been such a struggle.

"Are you?" he asked.

"I've had better nights. But hey, it could be worse. We could be fighting the archnephilim again." Even with my emotions a complete mess, I had to admit the situation wasn't as bad as that. Sure, I was still magically bound to someone for the rest of my life, and from the looks of it he hated me, but at least he wasn't a homicidal maniac.

"The scale of difficult nights does change when you put it that way."

The door at the end of the hall slid open and we stepped into the cool musty air of the garage. Gideon waited for us beside one of the JP's SUVs, his posture perfect, his expression hard. He tossed Jacob the keys and got into the front passenger seat.

I climbed in behind him so it would be harder for him to make eye contact. The buzz dimmed ever so slightly again. Yep, being near him affected my buzz, and that made me nervous. It hadn't before and I hoped it was because I'd had Gideon's mating brand for two weeks now and not because something within me had changed when the archnephilim had flooded me with power.

Except I already knew something had changed. My eyes still glowed and the damned buzz was harder to mute with nicotine.

"When we get to Rouge, I'll find out where Victoria is, and we'll get this over and done with," Gideon said, without looking at me. "Jacob might have claimed you, but given how that whole... *situation* came about, there might still be trouble. So keep your eyes open, Officer Shaw."

"Copy that."

I ate my sandwich as we drove in uncomfortable silence, heading deeper into the Supers' Quarter and turning onto the street designed for vampires that was covered with UV-blocking glass. The purple canopy stretching from rooftop to rooftop reflected the street like a dark mirror, hid the stars, and muted the glow from the sliver of moon peeking out from the clouds. It was less than an hour before dawn, and while the street wasn't packed, it was busier than the last time I'd driven down it. Shops and restaurants were open and the sidewalk patios were full as diners enjoyed the warmer than normal summer's evening.

Most of the people looked human, although there were some demons present, and while many were vampires, since over ninety percent of the vampires in Union City lived in the Quarter, there were probably a lot of humans in the mix as well. Most of the humans were blood bunnies, happy to give blood and be in the presence of a vampire—and given the sexual euphoria that a vampire could induce during feeding, I wasn't as skeptical about why someone would want to be a blood bunny as I had been before. There were probably also a handful of claimed humans in the mix as well, those who'd gone even farther than a blood bunny and submitted their will to a vampire, giving up all control of his or her life.

Jacob's claim inside me twisted, reminding me that I'd submitted to his will. It might have been to save him from being tortured by Victoria and not because I wanted to give control of my life to someone else or because I wanted the benefits of being claimed—such as enhanced hearing and seeing in the dark—but I'd still done it.

We turned onto the last street branching off the UV-protected road before it ended in a UV-protected park, and stopped in front of Rouge. The dance club was a large building with wide front steps and two towering Roman columns that sat at the edge of the UV canopy, and from the sound thumping out of the building was still open for business.

Gideon got out, but didn't climb the stairs as I expected. He stared at the club's blacked-out glass doors and a whisper of mist—had to be his grief—curled around me.

My throat tightened in sympathy. Zella hadn't died in her basement apartment under Rouge, but that fight had started it all, and her injuries had been so severe she hadn't been able to fight the archnephilim when he attacked Operations and killed her. And now we were returning to where she used to live and reminding him of what had been taken from him.

I wanted to tell him how sorry I was, how I wished Zella had been his mate. Maybe the mating brand would have been enough to save her. But his shoulders squared before I could work up the nerve to say anything and the mist vanished.

He strode up the stairs without looking to see if Jacob or I were following.

Jacob shot me a worried look, but there wasn't anything either of us could do right now save watch his back.

Inside, past the vestibule and the bouncer who'd taken one look at Gideon and bristled but didn't say anything, was a writhing, pulsing mass of people dancing, standing, talking, or making out in the booths or shadows clinging to the edges of the room. Strobe lights flashed over the dark walls and ceiling, heavy music vibrated into my bones, and the room's sweltering temperature came from a mix of natural heat, along with the empathic heat of joy, desire, and need wrapping tightly around me.

Sweat slicked my forehead and pricked under my arms and between my breasts. I unzipped my jacket and shoved my sleeves up, but it did little to cool me down. And in all honesty, I'd either have to leave or strip to my underwear to alleviate the heat.

Gideon wove his way through the crowd to the archway leading into the pub-style room at the back of the club, and headed straight to the bar. Jacob and I followed and leaned against it, staying close, while Gideon asked the bartender about Victoria's location.

I slid my attention over the room. The temperature was still too hot and now my insides were churning with fear. This was where everything had gone sideways last time. The polished wood furniture and brass accents gleamed in the light, its cozy English pub feel doing little to ease my discomfort. People played at four of the five pool tables and one of the three dart boards. A group in a large booth cheered at a baseball game on one of the big screen TVs, while more groups of varying sizes, taking up about half of the tables and booths, chatted and drank and ate.

If I hadn't been put in the position to make Jacob claim me, threading his essence into mine and control me body and soul, the pub would have looked like any old pub. But I knew how dangerous its occupants were, and I could see the intensity in their gazes and the unnatural stillness in the bodies of almost everyone in the room. I was surrounded by vampires. More than the handful from last time. And that terrified me.

I hooked my thumbs into the waistband of my jeans. I really wanted to wrap my fingers around the grip of my sidearm, but someone could take that as a threat and the whole point of this was to get in and out without causing a fight.

Jacob shifted closer to me, but I didn't know if it was to reassure me or enforce his claim on me to the vampires staring at us.

"Victoria is in her suite." Gideon's gaze jumped to me.

"Shit," Jacob said, his voice low. "This isn't going to be pleasant."

"I'll pay her price. You don't have to worry about it," Gideon said. The mist returned for a second then vanished as he turned and headed for the stairs at the back of the pub.

Upstairs, we headed down a wide hall with gilded frescoes on the ceiling and a marble floor. At the very end stood a set of intricately carved wooden doors, and a bulky vampire who stood guard. He was as tall and as broad as Gideon—so not nearly as big as Jacob but still imposing. His body covered a third of the carving, but not enough for me to miss that the image depicted a woman and two men in the throes of a threesome.

The guard opened his mouth to say something, but his eyes flashed wide, and he reached for the door handle instead, his body jerking as if controlled by someone else —and given that Victoria had been able to squeeze her fist and make Jacob drop to his knees in agony, it was likely she was the one in control.

"Come in, Gideon," Victoria called in her sultry alto.

The guard finished opening the door, revealing Victoria lounging in a massive bed that sat in the middle of the room, completely naked, the red silk sheets only covering one leg and only up to her knee.

She was stunningly beautiful, everything I'd imagined a master vampire to be, with pale skin, dark hair, red lips, and curves that would make a man drool. If she'd had horns, I would have thought she was a succubus. But she didn't, and the intense energy radiating around her, along with the mesmerizing darkness in her eyes, told every cell in my being that she was an extremely powerful vampire.

Two men, naked as well, were in the bed with her, one behind her kissing her neck as if we hadn't just entered and interrupted, and the other sprawled face down beside her, bloody rents scored into his back, blood smeared on his neck, and his body limp, but his expression dreamy and satisfied.

The room was as opulent as the hall outside suggested, with four marble pillars at each point of the bed, and massive frescoes that covered the vaulted ceiling and poured down the walls. The floor, what could be seen beneath thick Persian rugs, was marble, and the furniture was heavy and dark and swirling with orna-mentations and gold leaf. Floor-to-ceiling windows towered to my left and directly across from me, all with long gauzy curtains swaying in the early morning breeze, every one of them open.

"Have a drink, Gideon." She gestured to a sidebar against the right-hand wall, stocked with crystal decanters filled with liquids of various colors and glasses of all shapes and sizes.

Gideon met her gaze, no indication in his expression about what he thought about the master vampire receiving him without any clothes. "You know I don't drink on duty."

"Well, your other option is to join me." She ran her nails down the back of the guy beside her, drawing more blood and making him moan in pleasure. Her gaze drifted over Gideon's muscular body, pausing at his crotch before sliding back to his neck. She licked her lips. "I've always wondered what angel tasted like. Your choice."

"I'm just here to talk," Gideon said, his tone calm, casual. Which is exactly how I'd play the situation. Not react to the naked people and keep it relaxed. Without a doubt bad things would happen as soon as someone made demands from a woman like Victoria.

"Is that why you brought my offspring and his human?" A sensual smile lit her face. "They're your offering instead. How wonderful."

Her gaze locked with mine, capturing my soul and

making my pulse pound. The sensual smile was now edged with a deep hunger, and I really didn't want to be desert. Her smile deepened, revealing her extended fangs.

"She's really very pretty, in a human kind of way," she said, her tone rich, sending an involuntary shiver of desire through me. "I can see why you picked her, Jacob. Is she as tasty as she looks?"

Her gaze trailed down my body, slowly, sensually, but stopped when it reached my right forearm and the exposed mating brand. The carnal hunger turned wicked, and she slid off the bed and glided toward us, every step exuding sex and danger.

"Oh, Gideon," she purred, grabbing his right wrist and dragging a nail through the mating brand on his arm that matched mine. "I didn't know you liked to share. If I'd known, I would have tried harder to entice you into my bed."

"Victoria." He captured her hand around his wrist, and a hint of light billowed from his eyes. "We really just want to talk."

"No." Her eyes narrowed and her sensuality turned dark, now filled with the promise of exquisite pain. "You're here to ask questions. Demand answers. That's what you angels do. Well, there's a price for answers. Did you think you could get away with asking without paying."

"This is for the benefit of both of us," Gideon said.

She leaned her naked body against him, her other hand pressing against his chest. "I don't see how giving you answers benefits me."

"Because the humans found a feral vampire nest," Jacob said.

"Oh, they did, did they?" Victoria raised a sculpted eyebrow and pursed her lips. "And you want to know if it's one of mine making them?"

"Or if there's a new player in town," Gideon said, his tone still soft, almost seductive, but the muscles in his jaw flexed, proving Victoria was getting under his skin.

Her lips brushed his jaw, and her tongue darted out and licked the flexed muscles. "Pay the price, angel, and I'll tell you."

He inched his head away from her. "Which liquor do you recommend?"

"That's not on the table any more." Her hand slid down to the waistband of his fatigues.

"You know I'm not having sex with you," he said, his voice low.

"No, you'd rather have it with my offspring's human." She turned her piercing gaze to me. "Do you think she's already fucked him, Gideon? Or is she still fantasizing about what it would be like for my offspring to fuck her while he drinks her dry?"

I shuddered, my breath picking up with desire, as Jacob's claim brought the fantasy to the forefront of my thoughts.

"Or do you share? He bites her while you fuck her? You know she's thinking of him, that it's him who's driving her mad with desire." Her hand slid past Gideon's waist toward his groin.

He jerked back and grabbed her wrist, his body stiff, his eyes icy. "People are dying."

"Only humans," she purred. "Besides, I said I'd tell you if you pay the price."

The ice in his gaze shifted, grew pained, and the mist of his grief returned, edged with a strange flickering heat. He was actually weighing the idea of letting Victoria use his body to save lives.

Jeez, I knew he'd do almost anything to save people, I'd seen that fierce determination when he'd promised to protect me from the archnephilim, but he shouldn't have to make that decision, especially not with his heart still mourning his one true love, Zella. That wasn't fair to him, and while the smartest option was to just walk away, that meant more people would die.

And *I* couldn't let that happen, either. "How about you find out how tasty I am instead?"

CHAPTER 8

GIDEON'S EYES FLASHED WIDE, AND VICTORIA'S ATTENTION snapped to me, freezing me in place with her vampiric intensity. My pulse pounded a wild tattoo but my offer was the right call. It was dumb, but the right call. I couldn't let others die at the hands of the feral vampires, but I couldn't let Gideon give in to Victoria's demands. Yes, using sex as a currency happened every day, but Gideon shouldn't be forced into it, not if I could help it.

"Shaw," Gideon said, his voice sharp with warning.

Jacob shifted closer to me. He opened his mouth to say something, but Victoria shot him a glare and his body jerked, his expression tightening with pain.

"You answer our questions and you get to find out how tasty I am."

"So you'd rather I feed from you than fuck your mate?" Victoria threw her head back and laughed a sultry laugh. "What if I want both?"

Gideon stiffened. "That's not—"

"On the table," I said, cutting Gideon off. I squared

my shoulders and met Victoria's gaze. She was terrifyingly powerful, her intensity soul-consuming, but she wasn't an archnephilim, and I'd be damned if she forced my angel to sleep with her. "You either get to find out what's so interesting about me that your offspring and an angel want me, or we walk."

"I could crush you," she hissed.

"And then you'd have no hope in hell of getting into Gideon's pants."

"We're leaving." Gideon grabbed my arm and started to turn, but the room erupted into chaos.

Two vampires, their expressions filled with wild hunger, their fangs fully extended, rushed past the gauzy curtains into the room. They raced straight to the bed, one grabbing the dazed man before he could get up, the other vampire tackling Victoria's other man and sinking his fangs into his neck.

The men screamed. Victoria howled with rage and jerked a step toward them, but more feral vampires came through the open windows and threw themselves at us.

Gideon shoved me behind him and sent a blast of divine light at the closest vampire. She screamed, her face and hands burned, her skin red and oozing. Her body convulsed, but she didn't drop and instead jerked back toward Gideon, snarling. Jacob drew his Beretta, but his eyes widened at the non-effect of Gideon's blast, and he shoved the weapon back into his holster. With a snarl, he lunged at the vampire Gideon hadn't taken down, and ripped out her throat.

Victoria had taken out two ferals already with her bare hands and was moving, a blur of pale flesh and flying black hair, to the ones who'd killed her lovers, while her guard rushed into the room from the hall and joined the fight.

Gideon formed a sword of divine light in one hand and pushed me farther back with the other. "Stay back." Then he lunged into the fray.

I drew my Glock and fired at a vampire coming through one of the windows. The enspelled bullet slammed into his chest and blue lightning crackled over his body. He screamed and staggered, his arm tangling in the curtain and tearing it down, but the shot didn't kill him.

Shit. I stilled needed to make a kill-shot to take these things down. Head or heart. And while I was a good shot, I wasn't that good, certainly not when they were moving in a frenzy. There were over two dozen ferals still standing and I didn't know if more were coming. I only had ten of my sixteen shots left. I had to make them count, which meant I was going to need them to get closer to me to increase my odds of hitting my mark.

Victoria screamed, her vampiric speed slowing. Her chest rose and fell with wild gasps and blood rushed from gashes along her ribs. A chill tightened in my gut. These ferals could even hurt a master vampire.

Jacob ripped out the throat of another feral and lunged at another one when a gunshot roared into the room. It slammed through Jacob's chest, dangerously close to his heart, and likely would have hit it if he hadn't lurched forward a split second before to attack. It drew a strangled scream of pain, and he staggered. The vampire he'd been about to attack slashed at him with wicked claws, slicing his shirt and gouging deep rents in his chest.

I fired at that feral, aiming for the heart, hoping that even if I didn't hit, the enspelled ammunition would make it stumble long enough for Jacob to get away. Blue lightning snapped around the feral's body and it dropped to the floor, my shot striking true. But another gunshot roared into the room. Jacob wrenched to the side and the shot tore through the sleeve of his duster.

"Sniper," he yelled as he ripped out the throat of another feral. "Take cover."

Gideon decapitated a feral with his sword and glanced around the room, and in that second of taking stock, the sniper fired again. The bullet sliced through the right side of Gideon's upper chest near his collarbone with a spray of blood, drawing a scream of pain.

A hint of jagged electricity flickered in the mating brand, but it wasn't all-consuming like it had been before, which meant his injury wasn't fatal. Yet.

He twisted with the force of the blow and his light sword vanished. A feral vampire lunged at him, and he wrenched his hand up, his sword forming with the movement and impaling the vampire at the last second.

Two more gunshots roared into the room, one skimming Victoria's cheek. She stumbled, her enhanced vampiric speed making her lurch halfway across the room. The other hit Jacob's thigh. He staggered and the feral beside him raked her claws across his face.

Gideon ran his blade through that feral's chest and yanked Jacob to his feet.

I dove for the bed and ducked behind its meager

cover. But all the shots had come through the one set of windows and there weren't a lot of other pieces of furniture in the room that I could hide behind. The body of one of Victoria's lovers hung over the side, a massive swath of blood darkening the sheets and pooling on the floor.

Four feral vampires remained, more than two dozen bodies lay bleeding on the floor, and another gunshot erupted. The sniper fired again. This time the bullet tore through a gauzy curtain and exploded out the back of the head of Victoria's guard. The guy dropped, his eyes vacant and dead.

Gideon hauled Jacob back toward the bed while Victoria made a dash for the door. The remaining ferals dove for Gideon and Jacob, and another flurry of shots erupted, drawing a scream from Victoria and forcing her to wrench away from the door. Blood slicked her body from killing the ferals with her bare hands, but also oozed from two bullet wounds in her chest.

She dove for the bed as another gunshot slammed into the wall behind her, and she crashed to a stop beside me, bumping me into the blood pool. I fired another shot at a feral on Jacob, giving him time to kill a different one before turning to the one I'd hit. He and Gideon were only a few feet away from the bed, but with the ferals not pulling back, there was no way they could take cover.

Gideon killed another one and turned to the last remaining one, but another gunshot slammed through that feral vampire, into Gideon's chest, closer to his heart than the last shot, and out his back. He screamed and lightning erupted from the brand.

My muscles seized, agony screaming through me. Everything within me howled to save Gideon, help him, do *anything*, but what I really needed to do was duck back behind the bed. My head and shoulders were still exposed from the shot I'd taken to help Jacob. I was a target, and if I got shot that wouldn't help Gideon. Except I couldn't move.

Another gunshot roared into the room.

Time stuttered into slow motion. Gideon clutched his chest, his sword of light gone, and staggered for the cover of the bed, Jacob close behind him, while Victoria's eyes flashed wide. Frost swept over my hands and cheeks from a sudden fear-induced temperature drop, and the master vampire seized my arm and yanked me to the floor.

Searing pain sliced across my cheek and into my hair. My head hit the marble floor and specks of light snapped across my vision.

Time jerked back to normal. Gideon scrambled around the foot of the bed and dropped down beside Victoria, while Jacob dove over it and landed with a heavy thump beside me. The jagged lightning released its hold on my muscles, but still burned agony through me, and now strength bled out of the brand from me to Gideon.

"We have to get you to Amiah," I gasped, struggling to sit up and making the room spin around me.

His gaze locked with mine and for a second all the ice was gone and I was immersed in a perfect summer sky. God, he couldn't die. I couldn't let him die. Please.

"We have to deal with that sniper first," Jacob growled, drawing Gideon's attention away from me.

"I commanded my lieutenants to search the buildings across the street and find the bastard," Victoria snarled.

"And yet they're not going to find me there," a raspy tenor said from the far side of the room by the windows.

The frost on my hands crept over my wrists and down my neck.

Victoria shot Jacob a terrified look. "You said you killed him."

"I did."

"You know I can hear you," the tenor said in a singsong. "You did kill me, Jacob, but my century and a half is up and I'm back to take what's mine."

"I'll stop you the same as I did last time." Jacob glanced over the edge of the bed. "And now you've lost the advantage of surprise."

"How's your chest, Jacob?" Raspy Tenor asked. "Half an inch to the right and I'd be done with you."

Gideon drew in a ragged wet breath, his hands pressed tight to *his* chest, and the lightning from his brand threatened to seize me again. We needed to get out of there, but the only other door in the room was farther away than the hall door. We'd be bigger targets if we ran towards it. Perhaps if I shot this guy with my enspelled ammunition, we'd be able to make a break for the door. Which was ridiculous, given how both Gideon and Jacob had been shot and couldn't run at full speed. We'd be shot before we made it halfway there.

I peeked over the edge of the bed to see who we were dealing with, then quickly dipped back down. Raspy Tenor looked like another Wild West gunslinger. He was lean, a complete opposite to Jacob's bulky build, but just as tall. His eyes were black, and he radiated the terrifying intensity I recognized as vampiric. The intensity, almost as strong as Victoria's, made my gut clench in fear.

He too wore a black duster that looked an awful lot like Jacob's, and a black hat, the wide brim pulled so low that if I hadn't been sitting on the floor looking up at him, it might have shaded his eyes from sight.

The only things that didn't say he'd just stepped out of history was the modern sniper rifle slung over his shoulder and the SIG Sauer P210 in his hands trained at the bed.

"Still with Mommy, I see. Has *she* hooked up with the angel or have you?" The soles of his boots shushed against the carpet. He was moving, drawing closer to the head of the bed. "And you've found yourself another human. How cute."

Jacob drew his Beretta and shifted his attention to the head of the bed as well. "Give up now and I'll make your death fast."

"But I've barely been back, and I'm having too much fun." Raspy Tenor rushed around the bed, his SIG raised to fire, but Jacob shot first. His bullets drove through Raspy's chest, making the other vampire jerk. It threw off his aim, and his shot hit the wall behind us. Blood rushed across his chest and splattered onto the rug.

"Run," Jacob barked, and I jumped to my feet.

I wrenched against his claim, staggered, the jagged electricity from Gideon's brand slicing through Jacob's command, and forced myself to grab Gideon's arm and help him stand. Victoria rose to her knees, glared at Raspy, and squeezed both of her hands into fists.

Raspy hissed in pain against Victoria's mental control, but didn't drop, and snarled back at Jacob as bullet after bullet slammed into him.

Jacob scrambled to his feet, grabbed Victoria under the arm, and hauled her up, still firing one-handed.

She wrenched out of his grip and stood her ground. "You're still my offspring. I still control you."

"Keep on trying, bitch."

Jacob's Beretta clicked. Out of ammo.

Raspy snarled, revealing his fangs, and fired his SIG.

Gideon wrenched me close and put his body between me and the danger. Victoria screamed and I shoved Gideon's arm aside and fired my gun, hitting Raspy in the chest. He didn't even bother getting out of the way. Blue lightning crackled around him. He dropped to one knee and his eyes widened.

I aimed to fire again, but the door crashed open. Five vampires—Victoria's lieutenants?—rushed inside, exuding dangerous ferocity, their fangs extended.

Raspy sneered. "Next time I won't miss, Lockwood." He bolted with his enhanced vampiric speed to one of the windows and leaped out.

Victoria's vampires rushed after him. A gunshot roared outside and someone screamed.

Victoria turned to Jacob and clenched her fist, making him groan in pain and sag to his knees.

"You said he was dead," she snarled. She was even more ferocious than her lieutenants. Blood gushed from another gunshot wound in her chest—Raspy's last shot—mixing with the blood splattered over her naked body.

Jacob gasped for breath. His blood oozed from the

gashes on his face and chest, shallow enough that his vampiric healing was already starting to close them. But the gunshot in his thigh still bled profusely.

"I didn't know his soul was bound to the demon's seal," he said.

"Victoria," Gideon gasped, his breath wet and rattling. He pressed his palms to the wound in his chest, blood oozing between his fingers, and dropped to his knees before I could even try to ease his descent. His head dipped forward as if it was too hard to keep up. "Please."

I holstered my Glock, wrenched off my jacket, and pressed it as best I could to both the entrance and exit wounds near his collarbone. He was losing a lot of blood, and while an angel did heal faster than the average human, it wasn't anywhere fast enough to save him from bleeding out from the two gunshot wounds.

Strength rushed from me into him, and the room started to slowly spin and darken. This was worse than when the archnephilim had hurt him, his injuries were more severe, and I was still weak from earlier that night.

If we didn't get him to Amiah, he would die. And he just couldn't die. Please. He couldn't. My soul would shatter if he did. I wouldn't be able to keep living. It was because of his brand binding us together, and I didn't care. All that mattered right now was him.

I sank to my knees beside him into a growing pool of his blood, all my strength going into holding my jacket to his chest and into the brand to keep him alive. I had to stand, had to find the strength from somewhere to get him out of there.

"Jacob, help me," I said, my throat so tight I could

barely get the words out. Gideon wasn't going to die. I wouldn't let him die.

A flicker of power snapped beneath my skin. Like my buzz but more powerful, almost like the fire that had unfurled in my back when the archnephilim had tried to make the wings I didn't have manifest. I strained to stand, but the power turned into my stuttering angry buzz and the room twisted with exhaustion instead.

I couldn't do it without his help or Jacobs. "Come on, Gideon. Stand."

A burst of my strength swept into the brand and he shuddered, his head turning just enough to capture me with a single summer-sky eye. He raised a bloody hand to my cheek. His fingers whispered over my skin and my pulse stuttered, every cell in my body yearning for him.

"The team needs you," I said. "You don't get to die on them." Or me.

"I'm trying not to," he said, each word a struggle, each breath getting harder. The muscles in his jaw clenched. "I just need a minute. I'll be fine."

"Not unless you get help, so stand up." I imagined more of my strength flooding into him.

He groaned, his muscles bunched, and he stood, the movement sending jagged electricity screaming through me. I rose with him, but we were both unsteady and started to tip.

Victoria swore and both she and Jacob rushed to help us, Jacob grabbing Gideon, Victoria grabbing me.

"You should be healing faster than this, angel," Victoria said, her tone concerned but her gaze filled with hunger and lingering on his bloody shoulder.

Gideon leaned into Jacob. "It's been a rough night. I'll be fine in a few minutes."

"Or you're going to end up dying in my suite. And I can't have a JP agent dying in my suite." She released me, jammed a finger into one of her already healing bullet wounds, and coated it in blood. Then she grabbed Gideon's jaw with her other hand, forced his mouth open, and wiped her bloody finger over his tongue.

He gagged, jerking away from her, and she let him go —with her strength she could have held him there, probably even crushed his jaw.

"That should be enough to keep you alive long enough to get back to the Joined Parliament Operations Building."

Light billowed from his eyes, and the jagged energy coming from the bond eased to the same level as my buzz. Thank God. While I still swayed, the room slowly spinning, it was now a little easier to stay upright. It was certainly less painful.

"That wasn't necessary." Gideon glared at Victoria, clinging to Jacob to keep standing. Blood still rushed from his wounds, but the brand told me whatever Victoria had done, it had helped.

"Yeah, I know, now your pure angelic essence is tainted by vampire blood." She turned on her heel, strode to her bar, and poured herself a drink. "You're welcome. Now get out. You're not one of mine, so the healing properties of my blood won't last long."

"I didn't even know you could do that for non-offspring," Jacob said.

"One of the perks of being as old as dirt," she snarled.

"Thank you." Jacob wrapped an arm behind Gideon's back.

"I didn't do it out of the kindness of my heart." She took a long drink and leveled her intense gaze on Jacob. "We're not done with our conversation. If Logan Dunn is back, so is the danger of his demon. I can't have you distracted because your human has died because her angel has died." She rolled her eyes. "And I know you'll be useless if that happens. You were useless the last time. Now clean up this fucking mess."

CHAPTER 9

WE STAGGERED OUT OF VICTORIA'S SUITE, TAKING THE back stairs—as instructed—and climbed back into the SUV. I didn't know where Raspy Tenor was or Victoria's lieutenants, but the master vampire had been right, the effects of her blood were already starting to wane, and the jagged spikes of electricity were back to slicing through me.

Jacob drove while Gideon sat in the back, his eyes closed and his hands pressed against his chest wound. I crouched on the bench beside him, keeping pressure on his shoulder.

"It's going to be okay," he said, his voice soft, his eyes still closed, his breath shuddering gasps.

"Until you get shot again." God, here I'd been afraid I wouldn't be able to survive my job when I should have been afraid I wouldn't survive his.

"I'd have been good enough to get to Amiah if I hadn't been shot earlier this evening."

"That doesn't make it better." A stronger zap of electricity sliced up my arm and across my chest. I jerked and swallowed back a moan of agony.

He opened his eyes, captured me with his gaze, and I was falling into a summer sky again. This was where I belonged, wrapped in his pure warmth, wrapped in his arms.

A hint of clouds passed over his summer sky, dimming his angelic light, and he turned his head away from me and closed his eyes again. A chill bled into my heart, filled with the empty ache of losing the momentary connection we'd had. The connection had been so quick, only a few seconds. Losing it shouldn't have felt like I was suddenly lost in a vast sea of ice.

Jacob pulled into Operations' garage, and Amiah and another woman in scrubs—I think her name was Cassey—rushed out the door with a gurney to greet us. I scrambled out of the SUV to get out of the way. The garage dimmed and twisted, and I clung to the side of the vehicle to keep standing. Jacob helped Gideon out and onto the gurney.

Amiah shot me a withering glare then hurried Gideon inside, down the hall, and through the frosted sliding glass doors into triage, taking my heart with them.

Jeez. What a complete mess.

"Come on," Jacob said. "You should get looked at, too."

Jacob's command rushed through me, and I stepped away from the SUV. The garage twisted, and I staggered. Jacob caught me before I fell to my knees and lifted me in his arms.

I leaned my head against his shoulder, mindful of the

gashes across his chest—although they looked like they were mostly healed—and the bullet wound near his heart—not bleeding as profusely as it could have. I closed my eyes, not wanting to deal with the world whirling around me. In his massive arms, cradled close against his broad chest, I felt small, delicate, and safe. The vampiric intensity that terrified me in the other vampires comforted me, centered my soul, and I knew, without a doubt, I also belonged there, in Jacob's arms.

Because of his claim.

Except a part of me wasn't sure the rightness of being held by Jacob was completely because of the claim.

"How badly are you hurt?" he asked, his voice rumbling through me as he headed down the hall with uneven steps, his gait still affected by the gunshot wound in his leg.

"It's the brand making me dizzy." And sore and exhausted and heartbroken.

"He'll be okay."

A sliding door shushed open, and a jagged spike of electricity sliced through me. My eyes wrenched open and locked on Gideon as he convulsed and screamed. He lay on the gurney, his hands clutching the sides. Someone had cut off his shirt exposing his chiseled chest, the sculpted muscles smeared with blood. The shirt lay on the floor in a wet heap along with my jacket and an unnervingly large pool of blood. Light flared from Amiah's eyes with a sudden blast of her healing magic, surging through his body with an excruciating pain I was all too familiar with.

"Push the Midazolam," Amiah said. She captured

Gideon's face with her gloved, bloody hands and met his gaze. "I've slowed the bleeding, but that's all I can do until my magic recovers. You'll heal faster if you're unconscious. Do you understand?"

"Essie," Gideon said, his voice so soft I wouldn't have been able to hear it if Jacob's claim hadn't enhanced my hearing.

"Gideon, do you understand?"

He gave a tight nod and gasped, his face tightening in pain. "No more than four hours. I can't be down longer than four." His eyes rolled back as the sedative took over, and the jagged electricity snapping from the brand eased, blending back in with my buzz.

"Hang a bag of O-neg and finish packing these," Amiah said to Cassey then turned to us, her expression exhausted and pained. "How bad is your face, Jacob?"

Jacob sat me on the bed beside Gideon and pressed tentative fingers to the gashes in his face. "Mostly healed. The gunshot in my chest and leg are the worst."

"Can you get by without my magic and just a blood bag or two?"

"Yeah." He turned to the small fridge where they kept the blood, pulled out a bag, and shifted away from the gurney.

"And you?" Amiah asked me, peeling off her gloves, tossing them in the hazardous waste bin, and pulling on new ones.

My cheek was still bleeding, I could feel my blood oozing down my skin, hanging on my jaw before dripping onto my shoulder, but it wasn't gushing and I was just too tired to care. "I'm fine."

She rolled her eyes at me. "You're not fine, but you're clearly not going to die, either."

She doused a piece of gauze in saline, grabbed my chin, turning my head and angling it up to give her easier access to my face, and wiped at the blood.

"So much for your promise not to get my guys killed."

I didn't recall making that promise to her, even if I'd made it to myself, and I was just too tired to argue with her.

The other doctor grabbed a blood bag from the fridge, hung it on the pole by Gideon's head, and attached it to his IV. Then she wheeled his gurney down the hall, deeper into the building where I knew there were patient rooms.

Amiah turned my head even farther. The gauze rasped against the gash in my cheek and into my hairline with biting pain, and I ground my teeth, trying my best not to show it.

Out of the corner of my eye, I saw Jacob slip the blood bag back into the fridge and leave through the sliding glass door. Guess he needed more than just a bag or two. I'd heard that while a vampire could live just fine on bagged blood, drinking from the vein had better healing properties. He was probably off to find a blood bunny to recover faster, and I wasn't going to think too hard about that because even just acknowledging that made his claim twist inside me to volunteer my blood.

I squeezed my eyes shut and concentrated on just breathing. Everyone was still alive. It was going to be all right.

"I'm not going to bother with stitches," Amiah said.

"Jacob's claim on you is helping speed up your healing and they're just going to get in the way when I have to heal you properly." She taped a piece of gauze to my face. "If you bleed through this, just replace it."

She peeled off her gloves, tossed them, and headed down the hall in the direction they'd taken Gideon, leaving me alone in the small triage room. The agony from Gideon's brand was gone, more or less, my buzz now the strongest biting sting between them, and I was exhausted.

I laid back on the gurney and closed my eyes, but without a pillow, it wasn't particularly comfortable, and all the bruises and strains from the last few hours throbbed even more. All I really wanted was to sleep— well, have a shower since I was once again covered in someone else's blood, and then sleep, but I had no idea where Kol had taken my clothes and had no idea who to ask to find out.

The whirr of air through the vents and the hum of equipment plugged in and ready for use wrapped around me, lulling me, but I still just couldn't get comfortable.

With a sigh, I climbed off the gurney and settled on the overstuffed leather couch in the waiting area. At least there I could get some support for my neck. A small part of me felt guilty for getting blood on the couch, but the rest of me was too tired to care.

The buzz gnawed at me, and even with my eyes closed it felt like the room was spinning. I tried to concentrate on just breathing. My face— hell, my whole head throbbed, radiating from the slice in my cheek, that, now that I thought about it, had been a near-miss with a bullet, thanks to Victoria yanking me out of the way.

Because once again the brand had locked me in place.

How the hell was I going to convince Gideon to be more careful? I was a liability on the team if I was out of commission every time Gideon was.

But the idea of benching myself made me want to scream in frustration. That, and the chief would be furious if I wasn't seen in the field working with the team, and he'd fire me. And damn it, I liked my job. I was a good cop. Another day, another time, and it would have been a different car answering that domestic and running into that vampire nest. It was just my shitty luck that it had been me.

But was it shitty luck? As much as I wanted to have a fully human life and live exclusively in the human world, I wasn't just human. My essence, while perceived as human by supers, couldn't possibly be wholly human and maybe supers were unconsciously drawn to that—

Or I was unconsciously drawn to them.

I'd thought I hadn't allowed myself to completely live in the human world because of the fear of being discovered, but maybe a part of that was because I didn't belong in their world.

Of course, I didn't belong in the supernatural world, either. I was still half human, and I was a nephilim with almost no magic, and certainly not any useful magic.

The sliding door to the hall shushed open.

"You're still here?" Jacob asked.

I peeled my eyes open. They were gritty and sore from my contacts enspelled to hide the glow in my eyes, but I managed to focus my blurry vision on him as he knelt beside me. He'd changed his clothes, and the gashes in his cheek were gone, not even a hint of a scar, but there was still a strain around his eyes.

"Is the brand keeping you here?"

"No." I struggled to sit up, and he captured my arm and helped me. "I didn't know where else to go."

"I'm sure you've been assigned a room."

"So am I. Kol took my bag somewhere, but we left for Rouge so fast I wasn't told a room number or given a key."

He pulled out his phone and sent a quick text. "If they're in the middle of a hunt, he might not get back to me right away." He sat on the couch beside me, his weight lowering his side of the cushion and sliding me against his side.

I leaned into him, unable to help myself and too tired to fight it.

"Do he and Marcus know about Gideon?" My pulse tripped, speeding up. "Do they know about that sniper vampire? It looked like he was in charge of those ferals. If he isn't the one making them, then he's in league with whoever it is."

"I'm pretty sure the ferals are Logan's." His gaze slid to my gauze-covered cheek, his vampiric intensity crackling in his eyes for a second, then he pulled his attention back to his phone. "They've been warned, but Gideon will want as much information about the situation as possible when he's back on the job."

"In four hours," I said.

"Just under three now."

Jeez. I'd slept for an hour and I still felt like crap. "So what *is* the situation?"

He glanced back at me, his gaze returning to my gauze-covered cheek before jerking away again. He shoved off of the couch, strode back into the triage area, and grabbed a package of gauze and a roll of tape. "Why don't you clean up in my room? I'm sure by the time you're done, Kol will have gotten back to me."

"Sure." I stood, my muscles aching with the movement, my body still heavy with exhaustion and the room still ever-so-slightly spinning. "You know I'm still going to find out who this Logan guy is."

"I wasn't trying to avoid the conversation." He watched me shuffle toward the sliding door, determined to keep my balance. "Let me carry you."

The part of me he'd claimed thrilled at the suggestion. "I'm just stiff."

"And it hurts just looking at you." He shoved the gauze and tape into his pockets and picked me up.

"At some point I'm going to have to stand on my own two feet." But I leaned into him, savoring the feel of his bulky muscles pressed against me. A hint of heat radiated from his body, but not as much as I would have expected if he'd just fed.

"Given how you looked when we met you at the ferals' nest and again after Logan's attack, I'm surprised you're conscious." He strode into the hall and headed toward the elevator. "Almost all of that was the mating brand, wasn't it?"

"I wish Gideon would stop getting shot."

He chuckled, the sound a low rumble that sent my

cells vibrating in resonance with his essence and making the claim surge warm within me. "I'm pretty sure he'd like to stop getting shot, too." His expression turned grim. "I haven't seen him have such a rough night since the war. I also haven't seen him as brash since then. He's usually got a tighter control of his emotions."

"The love of his life is dead and he's permanently stuck with me. I doubt that's what he imagined for himself." Add in that his emotions had already been strained because the archnephilim had been murdering his squad members who'd survived the war with him, and that would be enough to break anyone's control. Even an angel's.

"It's not being stuck with you that makes the situation hard."

"It's because I'm not Zella." I fully understood that. I didn't want my soul forever bound to someone I didn't know or love.

"In part." Jacob reached the elevator and hit the call button with his elbow. "But you and Marcus are also a thing. He respects that."

Just thinking about Marcus made me want to scream in frustration, and given how cold Gideon had been toward me, I didn't believe for one second it was all about respecting whatever I had with Marcus. That, and no matter how much I ached for Marcus, he was determined to push me away. Which I had originally thought during the mess with the archnephilim was for the best, and now... not so much.

The elevator door slid open and Jacob carried me inside.

"Marcus and I aren't anything," I said.

"He's worried about you."

The door slid closed, reminding me of the last time I'd been in this elevator with Marcus and sending a shiver of desire sliding through me.

Jacob's grip on me tightened. "We all are."

"I'm determined not to be a liability on the team." Or to at least minimize my powerlessness against supers as much as possible.

"You're hardly a liability," he said, his rich voice sliding another sensual shiver through me. "You took down that archnephilim almost entirely by yourself."

"So, hey." I forced a laugh, determined to not acknowledge my growing desire for Jacob. "What's to worry about, then?"

Jacob's gaze locked with mine filled with—? Hunger? No, need? Longing? Desire? The emotions flitted across his expression, stealing my breath. His pupils dilated, and the temperature in the elevator shot up. It was desire in his eyes, one matching the desire sliding slow and sensual within me.

CHAPTER 10

I DIPPED MY GAZE TO HIS LIPS, WONDERING WHAT THEY'D feel like against mine. I already knew the bone-melting bliss of his bite and couldn't help but think back on Victoria's words. How would it feel to ride that bliss while he pushed inside me?

But I didn't know if I wanted to sleep with him because he was damn hot and because I felt safe in his arms, or because of his claim.

Except I couldn't feel the claim in my chest at all. Not even a hint of a twist. There was just the unfulfilled desire I'd been aching with since I'd left Operations a week and a half ago.

The elevator door slid open, and Jacob wrenched his gaze away from me.

He cleared his throat and strode down the fifth floor hall, lined with dark wood doors each with a card reader lock. "You're right. There's nothing to worry about."

But the raised temperature didn't decrease.

We passed the room I'd had last time, turned right at

the end of the hall, and stopped at the first door. This one didn't have a card reader but a fingerprint pad. Jacob unlocked the door with his thumb and opened it without jostling me.

Inside was a small apartment with a kitchenette smaller than the one in my apartment—and mine was small. It sat along the left side of a living room area that had a huge dark brown couch, a floor-to-ceiling bookcase packed with paperbacks, and a mahogany desk in the back corner by the large bay window. The room was done in creams and yellows, with hints of oranges and reds, reminding me of a warm summer day with the sun high in the sky. Midday, something he wouldn't have seen for a long time until the JP had given him the enspelled silver bracelet that protected him from the sun.

He headed through the only other door in the apartment and stepped into a bedroom the complete opposite in coloring, in varying shades of gray. A California king bed with a dark gray comforter and black sheets took up most of the space, which didn't surprise me given how big he was, but the large clear-front gun case beside it, displaying a variety of antique pistols and rifles, did. A leather hat with a wide brim, similar to the one Logan wore, hung on the corner, and I couldn't shake the feeling that their connection was more than just being Victoria's offspring.

The bathroom, just off the bedroom, was similar to the one that had been in my assigned room, with creams, grays, and blue with chrome fixtures. It was probably the standard design for all the rooms. The only difference for

Jacob's was instead of a tub-shower combo, he had a large standup shower.

He set me on my feet, leaning me against the glass shower wall, and shifted back, his arms crossed against his broad chest. "You good if I leave and figure out where Kol put your bag, or do you need me to stay?"

The claim returned with a vengeance, twisting in my chest. *Stay. Don't leave me. Tell me what to do. Let me please you.* Damn, for a second there I'd thought it was finally easing up.

Jacob frowned. "Essie?"

"Can you please tell me to clean up," I forced out.

"Do you think you'll pass out?"

I opened my mouth to say no but "I'm not sure" came out instead.

Why the hell had I said that? I was fine walking in triage—

Except I hadn't been fine. I was sore and exhausted and dizzy. I was still God damned dizzy.

He pursed his lips and frowned, his gaze boring into mine for an agonizing second as if he could see into my soul, then gave a tight nod, coming to a decision.

"Okay." He shrugged out of his duster and pulled off his T-shirt, exposing a muscular chest with a fine dusting of pale hair that trailed down his washboard abs and into his pants.

My pulse stalled and the desire I'd felt in the elevator flared hot and entwined with his claim.

He pulled off his boots and socks, started the shower, and turned back to me. The temperature in the bathroom increased and turned humid—too soon to be from the heat of the shower.

The need to touch him and be touched by him was overwhelming. I reached out and pressed a hand above his no-longer beating heart. His breath came up short, and the muscles in his jaw clenched.

This was a bad idea. I could shower myself. It would be fine.

I straightened to prove to him I was fine—no matter what the claim had made me say—and the bathroom twisted and darkened.

He grabbed me, wrapping an arm around my waist, and pulled me close to him, steadying me. "I got you."

God, he did, and I wanted more.

I needed a distraction.

"Tell me about Logan." Maybe talking about the reason I was dizzy and exhausted from Gideon's brand would cool me off.

"Good idea." He leaned me back against the wall, grabbed the bottom of my T-shirt, and tugged it off over my head.

I locked my gaze on the wall. If I looked in his eyes—or watched us in the mirror over the sink—I'd give in and kiss him, and that would just make a complicated situation more complicated. It was the claim. The claim. It had to be. Maybe if I said it enough times I'd completely believe it.

"Logan Dunn and I are blood brothers."

He knelt, his warm breath feathering down my chest and stomach, and helped me take off my runners and socks. Then he reached for the button on my jeans and my breath hitched.

I grabbed his hands before be could undo my pants, my gaze leaping back to his dark eyes.

"I know the affects of the claim," he said, his voice a low rumble.

And in that moment, with that look in his eye and the heat of his emotions, I wondered if the affects went both ways.

"But I'm not going to let you pass out in the shower." He pushed my hands away, undid my pants, and pulled them down. "We can keep this professional."

The claim tightened at his command, fighting my desire. He'd said to keep this professional. That would please him. Except my yearning still heated my skin.

I stepped out of my pants and turned my back to him to take off my bra and underwear. Perhaps if I wasn't looking at him, I could embrace the claim's command to keep it professional, except I could still sense his massive body close behind me.

"You and Logan were blood brothers?" I reached to unhook my bra, but his hands got there first, releasing the clasp and sliding the straps from my shoulders. "Is that because Victoria sired both of you?"

"We were blood brothers before we were turned." He tugged down my underwear and I resisted the urge to press my naked body against him. "His family took in my unwed mother when she had me and her father, my grandfather, disowned her."

"Because she had you out of wedlock?" I forced

myself to move to the shower's entrance, still clinging to the shower wall to keep standing.

Jacob stayed close, his hands on my upper arms to steady me and catch me if I fell.

Darkness shuddered at the edge of my vision, but I managed to slide inside, shuffle to the other side, and lean against the white tiled wall.

"No, because she had a Cheyenne's baby out of wedlock." He leaned closer and reached past me to grab a shower pouf from the hook at the bottom of his shower caddy. His bare chest pressed against my shoulder, and I struggled to stand perfectly still. He filled the pouf with soap, handed it to me, and moved back to steady me, only his hands in contact with my skin, barely skimming my hips, making the claim thrill that we were managing to keep it professional. And yet my body continued to ache with desire for him.

"Logan and I did everything together." He blew out a heavy breath that rushed across the back of my neck.

I bit back a moan and concentrated on washing myself as fast as my dizzy head would let me.

"We were getting into trouble from the very beginning, and when his family was killed, we swore a blood oath to avenge them." His grip on my hips tightened. "That was the night we learned he was a witch. Magic had burst around us the moment we'd cut our palms and pressed them together. Scared the shit out of both of us."

"So he didn't know he was a witch?" I shuffled into the spray of water to rinse myself off. Jacob shuffled with me, drawing close enough that my back brushed his chest. I bit back another moan. Even with the compulsion from the claim to keep it professional, I wasn't going to be able to last, because in truth, my aching desire was a need to be held, to lose myself in the physical and release all my churning worries just for a moment. I wanted Marcus but he was pushing me away. I pushed away from Gideon, because I was afraid of what would happen with his mating brand if I actually got to know him.

And if I was smart, I'd keep my distance from Jacob, but even as I thought that, I leaned back, pressing my body against his. His hands slid across my skin, one wrapping across my belly, the other cupping my breast, and pulled me close. My head tipped back against his chest and this time I did release the moan. God, he felt so good. To hell if this was the claim making me desire him or not. I was going to shatter if I didn't release the pressure inside me. Right now I could live with having claim-induced sex with him.

"Essie," he murmured, his lips pressed to the back of my head.

"Kiss me."

"You don't mean that," he said, but his hands didn't move from my body.

The shower spray beat against my hypersensitive flesh, and I rubbed against him, savoring the feel of his hardened erection underneath his wet jeans rough against my skin. "Kiss me."

He groaned and his hand on my breast tightened as the one on my waist trailed lower. His fingers reached the crux between my hip and thigh, and his lips dipped to the sensitive spot just behind my ear.

I trembled with anticipation and tipped my head,

offering him better access. A groan rumbled low in his chest and his lips grazed against my neck. My pulse picked up. The last time he'd bitten me there, I hadn't known how good it would feel. I hadn't wanted to give him control of me and my body, and a part of me had fought it. Now he already had control. There was no point in fighting, only in losing myself to the sensations and forgetting about everything else.

A shudder swept through him and he released my breast, yanked the soaking wet gauze from my cheek, and slowly, firmly, raked his tongue along the wound.

Sensual heat shot straight to my core, and I gasped. I was already wet and yearning, trembling with need. There should have been pain, that should have stung, but there was only bliss, curling tighter in my womb. And all he'd done was lick me. God! I squirmed in his grasp, rubbing myself harder against his erection. He needed to take those jeans off, but his hand returned to my breast and his embrace controlled me. I couldn't turn around to kiss him or unbutton those pants.

He raked his tongue across the wound again, and his fingers on my thigh brushed through my curls and skimmed my folds. The heat jerked taut within me.

"Oh, yes," I gasped. My thoughts whirled. *Take me, control me, satisfy me.* And I wasn't sure if it was the claim or not. All my aching heart and soul was gone, burned away in a blaze of pleasure.

He pressed his lips to my wound and sucked as he slid a finger inside me. My climax shuddered already on the edge from his magic. He added a second finger, filling me, and rubbed circles on my clit.

I moaned, my breath fast, and he took another pull on my cheek. His thumb pressed hard against my clit, the circles faster, matching the pace with my breath and pulse, and his fingers worked inside me building the heat into a tightly formed supernova that exploded with a cry of pleasure.

He held me tight as I rode the wave, his lips still pressed to my cheek, but instead of sucking, this time a wave of warmth seeped across it, his miniscule bit of healing magic closing my wound just enough to stop the bleeding.

"Thank you," he whispered against my cheek, then lifted me and carried me out of the shower. He set me on my feet long enough to wrap me in a towel, and carried me to his bed. Now I couldn't tell if I was dizzy because of Gideon getting shot or Jacob bringing me to climax.

He pulled back the covers and laid me on the bed. "I'll go find your clothes."

I grabbed his hand before he could leave and tugged him back to me. "I meant what I started in the shower."

His pupils dilated, his desire raw in his eyes, and the temperature, still hot and humid with desire, spiked to sweltering for a heartbeat. "You won't know that until the power of my claim has eased enough for you to say no to it."

He tugged his hand free, grabbed a dry pair of pants and a T-shirt from his closet, and left.

I groaned. He was right, and yet I didn't want to fight my attraction to him. Just like I didn't want to fight my attraction to Marcus.

Jeez, and they weren't the one I was supposedly destined to be with.

I tugged the sheet and comforter over me and curled up in Jacob's bed. It smelled like him, masculine, rich with a hint of freshness that I now knew came from his body wash. My skin still tingled from my climax, and I closed my eyes and embraced the sensation. There was nothing I could do until Jacob found me a clean set of clothes, and for just a few minutes, I didn't want to worry about Marcus and Gideon. So I focused on Jacob's arms around me, his wet body pressed against mine, and his hands on me.

I imagined him finishing what we'd started in the shower, his power sliding through me as he drove into me, bringing me to climax again, my name on his lips as he came.

"Essie." A sensual rumble of his deep, resonant voice that fed his claim, entwining his essence more than it already was with mine, and attuning me perfectly to him.

"Essie."

God, I felt so good.

A weight settled on my shoulder, and another, bigger one on the bed.

"Essie," Jacob said, his voice clearer, no longer soft and dreamy.

I opened my eyes and met Jacob's gaze. For a second I'd thought he'd returned to take me up on my offer. There was a tenderness in his expression I hadn't seen before, one that warmed me to my core. But he drew his hand away from me and shifted back. He still sat on the edge of the bed beside me, but the distance between us was clear.

Which, as much as I was disappointed, was probably for the best. I'd had, if not a full reprieve, at least some reprieve from the emotional mess with Marcus and Gideon. But I wouldn't be able to ignore it. As much as I might want to at the moment.

"How do you feel?" he asked.

Still a little boneless and definitely satisfied. But that wasn't what he was really asking about.

I stretched, testing my aching muscles, which weren't nearly as achy as they had been before or should be after lying down for—?

I had no idea how long I'd been out. If Jacob had just contacted Kol and found my bag, it should have only been a few minutes, but my eyes felt gritty, as if I'd slept with my contacts in for at least an hour.

"How long have I been asleep?"

"Almost three hours." He shifted back even farther. "Try sitting up. See if you're still dizzy."

"You let me sleep for three hours." I held the comforter to my chest and eased into a sitting position. The room remained perfectly steady. There wasn't even a hint of exhaustion from the brand, only the gentle hum that I recognized as Gideon's magic felt between the skin-crawling bites from my buzz.

"Recovering was the best thing you could do. You should get dressed." He stood, headed to the doorway to the living room, and leaned against the frame with his back to me. "Kol and Marcus will be back in about ten minutes and Amiah is about to wake Gideon."

My duffle bag sat beside the bed with a keycard and my holstered Glock on top.

"You found out which room I was assigned?"

"Same as before."

"Well, that'll make it easy to remember the next time Gideon gets shot and I'm too exhausted to think straight." I set the Glock and the keycard on the nightstand beside a paperback with a planet and a spaceship on the cover, and opened my bag.

"If that happens, you don't honestly think anyone on the team is going to let you stagger up to your room by yourself?"

Probably not. It depended on what condition the rest of the team was in and if Marcus was still doing everything in his power to push me away.

Except I knew that wasn't true. If it really came down to keeping me safe, Marcus would step up in a heartbeat.

"So what's the plan?' I dressed in the only other set of clothes I had at Operations, and did a quick search for my shoes. They sat beside the bathroom door without a drop of blood on them. "You cleaned my shoes, too?" And I hadn't noticed him return to the room to grab my stuff from the bathroom.

"And sent your other clothes down to be laundered." He jerked his chin toward my shoes without fully looking into the room. "Come on. Let's get you to Amiah to take care of that gash on your cheek."

"Bathroom first, then I'm all yours." *Fully and completely*. I pushed back the claim's urgings, palmed two nicotine patches from my bag, and hurried into the bathroom.

I raked my fingers through my hair, trying to get some of the tangles out, and retied my ponytail, all the while trying to not think about being in the shower with Jacob. The gash in my cheek had stopped bleeding—thanks to Jacob's magic—but it still throbbed and stung.

At least I didn't look so exhausted. It had only been three hours, but it felt like eight. I was back to myself and ready to face my new terrifying job.

I could do this.

I'd squared off with the archnephilim and won. I just needed to be smart about how I worked and dealt with supers.

I peeled off the old patches—and I wasn't going to ask Jacob what he'd thought of them—and slapped on two new ones, then shoved my feet into my runners, pocketed the keycard, and clipped my holster to the waistband of my jeans.

We took the elevator back down to the main floor and strode into triage to find Amiah and Marcus in a tight embrace, the temperature in the room sweltering. Desire. But I didn't know whose. Amiah's cheek was against his shoulder, her hand over his heart, and her eyes closed. His arms were wrapped protectively around her and his lips pressed against the top of her head.

CHAPTER 11

Marcus's gaze lifted and captured me, stealing my breath and making my chest ache for him. For not having him. For everything between us. His eyes were filled with the ferociousness I recognized as his wolf, but I didn't know what it wanted. Hell, I never knew what it or Marcus wanted. Maybe he'd been pushing me away because of what he had with Amiah. Maybe I was imagining the heat between us—

No, the attraction sizzling within me had been there from the moment I'd seen him, and I could see it simmering in his eyes right now. But that didn't mean anything. Just because you were attracted to someone didn't mean you had or even should have a relationship with him.

Except my soul hurt just thinking about him moving on. He'd said in the elevator that I was his. That he didn't care if I had Gideon's mating brand or not.

And then he'd given me up.

Because that was what I'd wanted.

If I cared for him, I'd give him up. But I didn't want to. I'd been dreaming of him for years, of the desire burning between us and his ferocious passion, and I didn't want him to focus that passion on anyone else. He was supposed to be mine.

"Is Gideon up?" Jacob asked.

"He's waiting in the cafeteria," Amiah said, not moving from Marcus's embrace. She sounded exhausted, and if I concentrated past my jealousy, she looked exhausted, too. Sure, she might have gotten as much sleep as I had this morning, but then she'd had to get up and heal Gideon again. I might not like her in Marcus's arms—which was really none of my business since Marcus and I weren't anything, honestly, really—but I did feel bad about her barely being able to recover before needing to use her magic again. "I'm just waiting on Officer Shaw."

"My cheek has stopped bleeding. I'll be fine." That, and I didn't want her to ruin the effects of my new nicotine patches.

"It doesn't look fine," Marcus growled.

"I didn't say it *looked* fine, only that I'll *be* fine."

"It has to still hurt, Essie," Jacob said.

"Jeez. Guys. On the scale of fine to dying, I'm fine."

Amiah pushed out of Marcus's embrace and sat on the arm of the couch. "Just come here."

Marcus glared at me as if he was daring me to refuse medical attention so he could let his wolf loose.

"Fine." I stepped up to Amiah. "I don't care if I have a scar."

"Good, because given how Gideon seems to be a

bullet magnet at the moment, I'm doing the bare minimum with everyone else."

"Works for me."

She pressed a finger to my cheek and a flash of heat exploded across my face. I gasped and staggered back, bumping into Jacob's broad chest. He grabbed my upper arms and steadied me, then quickly stepped back as if he didn't want to stay too close to me.

"Let's go," Marcus growled, and he headed deeper into the hospital section of Operations, taking the smaller halls to get to the cafeteria.

Given that it was just after ten in the morning, the cafeteria was empty with the exception of two women—one with the glowing eyes of an angel, the other looking human—who sat at a table in the sunroom side. Gideon and Kol already sat at the six-person table, with three mugs in the center, along with a carafe that smelled like it contained coffee, and half a dozen tinfoil wrapped some-things that smelled like eggs and bacon.

Gideon was eating one of the wrapped somethings—best guess a breakfast burrito—looking as if he hadn't almost died last night. His gaze jumped to me.

Just like Marcus, he could stall my pulse with a glance. His summer-sky eyes were icy. Any warmth I'd glimpsed last night was gone. And just like Marcus, that made my chest ache with a yearning that could only be compelled by his mating brand etched onto my arm, because we didn't really know each other.

His attention slid to my cheek and his eyes narrowed. "You should get Amiah to heal that."

I brushed my fingers over the gash. I hadn't bothered

to look in a mirror to see how much she'd healed it. I was just grateful her magic hadn't manifested as searing lightning and that my nicotine patches still kept my buzz manageable—and hey, now that I stood only a few feet from Gideon, my buzz had quieted even more. Besides, my cheek no longer throbbed and didn't sting when I touched it, so I considered it a win all around.

"It's fine."

"It's not fine," Gideon said.

"I've already had this argument with Marcus. I'm not having it with you." I sat in the chair beside Kol and across from Gideon, and grabbed one of the breakfast burritos from the pile at the center of the table.

Marcus and Jacob sat on either side of Gideon. Now all three of them could glare at me. Wonderful.

Kol shifted in his seat, his attention sliding from Jacob to me, his eyebrows raised.

And just great. The incubus had figured out something had happened between me and Jacob. I wondered if he'd felt the sexual energy of my climax when it happened, or if he was just now noticing the residual energy that probably still clung to me.

He jerked his gaze away from me and took a long sip of his coffee.

"Jacob, why don't you tell us what's going on?" Gideon said.

My pulse stuttered, my mind jumping to what we'd done in the shower, and Kol choked on his coffee.

Gideon frowned at him. "I'm assuming that vampire at Victoria's is connected to the feral vampires."

"Logan Dunn." Jacob poured himself a cup of coffee,

didn't add anything to it, and hunched forward over the table, the cup captured between his palms.

He still had the tightness around his eyes that I'd seen last night, and while I was sure he'd eaten—now that I was paying attention and not still fantasizing about how he'd made me feel—he still looked worn down.

"He's making them," Jacob said. "He was a witch before he was turned and afterwards he made a deal with a hellfire prince."

Kol's eyes widened and the room's temperature dropped. "Oh, shit."

"We'd know if one of the princes was free," Marcus said, reaching for a breakfast burrito and digging in.

"Ibizual isn't free. That was Logan's deal. A taste of the power promised by the prince for his freedom and then the rest of the promised power upon release." Jacob ran his thumb over the rim of the mug. "Logan is supposed to be dead."

"That's what Victoria said," Gideon said.

And was probably why Jacob hadn't mentioned him when we were last sitting around this table trying to figure out who was making the ferals.

"If the seal imprisoning Ibizual is weak enough," Kol said, "he would have the power to bring a vampire back."

Jacob raised his gaze to Kol, and a hint of misty grief curled around me. "Even if that vampire was burned to ash?"

Or the mist could be guilt. Probably a combination of the two. Jacob had said he and Logan were brothers, they'd grown up together, and in the end Jacob had killed him.

"If Ibizual had claimed that vampire's essence, then yeah, he could." Kol's hands trembled, and he gripped his mug tighter. "There's a reason demons imprisoned the princes two millennia ago, and why Lucifer didn't try to free them to escape the Realm of Celestial Darkness."

"So we have to assume Ibizual is attempting another escape," I said between bites of burrito, hoping Jacob's mist would ease up before it gathered on my cheeks and drew suspicion. "I can't imagine any other reason to bring Logan back."

"I agree," Gideon said. "Logan said his hundred and fifty years were up. Any idea what that meant?"

"I think it has something to do with the key to break the seal on Ibizual's cage. It's also why he came after me. We're magically connected. I felt where the key manifested the last time. He must believe I'll feel it this time, too."

"Does this magical connection allow you to find him?" Marcus asked.

"No. But he can't use it to find me, either." Jacob glanced at Gideon. "From my guess on the decay of the bodies we found in the nest, he's been back for about a month and a half. The new moon is tomorrow, which means the key will manifest in this realm tonight."

"Of course it will," Marcus said, finishing his burrito and taking another one. "Because a bunch of ferals and a witch-vampire-sniper just isn't enough."

Gideon shot him a dark look. "Is he as good a marksman as you, Jacob?"

"We were close in skill, but I was always better," Jacob said.

"That doesn't make me feel better," Marcus said around a mouthful of food. "You're the best marksman I've ever seen. Even if he has half of your skill, he'd still be damned good."

"Okay." Kol took a steadying breath, but his fear still dropped the temperature, mingling with Jacob's mist. At least it wasn't absolute terror, and I didn't have to hide the frost on my hands, although much more and the mist might start to freeze in the air around me. "You beat him before. You can beat him now."

"Except I didn't really beat him. He's still alive." Jacob pursed his lips, the tightness around his eyes deepening and his mist thickening. "We fought over the key until sun up. I got in a lucky strike and managed to get to cover before I burned up. Then I watched the sunrise turn him to ash and stared at that ash until the sun set."

I wanted to reach across the table and grab his hand, let him know it would be okay, and it wasn't just the claim tugging at my heart. But the horror of the situation was that he'd killed a man who'd been his brother and now he was going to have to do it again. I couldn't even begin to imagine what that felt like. That, and he hadn't mentioned that specific detail to the guys, and I didn't know if he wanted them to know.

His gaze lifted to mine as if he could hear my thoughts. "Am I going to have to kill him every hundred and fifty years?"

"We need a witch who knows about the cages," Gideon said. "I'll talk to—" Despair flashed across his expression, exploding in a mist so thick I couldn't see across the table before it vanished, and his expression hardened into an icy mask. He'd been about to say Zella. She'd been an angel able to cast spells and, from the fact that he'd instantly thought of her, must have had knowledge, or a way to find information, about the cages imprisoning the hellfire princes.

And now I wanted to hold *his* hand. But I was a reminder that no matter how much he'd loved Zella, they were never meant to be.

"Bane might know," Marcus said, his tone even, as if he hadn't noticed Gideon's reaction, even though I'm sure everyone at the table had.

Jacob shook his head. "We've already asked him to get us that coalescence snare at the last minute to deal with the archnephilim. He'll raise his price if we come to him again so soon with another rush job."

"Then he raises his price," Gideon said.

Jacob opened his mouth to argue, but Gideon stopped him with a sharp look before he could speak.

"Even if you weren't connected to this, we'd still need the information. We need to know everything we can about Ibizual and his cage, and most important, we need to find out if we can prevent Ibizual from bringing Logan back again. There were over two dozen bodies in that nest and at least a dozen ferals at Rouge. That's already thirty-six people he's murdered at a minimum. We need to permanently stop him before he kills more people."

"And Marcus and I think we've found another nest," Kol said.

Gideon gave him a questioning look.

"The place reeks of human decomp," Marcus said.

"We didn't go inside to confirm, just in case there

were a lot of ferals, but if it's anything like the first one, there's another pile of bodies in there," Kol said.

Gideon turned his hard gaze to Marcus. "Call Bane and get him on this. And I don't care what the price is. The JP will understand the expense."

Marcus pulled out his phone and tapped out a text.

"We also need to clean out that nest," Jacob said.

"Do you think Logan will be there?" Kol asked.

Jacob shook his head. "I doubt it, but he's clearly making himself an army and it'd be better to deal with them now when they're at their weakest than tonight when they're stronger and the key is manifesting."

"Okay." Gideon folded his burrito wrapper into a perfect square and smoothed out the foil. "We clear out that nest now. With luck, there'll be a clue there pointing to Logan's location. Regardless, tonight we'll secure that key then wait it out until the new moon has passed."

"Any idea what kind of magic the hellfire prince gave Logan?" Kol asked. His fear had eased up a bit, but the coffee in his mug still quivered, revealing the tremor in his hands.

"He has power over the dead," Jacob said.

"Of course," Gideon said. "That's how he resisted Victoria's power over him."

"Does that power over the dead include you?" I asked.

Jacob met my gaze, and I knew instantly the answer was yes.

Gideon stiffened and Marcus swore.

The claim started screaming, but I shoved its voice to the back of my head. "Is there a way to protect yourself?"

"I don't know. It happened so fast last time, I didn't

have to figure much out," he said. "And I'd thought I wouldn't need to think about it ever again."

"Get Bane on that, too." Gideon stood. "These ferals are hard to kill and blades are our best bet. Marcus, take Officer Shaw down to the armory and get her situated."

"Essie isn't coming," Marcus growled.

And after the fight at Rouge, a part of me wholeheartedly agreed with him. But another part knew they'd need all the help they could get.

The muscles in Gideon's jaw tightened. "Our orders say differently."

"Fuck our orders." Marcus stood and met Gideon eye to eye—or almost eye to eye since Gideon was a few inches taller than Marcus. "She's not running in there with a fucking sword decapitating ferals."

Put that way... Yeah, that seemed like a terrible idea. "Can any of the ferals be saved?" Maybe there was a way to prevent a bloodbath.

"No." Jacob downed his coffee and squared his shoulders. The grief and guilt he'd felt earlier had been shoved down and he was back to business. "The magic that makes a feral is incomplete. Their minds are gone, and they're driven only by the command of their sire and their base feral hunger."

"Like Michael's nephilim," Kol said.

"Michael's nephilim were worse." The light in Gideon's eyes darkened. "We say they were animals because of their merciless brutality, but when Michael didn't have full control of them, they could think for themselves. And when they could, they still slaughtered humankind. That's what truly made them monsters."

The room's temperature rose, Gideon's anger burning through Kol's fear, and my fear tightened within me.

This was why I had to resist the pull of the mating brand. I couldn't let myself forget that. It was bad enough I had to work with the team to keep my job. Letting myself get closer to Gideon would just increase the risk of him discovering the truth. At least my only magic was my screwed-up empathy and now my glowing eyes. The eyes I could say glowed from blasting all that divine light into my body, and because of the mating brand, it hadn't faded. As for the empathy... I might be able to pass that off as having a bit of supernatural DNA somewhere in my family tree.

It was a risk, but it let me keep my job, and it let me stay with the guys—

Holy shit. As terrifying as being a JP agent was, I didn't want to leave. I didn't want to go back to my old life. I couldn't go back. And while I could argue that was because I was magically connected to Gideon and Jacob, that didn't address my desire to face my fears and explore what could be between Marcus and me, or the friendship I wanted with Kol.

That, and a part of me, a small voice in the back of my mind, wondered if Gideon would really despise me if he knew the truth. Fate claimed we were soul mates. Was that enough for him to see me differently?

"—kindest option for a feral is a quick death," Jacob said, and I jerked my attention back to him.

He frowned at me. All the guys were staring at me. Did they know what I was thinking? Was my realization clear on my face?

A blush of embarrassment crept up my neck even though I had nothing to be embarrassed about. "If they can't be saved, load me up with an assault rifle with enspelled ammo and I'll cover your backs."

"Only a kill shot will take them out," Gideon said.

"A non-kill shot will make them stumble." I met his gaze. "I believe I saved your ass at least once in Rouge with that technique." *I also saved your ass by feeding my strength into your body when you were shot.*

"Marcus, take Officer Shaw to the armory and set her up with an M4 and a vest."

"One point for the human," Kol said under his breath.

Gideon shot him a fierce glare, then rolled his eyes and shook his head. "Be in the garage in ten minutes, and I better see everyone with a sword and a vest." His attention jerked to Marcus. "Even you. Your wolf isn't going to be an asset in this."

Gideon grabbed his empty burrito wrapper and coffee mug, set them on the stainless steel counter by the kitchen door, and marched out of the cafeteria.

Jacob shot me a worried glance and followed him as Marcus rolled his burrito wrappers into one ball and tossed it into the garbage can twenty feet away.

"Let's get this over with," he growled, standing and heading to the stairs.

I stood to follow, but Kol grabbed my wrist, his hand hot against my skin from his heightened demonic body temperature and the air still a bit chilly from his fear.

"What the hell are you doing?" he asked.

"My job?" Jeez, I hadn't thought Kol would fight me on this like Marcus.

"Jacob isn't your job." A hint of hellfire flickered in his gaze and a trickle of sensual heat slid up my arm before his eyes narrowed and it vanished with a flash. "You might have washed away the scent so Marcus can't smell it, but I can still feel the residual energy radiating off the both of you. If I'd been here when you guys had—" His gaze jumped to Marcus, who was now at the top of the cafeteria steps. "Jeez, I could have been anywhere in the building and it probably would have brought me close to full."

"We didn't have sex," I said, keeping my voice low. It had been awfully darn close, but technically there had been no intercourse.

He raised his eyebrows, clearly not believing me. "The situation is complicated enough."

"No shit. And Jacob's part of that complication."

"He is now."

"He was before. You know what his bite feels like. I fed that into you when I was saving your life." That was when the archnephilim had nearly killed them and I'd been desperate to save them. I shuddered at the memory of that moment, along with the memory of being in the shower with Jacob.

Kol's breath hitched and the hellfire in his eyes flared. "Jesus."

"Stop making eyes at the incubus, Shaw, and get a move on," Marcus barked from the top of the cafeteria steps.

Kol's attention jerked to Marcus, but his volume didn't rise. "You have to stop. Marcus is going to lose his shit when he finds out."

"Well, I'm going to lose my shit if Jacob's claim doesn't ease up. If Jacob was any other kind of guy, I'm sure we would have finished what we'd started last night." Which was one of the reasons I was attracted to him and knew that wasn't because of the claim.

"I need this team," Kol said.

"For fuck's sake, Shaw," Marcus snarled.

"You have to work it out with Marcus."

And that was the truth. If I wanted to stay with the team, I'd be miserable if Marcus was constantly trying to push me away. Except how did I convince him I was there to stay, that I wanted to be a part of his world, when the brand on my arm said I belonged to Gideon?

CHAPTER 12

I HURRIED UP THE CAFETERIA STEPS TO MARCUS, AND HE jammed his thumb against the elevator call button, the air around him searing with his frustration.

"This is the stupidest thing you've ever done," he said.

"I'm pretty sure shooting an enormous blast of divine light into myself to kill an archnephilim was the stupidest."

"Yeah, and how many lives are you down to now, kitty?"

The elevator door slid open and we got in.

Marcus hit the button for the basement and desire unfurled low within me at the memory of what we'd done in there only a few weeks ago. Add that to his emotional heat, and I was instantly covered in sweat.

"You'd rather I be fired from the force?" I asked, determined to ignore my attraction to him.

"I'd rather you be alive."

"I could be killed just as easily walking the beat."

The door slid open, revealing the study area straight

ahead with a wide wooden table and a couch illuminated by two hanging fluorescent lights. Across from the couch stood a security door with a keypad lock, and through the safety glass window, I could see a long rack filled with different kinds of rifles.

"No, pretty sure chasing down supers is more dangerous than walking the beat." Marcus headed to the security door and pressed his thumb to the fingerprint pad.

"It would be less dangerous if I knew you had my back."

"If I have your back, then I have all of you." He opened the door and stormed inside. "And I already know I can't have all of you."

"Marcus I—"

He wrenched around, his gaze jumping to Gideon's brand on my arm, his wolf darkening his green eyes, making him look dangerous.

I crossed my arms and glared back at him. "You said you didn't care about the brand."

"And you said you wanted your life back."

"What if I was wrong?"

Horror flashed through his expression and the room's temperature plummeted. "Don't ever say that. You don't belong here. You deserve a normal life, a normal husband, normal kids, normal friends, normal God damn everything."

I pressed my hand to the brand. "This says differently."

"You already know what I think about that." He jerked away from me, opened a wide locker beside him, and grabbed a bulletproof vest with the letters JP printed on the front and back in blocky white letters. He tossed it on the long narrow standup table that stood in the middle of the room, headed to the end of the rack with the rifles, and pulled down the M4 carbine.

And while I knew he didn't care that I wore Gideon's brand, he also knew, whether I wanted to be or not, I was always going to be bound to Gideon. "I—"

"We're not having this discussion," he said, setting the M4 on the table and heading to the shelves filled with boxes of ammunition and extra magazines. "Focus on not getting us killed."

"I'm not the one who's been shot twice in the last twelve hours." I drew my Glock and ejected the magazine.

Marcus set extra magazines, a box of enspelled 9mm, and a box of 5.56mm on the table. He grabbed one of the magazines for the M4 and started loading it. His frustration simmered around me as he filled the first magazine then started on the second one.

I reloaded my magazine, my fingers slippery with sweat, slid it back into my Glock, and reholstered my weapon.

The heat in the cramped armory kept growing. Marcus and I needed to clear the air, but I knew if I opened my mouth, he'd stare me down, so I started on filling the second 9mm magazine, my lips pressed firmly together.

I tried to concentrate on something else. Anything else. I didn't have deep enough pockets in my jeans for the extra magazines and was going to need to run up to my room to grab my duty belt. At least I wouldn't also have to bring along my Taser or flashlight. All the guys knew the effects of Jacob's claim, and if we ended up in a location with low light, I wouldn't need to hide my enhanced night vision. And if we ended up someplace with no light, the light on the M4's scope would do.

But Marcus's heat made staying focused on the task at hand impossible.

He popped round after round into the magazine, the muscles in his jaw getting tighter with each passing second.

"If things go south," he said, his voice low, "you get the hell out of there."

I couldn't tell if this was him compromising or not.

"Promise me," he growled.

"I'll promise if you promise."

He set the magazine on the table and captured me with his gaze. "I'm smart enough to know when to leave."

"You leave because you're afraid."

His eyes narrowed, his expression clear that he knew I wasn't talking about leaving a fight but leaving me. "I leave for you because you're too stupid to know you're supposed to be afraid." He stormed past me and out the door. "Put the ammo boxes away before you leave," he growled over his shoulder and headed for the stairs instead of taking the elevator.

I bit my lip, stopping myself from yelling after him again and reminding myself that he was just trying to protect himself.

And I wasn't too stupid to know I should be afraid. I was afraid. But some things shouldn't be avoided even if they were terrifying. Fate was determined to keep me in this world. And foolish as it was, *I* was now determined to stay, too. I wasn't going to fight it any more.

When this situation was over, I was going to need more training. Whatever it took to not be a liability to the team.

I shrugged into the vest, put the ammunition boxes back, and with the M4 in hand, headed to my assigned room. It hadn't changed since I'd last been there—not that I'd expected it would. It had looked like a hotel room then and it still did now, decorated in blue-grays and creams, with a queen-sized bed, a panel TV on the wall, and a couch near the large window that took up most of the back wall. My duffle bag sat on the floor at the foot of the bed and the clothes I'd been wearing last night were clean and folded on top—including my bra and undies.

I grabbed my duty belt from my bag, took off everything but my holster and two pouches for my extra magazines, and headed down to the garage.

All the guys were waiting for me, even Marcus, who'd only left to go up to his room a minute before me. They all wore vests, even Gideon—thank God—and Marcus and Jacob wore sheathed swords at their hips. Gideon didn't need one since he could make one out of pure light, and Kol had a pair of long daggers in sheaths strapped to his back and hidden beneath his shirt. Jacob also had his pair of 92 FS Berettas holstered at his hips, but had left off his duster, making him look a little less like a Wild West gunslinger, but not by much.

Jacob handed me an earpiece, his fingers brushing mine, making the claim sing and Kol scowl. We piled into a JP SUV, Marcus driving, Gideon beside him, Jacob in the back, and Kol and I in the middle, and headed to the second nest.

The tension and whirl of emotions from the guys made the air thick and hot, and I scrambled out of the vehicle the moment Marcus parked in front of a squat brown-brick subway station entrance. Three of the four doors were boarded up, along with a wide window that belonged to the attached variety store. This had been the last stop for the red line before explosive magic from Michael's nephilim army had destroyed the tunnels halfway between there and downtown. And while it was beyond the borders of my precinct, it was still less than three miles from the abandoned school.

All of the buildings on the street, two-story store-fronts with a smattering of three- and four-story office buildings, were boarded up. Redevelopment hadn't reached this far from the downtown core and until the city's human population rebounded, it probably wouldn't.

Gideon got out of the SUV and strode past me to the door that wasn't boarded up. The glass had been broken and lay in chunks, half on the concrete outside and half on the gray tiles inside. He glanced into the darkness, the glow in his eyes billowing. "I can't smell anything."

"Trust me, there are a lot of dead things in there." Marcus joined him, his nose scrunched in disgust.

"I don't doubt you," Gideon said. "You take point with Kol and get us to that nest. Jacob, you and Essie have the rear."

Marcus drew his sword, dipped under the handrail,

and stepped inside, his boots crunching on the glass. Kol followed, drawing his matching daggers, then Gideon, then me with Jacob close behind.

Inside the air was cool and musty and clashed with the flickering heat of the guys' emotions. I couldn't smell the decomp Marcus had mentioned, but I also didn't have the senses of a wolf. To my right, the metal grating in front of the wide entrance to the variety store had been forced open wide enough for a large person to get through. The space had already been picked clean by scavengers, anything metal that could be melted down and reused—including shelves and racks—had been taken, and most of the ceiling panels had been pulled down and the wires ripped out.

I swept my gaze over the empty storefront, pausing at the open door at the back—likely leading to the stock room—then along the wall to the front beyond Gideon's arm and the wide stairs leading down. There wasn't anywhere else to go.

We crept down the stairs. Someone had cut off the metal handrail and many someones had covered the tiled walls with graffiti. The air grew cooler, but it did nothing to ease the emotional heat from the guys. I didn't know if it was better or worse that the heat wasn't steady. I wasn't boiling, but the fluctuations made it harder to ignore.

The stairs led down to a wide platform with sunken subway tracks on either side. A colorful abstract tile mosaic covered the walls and the arched ceiling in a drastic difference to the austere brown exterior.

I scanned left and right, searching for any hint of movement. There was almost no light down there—the only illumination came from the stairs behind us and somewhere far ahead down the right-hand line—and while my vision wasn't perfect, it was still pretty good.

Jacob shifted closer to me. "You should switch on your light."

Marcus swore. "That'll fuck up my night vision."

"All of our night vision, and I don't want to waste power to make a light," Gideon said. "Switch the scope on your M4 to thermal, and I'll order gear for agents without night vision when we get back."

"How about not ordering the gear and not bringing Essie into near-blackout feral vampire nests," Marcus said.

"Let it be," Gideon said, his voice more low and dangerous than I'd ever heard before. "Officer Shaw is staying. Those are our orders."

"I'll be fine." I thumbed the switch on my scope to thermal. "Thanks to Jacob's claim, I can see as well now in this almost-no-light as I could before at night with a streetlight and no flashlight."

Gideon's back stiffened. If I hadn't been close and right behind him, I might not have noticed. "The claim is that strong?"

The emotional heat around me flashed hotter. I glanced at Jacob, who frowned, but I didn't know if the frown meant he was worried about how strong his claim was or if my night vision was better than it was supposed to be—which might give away my partial angelic nature.

A thread of fear curled small and tight in my gut, and I vowed to ignore it. It was Jacob's claim, not another side effect of having the archnephilim trying to awaken any nephilim magic I didn't possess.

If asked, I'd chalk it up to an unexpected effect of the brand and blasting all that divine light into myself.

But a part of me feared that excuse would only go so far and last so long. Being here with them was playing with fire, and yet just the thought of changing my mind made my chest ache with loss.

And now wasn't the time to deal with it.

I ground my teeth against my whirling emotions— and the heat from theirs and my God damned buzz— brought my scope to my eye, and glanced into the dark tunnel behind us.

Marcus led us forward and to the tunnel on the right toward the only other light source. We hopped off the platform, Marcus and Kol landing without a sound. Gideon's feet crunched slightly in the gravel, mine definitely crunched—even though I was the lightest in the group—while Jacob's didn't make a sound.

I was beginning to have a good idea why humans weren't on JP teams. Aside from the fact that they barely stood a chance against the more powerful supers, a lack of night vision and the inability to move silently over noisy terrain made the human the weakest link. Which stung my pride. I might have made one error in judgment when I was a rookie and turned Marcus into a werewolf, but I'd never before been the weakest link. Even when my buzz had first manifested and been out of control, I'd still managed to hold myself together and do my job.

I scanned the tunnel behind us. No sign of movement or heat signatures—and the scope would still pick up the ferals even if they hadn't recently fed and had low body temperatures.

The tunnel gently turned and ended fifty feet down at a cave-in, the pile of concrete and earth from the ceiling scorched black from some kind of magical attack. Sunlight streamed through a hole edged with the ragged ends of a wide broken pipe and twisted tree roots. A narrow doorway, the metal door ripped from its hinges and lying on the ground a few feet away, stood to the right.

"The nest is probably less than a hundred feet this way," Marcus said, and he headed into the narrow access hall.

Ten feet down the hall, I could smell the bodies. The reek of decomposition thickened the air and clung to the inside of my nose. The temperature in the hall was even cooler than the subway tunnel and a starker contrast to the heat coming from the guys. Moisture clung to the walls, dripped from the seams in a pipe running along the ceiling, and pooled on the concrete floor.

We hit a T-intersection, turned right, and reached a narrow set of concrete stairs, its metal railing still intact. The stairs led down into a wide area, three stories tall, with a bright band of sunlight slicing from one of a dozen grates close to the ceiling into the mouth of a large sewage pipe on the third story. More pipe mouths peppered the walls, some caved in and shallow, but most black maws that I could only see a foot or two inside. They were all big enough for a human or bigger, and more than I could keep an eye on at any given time.

The floor was tiered, as if the area had been built in a

patchwork. A few of the highest ones looked like landings, while the rest had slopes, all directing to the lowest level and the widest, floor-level tunnel. Water pooled on the lower levels, and the reek of decomposition was nearly suffocating. Bodies littered half the landings, the piles more haphazard than the one in the school. There were easily three times as many victims here than there had been at the first nest.

"Eyes open," Gideon said, his voice low as he followed Marcus down the stairs.

I swept my scope to a pipe mouth on the other side of the stairs. Three heat signatures. Two more in the tunnel beside it. Another one in the tunnel beside that.

"They're in the tunnels," I said. "I've got six—" Four more in the next tunnel and two in the one above. "At least twelve."

"Jeez, Logan's been busy," Marcus growled, reaching the bottom and scanning the tunnels closest to the stairs.

Kol hopped over the railing, skipping the last five steps, and landed beside Marcus. "How the hell did no one notice this many missing humans?"

"Since the war, more people are living off the grid," Gideon said.

"And we did notice," I said. "Missing persons has seriously spiked in the last month or so."

A low growl rumbled around the chamber, echoing off the concrete walls and growing in volume until it felt as if it came from all around us. Then someone screamed a high-pitched howl and a woman, covered in blood and filth, with matted hair and a ripped T-shirt, barreled out of the tunnel across from the stairs. Her eyes were wild, her fangs extended, and her nails sharpened claws.

She rushed toward Kol, throwing herself at him, and he deftly sidestepped her attack, sliced her arm with one dagger, and rammed the other into the base of her neck.

With a gurgled scream, she collapsed to the ground, but more ferals started howling and the dozen I'd counted ran from their tunnels toward the guys.

Kol rushed to the center of the room to meet them, making space for Gideon, who summoned his sword of divine light and decapitated a feral as he marched to meet a group of three coming from a pipe only a few feet from the stairs.

Marcus snarled and stabbed at a feral rushing toward Kol. He sliced open the feral's side. The creature stumbled but didn't drop and changed targets, lunging at Marcus.

Jacob drew his Berettas and fired at a feral coming from a tunnel on the other side of the room. His shot hit right between the eyes. Blue lightning crackled around the feral's body. The creature screamed and died, his body crumpling to the floor, but two more jumped over it and rushed into the fight.

I kept scanning the tunnels, but there were heat signatures in all of them. I fired a three-round burst at a feral dashing toward Marcus. Lightning crackled around it as it stumbled but didn't drop, and Marcus swept his sword out and decapitated it.

Jacob fired again and dropped another one with a flash of blue lightning.

Someone above me howled, and a bulky feral

dropped from the third-story tunnel and crashed down on Jacob.

My pulse leaped. They weren't just on the ground level.

Jacob jerked out of the way, but the feral's razor sharp claws still slashed his hand and ripped the Beretta from his grip. He grabbed the feral by its leather sports jacket, pressed the muzzle of his other Beretta to its heart, and fired.

Lightning swept around the feral, and Jacob tossed his body into another feral who was moving faster than humanly possible. Many of them were, actually, which meant they were older than the ones I'd come across in the school, or Logan had figured out how to make stronger ferals.

I jerked my attention to the second- and third-story tunnels and counted more heat signatures. "Heads up. There are more in the second- and third-story tunnels."

"How many more?" Gideon asked.

"Two dozen— Three—" And those were only the ones close enough to see. Whatever Logan's plan, he'd definitely made an army of vicious creatures that were hard to kill. And while the guys were deadly efficient, more ferals kept coming. We were already outnumbered and our odds were getting worse.

CHAPTER 13

I SHOT A THREE-ROUND BURST AT A FERAL ABOUT TO JUMP from a second-story pipe onto Kol. The feral fell out of the tunnel and hit the concrete with a sickening crunch, but still staggered to his feet.

Jacob grabbed for his dropped Beretta but it was kicked down a ramp in the scuffle, while Gideon impaled a feral rushing toward Jacob.

The feral I shot lunged at Kol. He twisted out of the way but into the reach of a petite female feral. She grabbed his arm and wrenched him around with her enhanced vampiric strength. He rammed his dagger into her gut, but she didn't even flinch and slashed her claws across his face.

With a roar, Jacob shoved out of the grip of a feral clinging to him and shot Kol's feral in the head before turning back to the group surrounding him. His eyes were black and his vampiric intensity radiated around him, a palpable energy that sang to his claim entwined with my essence.

I wrenched my attention away from him and fired again at the ferals jumping from the pipes. Lightning crackled around all of them, but I wasn't the marksman Jacob was and only managed to drop one out of the five. More rushed from a tunnel on the other side of the stairs. I stepped away from the wall to get a better shot and sent a barrage into the group as they barreled toward Marcus, who snarled, his wolf still captured within his human skin, but barely. Blood splattered him from the ferals he'd killed and oozed from deep gashes on his arms and legs.

Out of the corner of my eye, I watched as Gideon's blazing sword swept through the dim light, leaving a trail in the air. He too was covered in blood, his expression hard and icy, as he moved with powerful precision, each strike meant to kill or maim then kill. He decapitated a feral, twisted and impaled another through the heart, then ducked low, twisting again, as a feral swiped at his back. His blade slashed through one of the feral's legs, drawing a scream and toppling it to its knees.

Another feral lunged for Gideon's back, but he was engaged with two others. I fired a quick burst, making the feral behind him stumble. His gaze leaped up to mine, and the heated electricity from his brand swept up my arm, then he wrenched his attention back to the ferals he was fighting.

Marcus roared and killed another. The bodies were piling up and blood slicked the concrete, making the footing dangerous. I scanned the tunnels for heat signatures.

Nothing.

I did another sweep.

Still nothing.

"I think we're at the end of it."

"Thank God," Marcus growled.

"God has nothing to do with this," a raspy tenor said, his voice carrying over the growls and screams of the fight.

"Take cover," Gideon barked.

Jacob tossed the feral he'd just killed and jerked his attention up, his gaze jumping around the chamber. "Too afraid to come out and fight me?"

"You don't scare me, Lockwood," Logan said.

Marcus shoved past a feral and headed to the closest tunnel's mouth. Kol did the same.

I bolted to the closest cover, an alcove with a pile of bodies, pressed my back tight against the damp wall, and searched the chamber for Logan's heat signature. Still nothing.

Gideon impaled a feral as he ran for the tunnel across from him, and a rifle blast roared through the chamber.

My heart seized and Jacob tackled Gideon, moving with his enhanced vampiric speed. Blood blossomed across the top of Jacob's shoulder. He wrenched Gideon to his feet, and they bolted the rest of the way to the tunnel.

I yanked my scope back to the tunnels where I guessed Logan would be. Still nothing. I had no idea how he was hiding his heat signature, but in the world of supers, anything was possible.

"Jacob, can you find him?" Gideon asked over the coms. "Shoot him?"

"No," Jacob said.

"We can't just wait around," Marcus snarled.

"I'll draw his fire," Jacob said. "I have the best chance of surviving."

"Not a headshot, you won't," Kol said.

"Then I'll have to move fast enough he can't hit me."

Jacob darted from the tunnel mouth.

"Son of a—" Marcus snarled.

Another rifle shot roared through the chamber, and I caught a flicker of muzzle fire from a floor-level tunnel—not at all where I expected a sniper to hide. Another shot and another flare of muzzle fire.

Got you. I aimed just behind the muzzle flare and fired. Lightning exploded around Logan, illuminating him in the tunnel, and he screamed.

"You damn bitch," he howled and jerked his rifle toward me, the temperature spiking.

I wrenched back against the alcove arch as he fired. The shot roared and concrete shrapnel exploded from the edge of the arch.

"Get on out here," he snarled, and a low growl rumbled through the cavern.

"Holy shit," Kol said.

Cold sliced through the heat.

"Essie, watch your back," Jacob yelled.

His claim twisted in my chest, and I wrenched around. The bodies in the pile were moving. A hand, the skin bloated and oozing, reached out from the bottom of the pile and grabbed for my ankle.

I jerked out of the way and shot at it as all the bodies on top rose and heaved toward me.

I fired again, then wrenched back around to face the

chamber even though the animated corpses were the biggest threat. All of the bodies with the exception of those the team had decapitated were rising up and rushing toward the tunnels where the guys hid.

Jacob's claim twisted tighter, and my body heaved around again. I scrambled out of reach of an ashen-skinned guy with cloudy dead eyes who wasn't decomposing yet. I fired again, scrambling to get out of the way, only to wrench back around.

God damn it.

"Jacob. Command," I yelled, straining against the claim. It wrenched me around again, and I stumbled to the side, losing my balance as I fought it. A rifle blast sliced across the side of my shoulder, and the claim wrenched me back to face the chamber.

I emptied the rest of my magazine into Logan's tunnel but didn't hit him.

"Essie, protect yourself," Jacob said as he bolted across the chamber toward Logan.

"Stay with the team, Jacob," Gideon said, but Jacob kept running.

Logan fired again, and Jacob twisted, the bullet slicing across the front of his vest.

"Marcus, cover him." The light from Gideon's blade blazed from the mouth of his tunnel.

Marcus surged into sight, but the animated corpses pressed close and clung to him.

The woman with bloated skin broke free of the pile and lunged at me. I jerked out of the way, but another corpse swiped at me. His claws sliced into my arm with burning agony, while another woman wrenched the M4 out of my hands.

"Marcus," Gideon snapped. "To Jacob."

"Trying," Marcus growled back, but he couldn't break through the press of bodies.

Jacob fired into the tunnel where Logan was, didn't hit, holstered his Beretta, and drew his sword without missing a step.

"Kol?" Gideon asked.

"Almost. There—" Kol dove through the press of corpses at the mouth of his tunnel, and they wrenched around and grabbed at him. One snagged his ankle, tripping him just long enough for another to tackle him.

I scrambled out of reach of another body, my mind whirling. Of the team, I was the closest to Logan's tunnel and the only one not completely surrounded by animated corpses, but what kind of backup would I be for Jacob?

Jacob rushed into the tunnel and half a dozen corpses followed him.

I drew my Glock and bolted after him, instinct propelling me forward. I might not be able to help with Logan, and certainly wasn't fast enough to catch a vampire running at full speed, but I could hopefully stop the corpses so they didn't slow Jacob down, making him lose Logan. I'd need to be close enough to get a good shot, but I could handle them long enough for one of the other guys to break free.

"God damn, Essie," Marcus growled over the coms.

"Officer Shaw," Gideon yelled.

"We can't let Logan get away." I barreled after Jacob and the corpses.

The one at the end, slower than the others because of the rotting state of its body, jerked around and rushed at me. I fought my panic and kept running forward. I didn't know if I needed a head shot to stop any of the feral vampire's now animated victims, but I wasn't going to take the chance that I didn't. *And please, God, let a head shot work.*

The corpse snarled at me. I shot it in the chest. It stumbled, and I shoved it against the wall and shot it in the head.

I raced away as the spell's lightning enveloped it, destroying whatever magic animated it. My feet splashed through water and my lungs burned as I strained to run faster.

I reached another corpse with a gaping wound in its chest—this one had been a feral that one of the guys had killed. I shot it in the chest and shoved it against the wall. It raked its claws at my face and I jerked back, but not fast enough. Fire blazed along my jaw. I finished it off and kept running.

"Essie, I'm on your six," Marcus said over the coms.

I bolted around a corner, and Jacob roared. My pulse seized in fear. He stood at the mouth of another chamber, fighting the four remaining corpses, and Logan had his rifle aimed at him.

I fired at Logan, hitting his shoulder with a flash of lightning, and his shot went into the tunnel's ceiling. Jacob slammed an animated corpse at another one, crashing them against the wall, and lunged for Logan.

"Essie, get out of here," Jacob yelled, swinging his sword at Logan, keeping close so the vampire couldn't use his rifle.

The claim twisted, but I clung to my willpower, fighting it. Marcus was close. I could handle these corpses until then. Just a few seconds. That was all I needed to last, because Jacob had to deal with Logan.

I reached the first of the still-standing corpses, shot it in the chest, but I had to wrench out of the way of a slash from another one before finishing it off. The new one, a bulky man with fangs, seized the front of my vest and jerked me close to bite my neck. I shoved the muzzle of my gun to his chest and fired. He screamed and collapsed in a blast of lightning, but the first one was back on me.

I scrambled aside as it swiped at me. Jacob's claim twisted tighter. I had to run, to leave, to get out of there—

God. Damn. No.

I could hear Marcus's footsteps pounding against the water-slick concrete. I just needed to stay a few seconds longer.

"Essie," Jacob barked.

"No." I fired two shots into the reanimated feral in front of me, making it stumble, and shot at its head, killing it.

Marcus rushed around the corner as Logan howled. The animated corpse closest to me lunged. I leaped back but my heel caught on a lip in the floor as an explosion erupted from the chamber's entranceway. I hit the floor, and massive chunks of concrete rained down on me, slamming against my chest and legs and pinning me to the floor.

"Essie," Marcus said over the coms. "Talk to me."

"I'm here."

"What happened?" Gideon asked.

"Cave-in," I said. Jacob, Logan, and I were in another chamber, this one only about thirty by thirty, with only one tunnel leading out. A hint of light came from a grate high above, but no light came directly into the chamber.

Logan laughed, the sound filled with dark glee. "This is wonderful." He blocked Jacob's sword swing with his rifle, and turned so I was in Jacob's line of sight. "Your human is here to watch you die."

"I don't think so." I fought to move under the press of rubble. My left arm was buried, but my right arm and head were clear. Except I couldn't get anything to budge and could barely breathe against the pressure.

"You think you're that much more powerful than me?" Jacob snarled.

"I know so." Logan leaped back, dropped his rifle, and raised both his hands, palms up. "I have Ibizual's power rushing through my veins."

Jacob froze, his arms raised mid-swing, and groaned in agony, his eyes wide.

Logan fisted his hands. Jacob groaned again and collapsed forward, his palms pressed to the concrete, his chest heaving with desperate gasps.

I searched the ground for my Glock. The gun lay a few inches from my outstretched hand.

"And with a touch—" He laid a hand on the back of Jacob's head. "—I can take your unnatural life."

Red energy swept around Jacob, and he screamed. His body went stiff, and Logan howled with glee.

I heaved against the rubble and strained to reach my gun. I was close. So close. My fingers grazed the butt and pushed it a fraction farther.

Shit.

"What the hell is going on in there?" Gideon asked.

"Essie," Marcus said, his voice clipped, "I'm coming. Hold on."

Logan leaned close to Jacob's ear. "I'll take every last drop of your essence," he snarled, "and then I'll take your human's."

Jacob's screams turned desperate.

My soul howled, frantic to stop this, to save him, and it had nothing to do with his claim.

There was no way in hell I was going to reach my gun. My only choice was to pray I could find enough juice for a light strike to break the spell on Jacob so he could fight back.

I flexed my hand back, pointing my palm at Logan, and screamed the divine light strike spell, hoping the force of my words would aid the force of my spell. A blast of light shot from my palm with almost as much power as I'd had when I'd fought the archnephilim.

The blast hit Logan and he jerked toward me, barely a hint of a burn on his neck and face, and that healing before my eyes.

He sneered, and my pulse froze.

"Wait your turn," he growled, and he seized Jacob's head and sank his fangs into Jacob's neck.

CHAPTER 14

FEAR CLENCHED COLD IN MY CHEST. THE RED ENERGY blazed brighter around Jacob and he convulsed as Logan fed on him.

I had to stop him, except my light strike wasn't powerful enough. I couldn't do this alone. Hell, I couldn't do this at all. "Marcus, help."

"I'm trying."

Rubble shifted behind me, but everything within me screamed he wasn't going to get through fast enough.

My mind whirled. There had to be something. All I had was the light strike, but I needed more power. The gold in Gideon's brand on my arm flickered. I'd given him strength to save his life. *Please, God, let him be able to give me power to save Jacob's.*

"Gideon, give me power."

"What?" he asked.

"I need power."

"How can I give you power?" he asked.

"You can—" Shit. There wasn't time to explain this. It had to happen now or Jacob was going to die.

I shoved back all my racing thoughts and concentrated on my connection to Gideon. I imagined drawing every ounce of magic I could get from him into my body and focusing it in my palm.

The electric hum from his brand grew stronger, but it wasn't enough. I needed more.

Come on. Come on. Give me your God damn power.

I mentally yanked with everything I had, and Gideon's power exploded into searing white lightning in my hand. I clung to it, forcing the pressure to build into a blinding agony until I couldn't hold it any longer and then blasted it at Logan.

It slammed into the vampire and smashed him against the chamber wall. He sagged to the floor, his face, neck, and shoulders blackened and bleeding. One eye was completely gone and the skin on his cheek burned down to the bone.

He stared at me, what remained of his face a mask of shock and horror. My whole body shook with electric tremors, and my buzz screamed to life, burning past the nicotine patches.

Rubble tumbled past my head and Marcus scrambled into the chamber.

Logan wrenched to his feet and bolted down the tunnel. Jacob collapsed, blood rushing from the gaping tear in his neck, and didn't move. *Please, God, don't let him be dead.*

Marcus rushed to me, splattered in blood, his body covered with bleeding gashes.

I waved him off. "I'm fine. Check Jacob."

He glared at me but hurried to Jacob, who, thank God, was now groaning, which meant he was still alive.

Kol bounded in next, looking as beat-up as Marcus. He heaved the piece of concrete off my back and left arm, and I gasped in a full breath, my chest aching but not enough to suggest I had broken or cracked ribs.

Gideon staggered in last, also covered in blood and gashes, but his complexion was gray and he clutched his brand. The light radiating from his icy glare flickered and heat from an emotion—I'd place money on anger—surged around me.

"What the hell was that?" he asked.

"One massive light strike, at least as powerful as a blast from a divine light ring," Marcus said. "I didn't think a human could cast a combat spell with that much power."

Kol pushed aside the concrete pinning my legs and helped me shift into a sitting position, my body throbbing and on fire with the buzz.

"They can't. She stole mine." The muscles in Gideon's jaw tightened. "Don't ever do that again," he said, his voice low.

"He was going to kill Jacob. I had to do something." Blood wept from a wide gash in my right leg and I could also feel it trickling down my neck from the slices in my jaw.

"I could have been in the middle of fighting ferals," Gideon snapped. The temperature rose even more, the heat making sweat bead on my forehead and flush my cheeks. "Marcus was almost through the cave-in. Taking all my magic without warning was reckless."

"Marcus wasn't going to be fast enough." I wasn't going to justify my decision to him. Okay, maybe I'd taken more than I should have, but I hadn't even known I could and I'd been desperate.

"You didn't know that. You couldn't see him. Marcus was right. You are a liability." The frustration and disgust in his tone stung. I saw that same look in his eyes that I'd seen in the cops gathered in the basement of the abandoned school. I was dangerous, a death sentence to anyone who worked with me.

I shoved myself to my feet and wobbled, my legs aching. Kol reached to steady me, but I gritted my teeth, fought for my balance, and shoved his hands away. "I made the right call."

"You made a bad call. I'm calling the chief when we get back to Operations and having you replaced."

If he had me replaced, the chief would fire me. Everything I'd worked for, everything I wanted, would be taken away. I'd be a pariah. Even if Gideon's brand did let me leave town, no police force would ever hire me again. God, and here I'd thought Gideon learning I was a nephilim was what would ruin my life.

"It wasn't a bad call," Jacob said, his voice weak, his hands clamped to his neck to staunch the bleeding. But blood still oozed between his fingers.

The fury in Gideon's eyes didn't soften. "She abused the connection of the brand."

"And you're going to destroy my career because of it?" I said.

"You're a danger to everyone you work with." He jerked toward me, using his taller, bigger stature to glare down at me.

"I'm not the one who keeps getting shot," I said.

"My problem. Not yours. Taking all my magic without warning could have killed me."

"And you getting shot almost *did* kill me. I just about had my throat ripped out by a feral because of you. Consider us even." The color drained from his face, and I jerked away and staggered to Jacob's side. "Let's get out of here."

Marcus stared at me with his piercing green gaze, his expression just as hard as Gideon's.

Well, fuck you, too. I'd reached the end of my emotional rope and just couldn't handle them any more. I hurt, inside and out, and the buzz—

God. It was so hard just to think straight.

Marcus shoved between me and Jacob and helped the vampire stand. Kol drew close to me, but didn't try to help me walk. Thank goodness, because I was just as likely to start yelling at him as I was Marcus and Gideon, because I was barely holding my frustration and anger at bay.

I grabbed my Glock, climbed over the rubble now partially blocking the doorway, and marched as best I could back to the SUV. Kol and Gideon gathered the rest of the discarded weapons, and without a word, we piled in and headed back to Operations.

If I'd thought the tension in the vehicle had been tight before, it was practically suffocating now, with drastic temperature fluctuations that made me sweat and shiver at the same time.

Gideon called ahead to alert medical of our situation and have a clean-up team head back to the abandoned subway station to deal with the remaining bodies. When we arrived, Amiah was waiting for us with a gurney and a scowl, and Marcus jerked the SUV to a stop just outside the garage's glass door. He climbed out, leaving the keys in the ignition.

"I'm shifting out the rest of my injuries. Kol, park this," he growled, and stormed to the far end of the garage and out the heavy metal door at the back to the rest of Operations' property.

Gideon and Kol helped Jacob out of the back of the SUV. The vampire was ashen. His hands were still clamped to his neck, blood still seeping between his fingers and soaking into his T-shirt. What the hell had Logan done to him? His neck should have at least stopped bleeding by now. The gashes on his hand from a feral's swipe hadn't healed either, and they were much shallower than the tear in his neck.

"I'm fine," he said.

Amiah huffed. "Get on the gurney so they don't have to carry you." Her attention jumped to Kol. "Can you manage?"

He wiped the blood off his cheek, revealing mostly healed gashes. "I'm good."

"Good." She turned to Gideon, raked her gaze over him, then turned to me, her scowl deepening. "Let's go, you two."

Gideon helped her push Jacob into the triage room

and I hobbled along behind. I was going to lose my job, and I hadn't even screwed up this time. Jacob would have died. I didn't understand why Gideon was so angry.

Of course, maybe it wasn't anger that was driving him. Having all his magic stolen for the time it took me to cast that light strike could have been terrifying. He was Mr. Icy-In-Control-Angel, and I'd made him helpless. That must have been terrifying.

And I was the target he could take that fear out on. I wasn't really a team member, I was just the human fate had bound to him, reminding him that the woman he loved was dead.

Well, I didn't want to be bound to him either. God, I wanted to scream out all my rage and frustration and heartache.

Amiah grabbed two blood bags from the fridge and shoved them into Jacob's hands. "Drink both of those."

"Sure." He moved to hop off the gurney.

"Here. Now. You don't get to leave until both those bags are empty." She wrenched around to me, grabbed my wrist, and agonizing lightning screamed through me then vanished so fast it left me dizzy. I had no doubt this was the barest minimum healing Amiah could do and my bleeding had been stopped and nothing more.

"Get out of here," she snarled at me.

Absolutely. The best idea ever. I needed to figure out how to save my job, and I couldn't do that with Gideon's fiery emotions and icy glare drilling into me.

I marched out of triage and down the hall to the elevator. My buzz gnawed at my senses, growing stronger the farther I got from Gideon, but the heat of his emotions didn't cool.

God damn. How was I going to fix this?

An achy cold thread seeped into my chest.

Could I even fix this?

I took the elevator up to my room, pulled off my bloody and filthy borrowed vest and clothes, and turned to take a shower, but stopped before turning on the water. I didn't want to stay there long enough to have a shower. I wanted to go home, get away from Gideon and Amiah and everyone. If I had a moment of calm, maybe I'd be able to figure a way out of this mess.

I scrubbed the blood and dirt from my face, neck, and arms with a washcloth, changed into my only set of clean clothes, reapplied two new nicotine patches, and shoved my dirty clothes into my duffle bag. I left the vest, the extra magazines, and the room's keycard on the bed.

I wasn't coming back. The only person on the team who wanted me there was Kol, and quite frankly he could spend time with me without me being on the team. In fact, me leaving would be better for him. He wouldn't have to worry about me fucking up the team dynamics.

Marcus might have been right that I didn't fit on the team, but he'd been wrong about me and the world of the supernatural. I hadn't been terrified like I thought I would be facing those feral vampires as part of the team. I hadn't frozen, hadn't broken down, hadn't done anything but stand my ground and do my job. Physically I might have been the weakest link on the team, but I'd still managed to hold my own.

I took the elevator back to the first floor and headed

to the garage, my buzz easing just a bit as I drew closer to the sliding glass triage doors.

"Good, now the second bag," Amiah said, her voice sharp.

"I'm fine," Jacob growled.

"The second bag."

And Jacob was alive because of me. They were *all* alive because of me, because I'd faced down that archnephilim and killed him. Of course, I'd thought I was going to die, too, but that was beside the point.

I strode out into the garage and headed to the door, my buzz growing with each step that I took away from Gideon.

God damn buzz. God damn Gideon.

I jerked back toward the glass door to the building.

This was giving up, and I hated giving up, especially when there was no victory in it. I was more than willing to do what was necessary and sacrifice myself for the good of the many, but this wasn't anything. It was just losing. The team might not be worse for my departure, but it wasn't necessarily better. They were still going to be stuck with a human officer and that human wouldn't have the few supernatural advantages that I had.

Except leaving protected my secret. The longer I stayed with the team, the better the chance that someone would discover the truth. And I needed to protect my secret. Didn't I?

I stormed back to the big garage door and the way out of Operations.

Gideon clearly despised nephilim. They were responsible for horribly disfiguring Zella and the archnephilim had been responsible for murdering her. His hate for me would turn into outright loathing if he learned the truth.

And Marcus would be furious. I'd been so adamant about protecting my perfectly human life, afraid to have anything to do with the supernatural world, and he'd sacrificed his feelings for me to give me that. Of course, he had also been an asshole about ensuring I kept my human life, but I knew that was to protect himself.

Except a part of me didn't want to be protected any more. For the last week and a half my soul had hurt. The man I yearned for had given me everything I thought I wanted, and it had been horrible.

I jerked back to the glass doors leading into the building.

God, Marcus. The look on his face when I'd said I'd been wrong about leaving. He'd been so angry, so horrified, that I'd changed my mind and wanted to be in his world. He thought I was weak. Maybe I was weak.

I wrenched back toward the way out.

I was not weak. I'd struck a serious blow to Logan when even Jacob couldn't. Another blast like that, and I might have taken him out and ended this whole mess.

I was not God damned weak. I spent my life in hiding, being afraid because I was a nephilim without magic, unable to defend myself against any supernatural beings but the weakest ones. I was practically human with the exception of my father, an angel I'd never met, who my mother had never mentioned by name. And I had just stood up against a vampire possessing magic from a hell-fire prince and struck a damaging blow.

Take that, Gideon and Marcus, and your Essie is too

weak, a liability to the team. God, I wanted to scream that at them. I, a human, took out an archnephilim. I, a human, seriously hurt Logan when no one else could.

I stormed back to the inside door.

I was God damn strong. And I belonged.

God, why the hell did I want to belong so much? Why did I care? Why couldn't I just leave? I *needed* to leave. Now. It was for the best.

I screamed. Jerked to face the way out. Jerked back to face the way in.

The brand filled me with yearning for a man who hated me. My heart ached for another man who was determined to push me away for my own God damned good, as if I didn't know what was best for me.

And I was stupid. So fucking stupid. I *wanted* to stay. I finally knew where I belonged, knew what my purpose was. Even at the expense of my own safety, this was where fate said I belonged.

And Gideon was going to end it all. Hell, he'd probably already made the call. There was probably a message on my phone from the chief, firing me. Don't bother cleaning out your locker. Don't bother showing your face at your precinct. Disappear, Essie Shaw. Disappear like you always did when things got dangerous or scary.

I screamed again, and my eyes burned with tears.

Except even if I could disappear with Gideon's brand on my arm, I didn't want to.

My throat tightened and my threatening tears made my legs tremble. What the hell was wrong with me?

Just leave. Just God damn leave.

I took a step closer to the inside door.

I couldn't go back inside. And yet I couldn't leave. I couldn't do anything, and even when I did everything right, it was wrong.

I jerked past the door, storming deeper into the garage.

Fuck Gideon. Fuck Marcus. And fuck my father for falling in love with a human.

Shaking with rage and heartache, I ducked into the hidden alcove made by the door leading into the building. It hid a black metal locker recessed into the wall, secured with a fingerprint scanner. I pressed my back against the concrete wall beside it and slid to the asphalt.

Fuck all of this. This was no way to fix any of it.

Tears streamed down my cheeks, and I didn't care. I had to release my frustration and heartache and fear or I was going to shatter. My throat and chest and heart hurt, squeezed tight with too much emotion that I couldn't release fast enough.

The door to the hall shushed open, and I clamped my hand over my mouth, trying to muffle my sobs. Any of the guys but Kol would see me crying in the garage as proof of how weak I was.

Jacob hurried into sight, and his claim twisted, ever so slightly, in my chest. He might have drunk Amiah's bags of blood and his stride had evened out, but there was something still wrong with him. I didn't know what. That tightness around his eyes that had been there all day? His still slightly ashen complexion?

He glanced back to the glass door, then rushed

deeper into the garage and not out the door to the street like I'd expected.

I pressed tight against the concrete wall, even though I knew he'd see me regardless if he glanced my way.

But he didn't look. Instead he rushed to the sewer grate a few feet away, dropped to his hands and knees, and threw up blood.

CHAPTER 15

MY ESSENCE LOCKED ONTO JACOB, FEAR RUSHING FROZEN through me as his back heaved and his body shook. He threw up more blood, again and again, until he was trembling and gasping and dry heaving. My breath caught in my throat, an almost inaudible gasp, and his gaze jerked toward me, capturing me with his vampiric intensity.

"Essie," he said, his voice a low rumble, making the claim vibrate with joy. "You shouldn't be here."

Him too? Of course he'd want me gone, too. He'd been forced to bind his essence to mine to protect himself from Victoria. I was a reminder of his weaknesses, and now I'd witnessed another one.

And yet I couldn't make myself stand up and leave him. Something was horribly wrong. He shouldn't have been throwing up blood. He needed it to survive. Amiah had told him to drink the blood to heal from whatever Logan had done to him.

Except he'd also snuck the blood bag he was

supposed to have taken after the first fight with Logan at Rouge back into the fridge without drinking it.

"You can't consume bagged blood," I said, the realiza-tion hitting me. "I thought vampires could."

"They can. I could—" His body stiffened with another dry heave, and he gasped for breath. "I could until I claimed you."

Oh, shit. "Is this something else I did?" I'd barely known anything about how a vampire's claim worked, only the effects it had on the human being claimed. Had I unknowingly screwed up his life by trying to save him then returning to my normal human existence? "Why didn't you tell me? Have you been starving for a week and a half?"

"Essie, it's all right." A tremor swept through him, drawing a ragged gasp.

I scrambled to his side, not caring if it was his claim compelling me or not, and rubbed slow circles on his broad back. "It's not all right. I made you claim me."

"You didn't make me do anything." He shuddered again and groaned. "I just didn't expect this. I knew my claim was strong, but I didn't think it was this strong. It doesn't feel like it is."

"So this is what happens when the claim is too strong?"

"I've only ever heard of it happening when a vampire has a strong claim on a super," he gasped. "But yes. I can't keep down bagged blood, and blood from a bunny isn't nearly as effective as it used to be." He groaned again, squeezing his eyes shut, his face etched in pain. "I need you, Essie. My essence has locked onto yours as yours has onto mine."

"You should have asked." If he needed me, I'd be there.

He captured me with his dark gaze, stealing my breath.

"Because it's rarely just blood with a claimed one," he said, his voice husky, the strain around his eyes so tight it hurt my soul. "And I won't put you in that situation." He jerked his gaze back to his hands, still pressed against the asphalt beside the grate. "I can wait it out."

"How long will that be?"

"I don't know. My essence has to work its way out of yours."

"You've bitten me twice now. That could be months." Could he survive without bagged blood for that long? I raked my gaze over his body. He looked like shit, and the tear on his neck was still weeping blood. He'd said the key that would break the seal to Ibizual's prison was going to manifest tonight. That meant he was going up against Logan again. He wouldn't survive another encounter like this.

I grabbed his arm to pull him to his feet. "We need to get you to a bunny."

"It won't help."

"You said a bunny's blood isn't nearly as effective, but it still does something."

"Whatever Logan did, it was powerful. A bunny won't help this time. If I'm going to recover, then I need your blood."

"Then take it."

The muscles in his jaw tightened and his gaze locked back onto mine, filled with not a physical hunger but a sexual one as well. "I can't. I won't be able to control myself this time."

A shiver of desire swept through me. Was I willing to have sex with Jacob to help him? A part of me screamed 'Yes!' I'd been willing to sleep with him earlier that morning in the shower before I knew it would help him, and my reasons then hadn't changed now. I still ached with unfulfilled desire for men who either wanted to push me away to protect me or hated me. Jacob could satisfy that need, and I could help him out at the same time.

"Do you expect a relationship out of this?" I asked. I didn't want another complication. I just needed a release or I'd shatter.

"No. Your heart belongs to Marcus and your soul to Gideon."

"I don't *belong* to anyone." Why was that the given in this mess? They didn't want me, and all they'd done was hurt me. God! I wanted to go back to screaming. "I'm so sick and tired of everyone acting as if I'm not an adult able to make my own choices. This whole situation is completely fucked up. At least let me help you. You say I'm the only one who can."

"Yes." He didn't sound happy about that.

"I'm not going to let you suffer. If Marcus and Gideon can't understand that, then I don't care what fate says, I don't belong with either of them." And they didn't want me anyway. I'd release the emotional pressure threatening to shatter me, and Jacob would be well enough to face Logan. In the long run, it might be a disaster, but in the short term it was a win-win. Once the situation with Logan was done, we'd figure out what to do about his need for my blood after that.

"I'm not going to let you make a decision influenced by my claim," he said. "You don't really want to do this."

"I'm volunteering, and your claim has nothing to do with it." Even if it was thrilling with ecstasy at the idea.

"The claim is making you say that. My control of you is too strong. You can't resist it."

Except I'd resisted it in the tunnel when he'd told me to leave and I hadn't. "Tell me to do something."

"Get away from me," he said.

The claim twisted. I jerked to my feet, but squeezed my muscles tight before I could walk away, crossed my arms, and glared down at him. "I can resist you."

"Give me your blood."

"Only if you ask nicely."

He jerked to his feet, his gaze capturing me, locking my soul in those black depths. "Feed. Me."

The claim clenched, stealing my breath and screaming through me. Help him. Feed him. Satisfy him. There was only him. There would only ever be him. And I had to please him.

"No." This was my choice. My decision. And magic wasn't going to coerce me. A part of me feared that the other guys would think Jacob had taken advantage of me because of the claim, but if I had to deal with that to save his life before he faced Logan that night, so be it.

He pulled out a switchblade, flipped it open, and held

it out to me. "Cut your wrist and feed me," he growled. His claim tightened until I couldn't breathe.

"You can't make me do something I don't want to do," I hissed back. "If you don't feed now, Logan will kill you tonight and Ibizual will be set free."

"So you're making yet another sacrifice." He closed the knife, shoved it back into his pocket, and captured my face with his hands. "Essie, you have to stop doing that. You don't have to kill yourself to prove yourself."

"I'm not trying to prove myself. I'm doing what needs to be done." I pressed my hands over his. "I make this choice freely. Let me help you." And help me release my desire for men who don't want me.

He pursed his lips together, but his gaze had shifted from soul-capturing concern to hungry.

My pulse pounded with hope and yearning and fear. *Say yes. Please say yes and save yourself tonight.*

"Okay, but not here." He released my face and grabbed my hand. "The feeding could make you dizzy. You'll need time to recover."

I grabbed my duffle bag and we hurried back inside as fast as Jacob's weakened body would let us, thankfully not running into anyone since I didn't want to have to explain why I was holding Jacob's hand or why my eyes were red and puffy. And I was grateful he hadn't mentioned them.

We took the elevator up to the fifth floor and headed to his room. His grip tightened on my hand the closer we got, and his stride became uneven. His breath came fast and his complexion was even paler than before.

Gasping, he unlocked the door and dragged me inside. His arm wrapped around my waist and jerked me close, my back against his chest, as he braced himself against the door. The temperature snapped to sultry, hot and humid and sensual. I didn't know if it came from his desire for me or my blood, and right now I didn't care. We were both going to satisfy a need, and I was good with that.

His other hand combed into my hair, capturing my head and tugging it to the side to expose my neck.

I dropped my duffle bag. My pulse leaped in anticipation and instant desire surged hot within me. With a growl, a low rumble that vibrated through his massive chest into my back, he sank his teeth into my neck.

Pain sliced through me, followed by a rush of sudden, bone-melting pleasure. My breath hitched, and I moaned. There was no need to keep it in or hide how he made me feel. The whole point of this was to help him and help myself.

His hand on my stomach dipped under my shirt and slid up my chest to my breast, putting us back in the same position as when he'd magically entwined his essence into mine.

He took a long pull on my neck, and the sensation seeped hot across my chest and into my core, drawing another moan. I slid my hands down his thighs and rubbed my body against his. His erection, huge and firm, pressed against me, and my pulse quickened.

His hand slipped beneath my bra and he kneaded my breast, drawing a searing line of desire from neck to heart. I arched my back, needing more, needing all of him. The desire that had wound tight within me from the moment Marcus had stormed back into my life clenched my heart and my core, and I ached for release.

Jacob took another pull on my neck. The ache curled tighter. My head spun, and I reveled in the sensation. There was only him, his need for me, and my burning desire to have him in me, filling me.

With a moan, he drew his fangs from my neck, and a flicker of heat, his vampiric healing magic, sealed the wounds shut. My soul throbbed with unfulfilled desire, disappointed that this was it. But with a growl, he picked me up, carried me into the bedroom, and laid me on the bed.

The hunger in his eyes, for me and not just my blood, stole my breath. He yanked his T-shirt off, exposing the vast expanse of his muscular chest and making my mouth water. I flicked open the button on my jeans. He hooked his fingers under the waistband and slid them and my underwear off, then crawled up the bed toward me, his gaze never leaving mine, his desire for me making my pulse pound. He pressed his hands against the insides of my knees, urging me to open for him, then licked his way up my thigh and blew a feathery breath against me.

I bucked as the sensation jolted through me, drawing a low sensual laugh from him.

"God, Essie, you're so beautiful." He brushed my folds with his fingers and licked the inside of my thigh, sending another jolt through me. "You have a vein here—"

"Yes," I said before he could finish, the thought of his

erotic bite rushing through me so close to my core making me tremble on the edge of climax. "Jacob, yes."

He teased his finger through my folds again, building the anticipation of his bite, spiraling my desire tighter. His powerful shoulder muscles bunched as his body settled between my legs.

"So here?" he teased, flicking his tongue against my thigh as he flicked his thumb against my clit.

I bucked again, another rush of pleasure shooting through me. "Yes, Jacob. Yes." Please. Yes.

His thumb circled my clit and his fangs sank slowly, agonizingly slowly into my thigh with a surge of need. I gasped, the sensation stealing my breath and thoughts. There was only the desire squeezing tight within me, hot and hard, building and building, and nothing else. No worry about what I was, no heartache over Marcus pushing me away or Gideon ruining my career. Right now there was only Jacob and my aching need, and it was perfect.

He sucked on my vein and slid a finger inside me, his thumb circling my clit, pressing harder and harder with each rotation. I writhed against him, craving release, and yet clinging to the pressure, waiting until I couldn't hold it back any longer, knowing I would come screaming.

Another suck and he added another finger, sliding them in and out of me. I ground into him, matching speed with his hands, driving him deeper into me, the pressure growing, squeezing, clenching—

Suddenly he froze, his hand, his mouth, everything absolutely still, and he squeezed his eyes shut. The ecstasy of his bite flickered, and a whisper of pain crawled up my leg.

My pulse stalled. Something was wrong. "Jacob?"

"No. Not now," he hissed.

"What?"

He groaned, but it didn't sound as if it was in pleasure. "Please, no."

"Jacob?" Was he regretting what we'd started? Every fiber of my being thrummed on the edge of climax, threatening to tear me apart. "I said yes. I meant it."

"Shit." He released his teeth from my thigh and a hint of healing magic sealed his bite shut. The room's temperature suddenly dropped, his desire vanishing between one heartbeat and the next.

"You're stopping?" The ecstasy his bite had induced twisted into loss. It still pulsed, close, so close to climax, but now the feeling was cruel, an unfulfilled tease. "Please." I needed him to finish what we'd started.

"God, I want you. I want to give you what you deserve." His body shook, and he jerked out of the bed. "But I have to go. Now."

"Go?" I sat up, the movement sending a shudder of desire through me, and I moaned.

The hunger in his eyes deepened, but his body wrenched toward the bedroom door. "Fuck." He grasped the doorframe, as if his body had a mind of its own and he was trying to keep himself in the room.

"Jacob?"

"Victoria's summoning me and I can't—" The muscles in his neck strained as he fought to keep hold of the frame. "I can't resist her. I'm sorry, Essie. We'll finish this. I promise."

His grip broke free of the doorframe, and he hurried out of his apartment, still shirtless, leaving me aching with want.

I squirmed, sliding my legs against his comforter, the movement ratcheting up my need, curled so tight that it was painful. Collapsing back on his bed, I rubbed my finger over my clit, desperate to relieve the pressure, but it was as if Jacob's magic had frozen within me, trapping me on the precipice and unable to crash over the edge.

The pain spread across my abdomen and into my chest, and I couldn't draw a deep enough breath, could only gasp. And each gasp made me quiver, ratcheting up my pain and need.

I ground my teeth and forced myself out of his bed. His magic would pass. I just had to ride it out. I didn't know how long he was going to be, but I knew if I stayed, surrounded by his rich, masculine scent, I'd go mad.

I dragged on my underwear and pants, the fabric sliding up my body drawing a moan, left Jacob a note to find me at home, and grabbed my duffle bag. I had to go back to plan A. Go home and then figure out what to do about my life once I was away from the guys. I could barely think straight right now and with Jacob gone, my thoughts were jumping to who was in the building that I could convince to help satisfy me. Which was a terrible idea.

Each step down the hall to the elevator sent tremors through me, but none of them strong enough to release me, and my head spun from the blood loss. I had no idea how I was going to make it out of the building, let alone down the street to wait for a taxi—since I wasn't going to wait for one here—but there wasn't any other choice.

The elevator dinged and the doors slid open, revealing Marcus, holding his vest, sheathed sword with belt attached, and boots. He wore baggy workout shorts and nothing else, and looked sexy as hell.

CHAPTER 16

MY BREATH VANISHED, BOTH WITH MY DROWNING NEED from Jacob and the attraction that always sizzled between me and Marcus. Every time I saw him, I thought he was hot, and right now, wearing only shorts because the magic to shift into his wolf consumed his clothing, he was mouthwateringly sexy. He wasn't anywhere near as bulky as Jacob, but his chest and arms were ripped, each muscle defined, making me yearn to run my hands over them and scratch my nails across his washboard abs.

His piercing green eyes captured me, and a feral hint of his wolf stared back at me. The air around me ignited into a heat stronger and more humid than the heat of Jacob's desire. Marcus's gaze raked over my body, amping up my need with just a look, making me yearn for him to touch me, then it settled on my neck. Jacob's magic was only strong enough to seal his bite shut, not enough to hide the evidence.

"Of course," he said as he stepped out of the elevator,

his voice so soft I couldn't get a good sense of his inflection. "You let him feed on you."

No point in denying it. "Of my own free will. His claim had nothing to do with it."

The temperature didn't change from sweltering, but I still couldn't read his expression, as if he was trying to hold his emotions at bay but couldn't contain his desire—no, with him, it was more likely anger and I just desperately wanted it to be desire.

"I saw you resist him in the tunnel. I know you could have said no if you wanted to."

"I didn't want to."

"I know you didn't." His expression... still so strange and impossible to read. "You willingly give of yourself to save people, Essie. It's just who you are, and Jacob needs you."

"What?" My already struggling thoughts tripped. I mustn't have heard that right.

"He's starving." Marcus stepped closer, and I shifted back. If he got too close I was going to beg him to take me, and I wouldn't be able to handle the rejection.

"It's his claim, isn't it?" he said. "It's stuck on you."

"Does everyone know? I got the impression Jacob was trying to hide it." I clung to my duffle bag, praying that would stop me from throwing myself at Marcus.

"I doubt anyone else has figured it out. He's certainly hiding it. But after the archnephilim, his scent changed. I couldn't smell the blood in him like I should."

"So this... *situation* is common?"

"No. I only read up on it when I saw a vampire

starving to death at Mercy Memorial during my transition," he said. "There wasn't much else for me to do during that time. The vampire's werewolf had been killed in the war, and she was unable to feed from anyone but the one she'd claimed. It's a terrible way for a vampire to go. Very very slow, and I suspect she's still in the hospital starving if she hasn't managed to make another claim."

"How come Amiah doesn't know about Jacob?" She'd been the one to help Marcus through his transition. She'd been at the hospital at the same time he had. She had to have seen that vampire, too.

"She's not looking for the signs and the claim on you is so new, if he can hold out, his body's singular focus on you will pass. We just needed to wait it out."

"But he keeps getting hurt and needing more blood than normal."

"Yeah." His gaze raked over my body again and his eyes narrowed.

I bit back a moan. *I will not beg. I will not beg.* He was determined to keep his distance, and I had to respect that, no matter how stupid it was. And I didn't think how well I'd handled myself in the ferals' nest would convince him I could be in his world. It probably had just made him more terrified for me.

"Tell me the truth, Essie. Did you finish?"

My desire twisted so tight I wanted to scream with frustration. "I think he got enough."

"But did you?" He raked his hand through his hair, mussing his dark curly locks, making me yearn to touch them, and looking uncomfortable. "Did you climax?"

"I don't think that's any of your business."

"I can smell the sex on you," he said. "Stop trying to hide it. It goes hand in fist with the claim and bite—that's just a given. But you look as jacked up as a zip addict."

I probably felt as desperate as one, too. Which was my own God damn business, and I would not beg him to help me. "Victoria summoned him."

"Shit," he said, taking my omission as a negative to his question. He stepped closer to me, and I lurched back, hitting the hall wall, making him stop, his empty hand raised, palm out, as if he was trying to keep me calm. "He mustn't know just how much the claim has changed the power of his bite for you. He wouldn't leave you hanging if he did. That's just not his style."

"What do you mean?"

"It's a side effect of a strong claim," he said. "Most consider it a bonus. The magic of his bite keeps building until released by a climax."

I trembled, throbbing at the word *climax*, desperate for release.

Then horror flooded me. I'd tried for an orgasm myself and it hadn't worked. "I have to wait for him to come back? If Victoria's pissed, she could hold him for days." She'd threatened to do that before.

Marcus shifted closer to me, and I gritted my teeth, fighting the need to throw myself at him.

"It doesn't have to be him, just someone to unlock your hold on it. It'll be okay."

"Okay?" I said, my voice rising with panic. "It's not okay. And how the hell are *you* okay with this? Why aren't you furious and pushing me away?" And making me cry with heartache. Wolves were notorious for their possessiveness.

Except the temperature around me was still hot, so he had to be feeling something. I just couldn't understand the powerful emotion combined with his calm understanding.

"Oh, my wolf fucking hates this, and I don't like it, either, but nothing Amiah is going to do for Jacob is going to help him. You had to let him bite you or he was going to die."

"So you've just changed your mind?" Now his calm was making me furious. And God damn, I needed a fucking orgasm. "What about a normal life and normal babies and normal fucking everything?"

"I was wrong, okay" he said, the ferocity of his wolf suddenly darkening his eyes. "You're neck deep in the supernatural world whether I like it or not. You won't listen to reason and you won't leave. There's no getting out for you now, and my wolf gave me a whole lot of shit while we were running off that mess with the ferals' nest. He doesn't give a shit that you belong to Gideon—"

"I don't *belong* to anyone."

"You keep telling yourself that."

"You God damn listen to it."

"My wolf doesn't care. He wants you— *I* want you. However I can get you. I can't let you go again, Essie. If you leave, I'll follow. If I have to share you with Gideon— and shit, I guess Jacob too now, so be it."

"Whoa, wait a minute." Except my straining-to-explode need thought that was a fantastic idea. All of them. Now.

I shuddered and hugged myself tighter. All that testosterone in one bed was a terrible idea, and I didn't think that was what Marcus meant.

"Life with supers is always a mess, whether we like it or not, and Essie—" He captured me with his gaze, and a surge of emotion, true, honest to goodness actual emotion, not wild temperature fluctuations, swept through me: sincerity, awe, determination, fear, and love. "You weren't a weak link in that fight in the ferals' nest. Hell, you almost killed that vampire, and I can't argue with my wolf any more that you can't hold your own in this world."

Marcus's fear deepened, and my soul cried that ferocious, powerful Marcus felt it so deeply.

"I need you, Essie. I'm done pushing if you're done running."

"I already tried to tell you I was done running in the armory, you jerk."

He gave me a rueful smile. "You did and I freaked out." His expression turned fierce, hungry, and he offered me his hand. "Let me help you release Jacob's magic."

I stared at his hand, aching, burning to take it. "I don't belong to you."

"No, I belong to you," he growled.

Jacob's magic swelled, teasing me, God, driving me insane. I gasped, and my knees grew weak.

Marcus dropped his gear and grabbed me by the hips, steadying me against the wall. My breath stalled, and the attraction that had been between us the moment we'd first locked eyes across the squad room in the precinct seared through me. "Fuck, Marcus."

"That's the offer."

I dropped my duffle bag and crashed my mouth against his, unable to resist any longer. I'd dreamed of having sex with Marcus for so long. I was sure he was going to change his mind about sharing and me being part of his world and everything, and I was terrified for that moment. But right now, he was offering me a release and there wasn't anyone else I'd rather be with.

He met my kiss with a hunger of his own, one hand tangling in my hair capturing my head, the other wrapping around my back and pulling me close to his body. His tongue swept into my mouth, plundering me.

I couldn't get enough of him. His desire, back to being felt as a change in temperature, seared me inside and out, and I clung to him, pressing against him.

His lips left my mouth and trailed down my neck—the opposite side of Jacob's bite—his stubble scraping my hypersensitive skin and sending a shudder through me, twisting my need to release tighter.

"Your room is closest," he growled into my neck, and he kissed his way down my body, setting every nerve within me on fire even though his lips were on my clothing and not my skin.

"I was leaving." My breath heaved, quick gasps making my head spin and ratcheting up my need. "Left my key in the room."

"Of course you did," he growled, grabbing his gear and my duffle bag in one hand. "You never make anything easy."

"Don't blame this on me." I captured his face and tipped his gaze back up to mine, groaning at the ferocity in his eyes, the need to have me, and the sight of his erection tenting his gym shorts. "You didn't want me here."

He rose, exuding lithe, dangerous power, and pinned me against the wall with his body. "And I was a fucking idiot."

I wrapped a leg around him and rubbed myself against him.

He groaned. "A real idiot. Come on, I'm not taking you in the hall."

"Don't want the others to watch?" I teased. I wasn't into voyeurism, and I was sure Marcus wasn't, either... of course he had said he was willing to share...

He brushed his lips against my ear, his breath teasing me with rushing pleasure. "First time is just for me."

I stared at him. "You *are* a voyeur?"

He grabbed my butt with his hand and nudged me. "Up you go."

I hopped up, wrapping both my legs around him, still amazed he could easily support my weight with one hand and walk, even though I knew werewolves were stronger than the average guy.

"Marcus?" I asked, clinging close to him and brushing my lips against his jaw, just below his ear. "Are you into having people watch?"

He groaned and picked up his pace. "No. I just wanted to see your reaction."

"And?" I flicked my tongue against that tender spot again.

"If I could think straight, I'd have thoughts about it."

He unlocked his door with his thumb, and dropped his gear and my bag the moment we were inside.

His room was set up the same as Jacob's, living area with kitchenette and bedroom with en suite bathroom. His color palette was more toward greens and browns and his furniture different with a different set up, but that was all the impression I took in before my desire jerked me back to Marcus and his body and how he made me feel.

He shoved a pile of papers off his desk and set me on the edge. I kicked off my shoes, and he grabbed the bottom of my T-shirt and yanked it off over my head. His mouth captured mine again, one hand on the back of my head to control me, the other sliding inside my bra and teasing my nipple into a taut, painful bud.

I needed a release so much I was certain I'd explode if it didn't come soon. My nerves, my soul, every cell in my body was wound tight, pulsing with desperate, hungry need.

He pushed the cups of my bra down and sucked my breast while kneading the other one. I arched my back, moaning. I needed more. God, please. I had to have more. Now.

"Marcus. Please," I gasped. "Don't play with me."

I grabbed for the waistband of his shorts, but he pushed my hand away.

"Not yet."

"Not yet? Do you have any idea how Jacob's bite is making me feel?"

He smiled against my breast. "I have a good guess."

"Then please…"

He undid the button on my jeans and grabbed the waistband. I raised my hips and he yanked the fabric, underwear included, down my legs. The material sliding against my skin made me buck, heat flooding my core, but still no climax. I needed him now. Had to have him filling me. God, I never thought this was what our first time together would be like. I thought we'd take our time, enjoy each other's bodies, not rush into it filled with desperate need.

He grabbed my knees and shoved my legs apart, spreading me wide for him, and the feralness in his gaze, the one that was all wolf, darkened his eyes. Then his attention jumped to Jacob's bite on my thigh and he growled.

My pulse stuttered. "You said you didn't care." This was a bad idea. Marcus ran hot and cold toward me at the best of times. Knowing I'd had Jacob between my legs—

"I don't." He leaned in and licked the bite. "I'm pissed he had the opportunity to give you what you needed, what you deserved, and didn't."

I shuddered, remembering the feel of Jacob's bite and his fingers pumping into me, then the image shifted to Marcus, sliding inside me, driving me to climax.

"Victoria didn't give him a chance," I said. "Literally forced him away half dressed."

"Serves him right," he said, his voice low, dangerous.

My breath hitched, and I fought to think past the pain and lust and need. I dug my hands into his scalp, grabbing his hair, and pulled his head up to look at me.

His piercing green gaze stole my breath. So too did his hunger.

"I want you in me. Now."

"I don't want you riding Jacob's magic when you come for me," he snarled, and he jerked my butt right to the edge of the desk and raked his tongue over my clit.

I gasped, my breath completely gone, the promise of a climax sparking within me, close, so God damn close, but not there.

He pushed my legs open as wide as they would go, opening me completely to him, and growled against my folds, the sound pure masculine desire.

I tightened my grip in his hair, writhing against him. "Yes, please, yes."

His tongue tormented me, his stubble rasping against my sensitive skin as his fingers dug into my thighs. My need was so tight I couldn't breathe, then he sucked hard on my clit and fireworks exploded behind my eyelids. Pleasure roared through me, making every muscle contract, and Jacob's magic flooded every cell in my body.

Marcus groaned, his nails biting into my flesh, his mouth grinding against my clit, his breath fast and hot against my skin.

Tremors raced through me, bolts of electricity that kept zapping me, making me twitch and gasp. I fell back on the desk, unable to keep my body up, unable to catch my breath or think straight.

"Holy fuck." Marcus sagged to his knees, his expression stunned. "I didn't think it felt like that."

I managed to rise up on my elbow to meet his gaze. "Regretting not coming with me?" I flashed him a wicked smile, teasing him, but the moment the words came out, I realized I wasn't done. Jacob's magic was gone, but I still wanted Marcus. Again and again if he'd have me.

His pupils dilated, seeing my desire for him. "I have protection in the bedroom."

He stood, wrapped an arm around my back, and pulled me close to lift me, but his erection, still tenting his shorts, brushing against me, drawing a gasp and a sudden, desperate need.

I scratched my nails down his chest, making him moan.

"I trust you're clean, and I'm on birth control." I didn't want to wait. Jacob's magic might be gone, but I still burned for Marcus. There was a different kind of magic between us that was just as powerful as Jacob's, and I'd been aching for Marcus for years.

He growled at that, leaned into me, and slid his hands up my thighs, the movement tender and so fucking sensual. His wolf darkened his eyes and his body trembled. I could tell he was trying to hold it back, keep it controlled. But I didn't want control. I wanted all the ferocious passion the sexual tension between us had been promising since the mess with the archnephilim had brought him back into my life.

I slid my hands over his and up his arms. "Marcus, let go."

The muscles in his jaw clenched.

"Marcus—" Screw words. Actions were better. I slipped my hands down the front of his shorts and shoved them off his hips, freeing his thick, straining erection.

My pulse tripped at the sight of it, and I wrapped my

hand around the base. His eyes rolled back, and he moaned my name.

"Let go, Marcus." I drew my hand along his length then pumped back down. "Please."

He shifted closer, aligning with my core, and I slid his tip through my wet folds, proving how ready I was for him, how much I wanted him inside me.

With a groan, he pushed his hips forward, sliding himself inch by agonizingly sensual inch into me. My heart pounded, my yearning ratcheted back up, as intense and aching as it had been with Jacob's magic.

His breath came fast, and his body shook. His control was astounding and driving me insane.

"You feel so good," he said, the muscles in his jaw and neck straining. He slowly drew out. I shuddered, my head dropping back, and closed my eyes, every nerve focused on the sensations.

He pushed back again. So. God. Damn. Slowly.

"Marcus, let go."

"I don't want to hurt you," he growled, his wolf right at the surface.

"You won't hurt me."

"Not me—"

I moaned and met his gaze. "He won't, either."

The struggle in his eyes deepened.

"I trust you. All of you. Please, Marcus." I was back again to feeling like I was going to burn up with desire. He was driving me mad. "Fuck me," I snarled.

His wolf snarled back, and he plunged into me with a fierce push. I gasped, and his eyes blazed with hunger. He shifted a nail into a claw long enough to slice through the front of my bra, exposing my breasts, and shoved me back against the desk. I clung to the edges as he drew out and plunged back in, each stroke adding more fuel to the already blazing fire within me.

He squeezed my breasts, and drew back out. Growled, then plunged back in, each stroke faster and more forceful than the last. His breath turned into quick needy gasps. So did mine. The pleasure was consuming. There was only him and his body driving into me and it was perfect.

His hand left my breast and he clutched my hips, his thumb finding my clit.

I cried out, pleasure zinging through me, twisting my need higher. He pounded faster and harder, grinding his thumb against my clit until my climax once again seized every muscle, this one more powerful than the last. I screamed his name as a wave of pleasure crashed into me. I rode it, clinging to it, as I ground against him, straining to hold on until he came. And then his body jerked hard against me, all his muscles contracting as his orgasm seized him. Mine surged, my hold on it shattering, and the sensation consumed me, lightning crackling through every cell with glorious, mind-blowing bliss.

"God, Essie, you're amazing." He collapsed forward, resting his head on my belly, his breath ragged.

I slid my hand through his hair. My breath was just as ragged, my muscle still twitching with aftershocks. My heart pounded, filled with joy, every cell in my body reveling in the rightness of being with Marcus.

This was where I was supposed to be. I knew it in my soul.

To hell with what fate said about Gideon and me. Marcus was who I belonged with.

"Marcus, I—"

Blazing white agony erupted in my head. All the muscles in my body jerked so tight I couldn't scream, couldn't draw breath, and could barely think.

CHAPTER 17

THE AGONY RIPPED EVERY OTHER SENSATION AWAY UNTIL there was only it, screaming through my head, threatening to consume my vision in darkness and suffocate me with pressure. It was coming. *He* was coming. With his massive power and devouring darkness.

Marcus jerked off me, captured my cheeks, and locked gazes with me. Worry filled his eyes and cold swept over my skin. "Talk to me, Essie."

But I couldn't draw enough breath to speak. I wasn't sure I could get my jaw to unlock to say anything even if I could.

The sense of black malevolence, pure evil, flooded me. The walls of his prison were weakening, and now he could slip a thread of magic beyond its confines. The seal holding it altogether, bouncing for eternity among all the realms of existence, was going to manifest in the weakest magical realm, the realm of mortals, and once again he had a chance to empower the spell he'd set over a millennia ago to free himself.

"We have to get you to Amiah." He pulled up his shorts and grabbed a throw blanket off the back of his couch.

God, I didn't want to go back to Amiah, and certainly not naked in Marcus's arms. Tears leaked from my eyes and I convulsed.

Marcus grabbed me before I fell off the desk and sat me up, leaning me against his chest.

"It'll be okay," he said, but his fear swept frost across my cheeks and up my arms.

Find it. The key was going to manifest. I had to get ready— No, Logan had to get ready.

I shuddered with cold and fear. Marcus wrapped the blanket around my shoulders.

Free me.

"No," I gasped. But somehow I knew *he* couldn't hear me. It was the compulsion from his spell, set into the magic *he*, Ibizual, had given to Logan. That had been his demon-deal to gain more power.

Secure the key tonight. Break the seal tomorrow.

"Essie, you need help." Marcus lifted me, cradling me against his chest, and headed to the door.

The agony released my muscles but still burned in my head. I sagged into his embrace, my skin stinging with the frost of Marcus's fear. "The key is starting to manifest."

Marcus froze, his hand on the door about to open it. "What?"

"I can feel the spell." I shuddered, sending agony slicing through my head. "I can feel *him*."

"I'm still taking you to Amiah."

"She won't be able to do anything." This wasn't the kind of injury Amiah could heal. It wasn't actually an injury. I pressed my palm over Marcus's heart, feeling his pulse race. "We—" I stopped myself. I wasn't part of the team any more. "The *team* needs to get ready."

Marcus's grip on me tightened, conflict pinching the corners of his eyes. He had a job to do, and yet he didn't want to let me go.

"You were convulsing," he growled. " You have frost on your cheeks."

"And you guys are going to get slaughtered if you don't come up with a plan," I snarled back and pushed against his hold on me, trying to break free. My throat tightened as my fear clenched my chest. I couldn't lose him—

No, I couldn't lose Gideon—

Jeez, I couldn't lose either of them.

Shit.

"Ibizual can't be allowed to escape." He'd consume everything and everyone.

"Fine." He set me on my feet, and I clutched the blanket to my chest, unable to get warm. "Can you tell where it's going to be?"

I sucked in a ragged breath and concentrated on the sensation inside my head. Thick, consuming darkness. It was a lot like the clinging, suffocating smoke from the archnephilim, but a thousand times stronger. It enveloped me, pressing against my senses, but there was no sense of location, or direction or anything. Only the knowledge that the key was coming. *Prepare. Find me. Free me.* The darkness squeezed tight. Agony sliced across my skull, and I convulsed.

Marcus pulled me back into his arms before I collapsed. The frost from his fear thickened on my face. His expression pinched tighter, and his wolf darkened his eyes. "Anything?"

"Not yet. Maybe Jacob knows. This is supposed to be his connection with Logan." And I could only assume the strength of his claim was the reason I could feel the power building to manifest the key.

Marcus leaned me against the door and grabbed his phone from inside his boot in the pile of gear he'd dropped the moment we'd entered his apartment.

I pulled the blanket tighter around my shoulders, my teeth chattering, and focused my attention on my clothes a few feet away by his desk. His gaze followed mine as he dialed Jacob's number.

"Marcus," Jacob said after the third ring, his voice clear thanks to the enhanced hearing from his claim. Question and uncertainty filled his tone as if he didn't know what kind of reception he was going to get.

"Do you know where the key is going to form?"

"No, I—"

Marcus retrieved my clothes and dropped them in a pile beside me. "Are you sure?"

"Shit. It's less than eight hours until dusk. I should be feeling something now." Tension tightened his tone. "I'm coming in. We need to figure out how to get eyes on Logan so we can stop him from getting the key."

Marcus's gaze locked with mine. "Essie can feel the key."

I sank to the floor and opened my duffle bag to grab my dirty bra, which was now better than my sliced-in-half bra.

"You heard me, right?" Marcus growled. "Essie can feel the key."

More like it was tearing into my brain. I dropped the blanket from my shoulders and shrugged out of my ruined bra.

"How can she—?"

"Jeez, Jacob. It's your claim on her. It so fucking strong she's bite-locked." He clenched his jaw, his wolf now more than just darkening his eyes but pushing through into his expression and body language with dangerous ferocity.

A blast of agony sliced into my brain, seizing my muscles as I tried to secure my bra clasp behind my back.

"I know the claim is strong, but she can't be bite-locked," Jacob said. "That only happens when a super is claimed or—"

"Or when your claim on the human is unnaturally strong. I know, it's rare, but she's bite-locked and you left her hanging." He jerked away from me and stormed to the far side of his living room to glare out the window. His frost vanished, replaced with sudden blazing rage.

"Marcus, I didn't know."

"How can you not know how strong your claim is? How could you do that to her?"

But Jacob didn't know I was half super, and I hadn't known there was a difference between claiming a human and a super. This was my fault, and now Jacob wasn't going to survive without me.

"I swear, I thought the strength of the claim was just a problem for me. I know your wolf has claimed her."

"He has," Marcus growled.

"My claim isn't an emotional bond. I'll keep my distance from her. I'll—"

"You'll fucking starve to death. Don't be an idiot."

"Marcus—"

"But if you leave her like that again," Marcus said, his voice low, dangerous, his wolf barely contained, "I'll rip your fucking throat out."

I managed to clasp my bra and pull on my T-shirt.

Marcus wrenched back to face me. "Now, what do we do about this key?"

"We have to wait until dusk to know which direction to head."

"Until dusk?" I had to deal with this agony until dusk? Realization made my stomach drop. Just because the key manifested didn't mean the pain would go away.

"How the hell did you function enough to find that key the first time?" Marcus asked, helping me stand so I could put on my pants.

"What do you mean?"

"Essie is in so much pain she can barely stand."

"Last time it hurt, but it didn't hurt that much. It's either because she's human, something to do with the claim, or something about the key manifesting that's different this time."

"So you have no fucking clue." Marcus blew out a heavy breath. "Wonderful."

"I'll call Gideon and Kol, and we'll meet in the lounge."

"Good. *You* can explain to Gideon why Essie is still involved."

Jacob groaned. "If she's the one who can feel the key, we need her. Are you going to fight me on this?"

I slid back to the floor to put on my runners.

"Essie handled her own in the nest." Marcus knelt and helped me with my shoes, his piercing green gaze capturing mine, the heat of his anger turning sultry. "And I've been reminded that I'm an idiot."

"Okay. I'll be there in ten."

Marcus hung up as another blast of agony seized me, making me convulse.

Find it. Free me.

I had no idea how I was going to last until dusk, or God, even longer. Gasping, I tried to stand.

"Stay there while I change." He stood and glared down at me. "You don't need to prove how tough you are right now."

I raised my hands in defeat. "Fine." Besides, I wasn't sure if I could stand.

He hurried into his bedroom, changed into jeans and a T-shirt, and returned to the door to pull on his boots. Then he picked me up, and he stepped out into the hall.

A few doors down, Kol stepped out of his apartment, and his attention jumped to us. A sultry smile lit his face, billowed desire through my chest, and stole my breath. God, he was so beautiful. He hurried to catch us, his gate not nearly as smooth as usual, as if he were trying too hard to be steady, and his eyes were glassy. If I hadn't known better, I'd guess he was drunk or high.

"Really? We're in the middle of a crisis and you overindulged?" Marcus said as we headed to the elevator.

Kol glared back at him. "Well, the next time you and Essie have magically enhanced sex, warn me. The first round burned through all my shields and I had no defenses for round two."

"We didn't have magically enhanced sex, we—" Marcus frowned.

Heat rose to my cheeks. "Would Jacob's bite count?"

Kol's eyebrows rose.

"Well, shit," Marcus said. "Releasing Jacob's bite-lock does count. But round two wasn't magical."

"I would beg to differ," Kol said.

I playfully slapped Marcus's chest, feigning anger. "So you're saying it wasn't magical for you?"

He rolled his eyes at me. "That's not what I meant."

"Then what *did* you mean?" I pressed, making Kol snicker.

"Essie," Marcus growled.

"Marcus," I growled back, and a blast of agony slammed into me.

I managed to gasp in a quick breath before all my muscles clenched, but the first convulsion pushed it out of me, and I was suffocating with agony and darkness, all of it threatening my consciousness.

"Holy shit." Kol's eyes grew wide, all playfulness gone. "What the hell is that?"

The pain released my muscles but continued to throb in my skull. I clung to Marcus, fighting to get my breath back. "The key is starting to form."

And every cell in my body was screaming that I had to get to it first. I couldn't let Logan release all that evil.

CHAPTER 18

W<small>E HEADED DOWN TO THE FIRST FLOOR TO A LOUNGE NEAR</small> the back of the building. It was a comfortable space, decorated in tans and creams with two over-stuffed couches and six matching armchairs. An enormous panel TV hung on the wall and past that, deeper into the room, stood a floor-to-ceiling shelf filled with books and puzzles and games near a large pale-wood table with half a dozen matching chairs. At the back wall, patio doors opened to a small patio enclosed with a tall privacy fence and two small wrought-iron cafe tables and chairs.

"This place has everything," I said, trying to distract myself from the agony pounding in my head.

"All essential JP team members live here, along with the almost dozen angels living in Union," Kol said. "We have a variety of amenities since we can't spend all our free time working out in the gym." He shot a hard look at Marcus.

"Says the demon whose body will never change."

Marcus set me on the couch. "How about you put your extra juice to good use so Essie can concentrate?"

"It is yours." Kol flashed a wicked smile, making Marcus stiffen.

His wolf darkened his eyes until he clenched his jaw and forced his beast back down.

"Well, mostly." Kol shrugged. "I guess round one is partially Jacob's and round two... whoever cast the spell you two used."

Kol settled in beside me, within reaching distance and not closer.

"There was no spell," Marcus said, sitting on my other side, also not touching me. Which was good, because if I understood what Marcus was asking, Kol was going to use his magical enthrallment to help me think past the pain by making me focus on other sensations. And I had no idea how I'd feel while turned on again by the incubus with Marcus's body brushing against me.

"You need to be careful with that. Sex magic can be dangerous."

"There was no spell." Marcus glared at Kol.

"What spell?" Gideon asked as he entered the lounge. His attention jumped to me and the icy look in his eyes grew harder.

"Nothing." Kol grabbed my hand and a hint of heat swept up my arm, muting but not eliminating the pain and making my mind jerk back to the memory of climaxing with Marcus inside me.

My pulse picked up, and I shuddered. So did Kol. Marcus's glare deepened.

"Sorry," Kol mumbled, and the heat dimmed until I almost couldn't feel it.

Gideon leaned against the side of an armchair and frowned, his attention on Kol. "What's wrong with you?"

"Nothing." But Kol's grip on my hand tightened. "What's the plan?"

"We have to wait until Officer Shaw can tell us where the key is," Gideon said, not sounding happy about that at all. "Then we go get it. We should be prepared for more ferals."

"We've killed a fair number already. How many more do you think Logan made?" Marcus asked.

"Assume there's more," Jacob said, striding into the lounge. He still wore his dirty pants from the fight with the ferals, one leg with a wide blood-encrusted gash mid-thigh, but he'd put on a shirt. I could see the question, the need to talk in his eyes, but his glance at Marcus beside me told me he wanted to talk in private.

And yeah, we had a lot to figure out, now that everything was completely complicated.

"There's always more." Jacob sat in an armchair and turned his attention to Gideon. "And Essie won't be able to tell us where the key is. It doesn't work that way. She has to lead us to it."

"Of course she does." Gideon pinched the bridge of his nose. "So we know the key won't form until dusk, we know Logan will have more ferals, but we have no idea how many or where they are. Do we know *anything*? What about Bane and information on hellfire princes and their cages?"

"I haven't heard from him yet," Marcus said.

"Victoria said she can't sense Logan, but she did gift me with a little extra magic, so hopefully it will be harder for him to control me."

"Do I want to know what that cost you?" Gideon asked.

"The terms are reasonable," Jacob said. "I'm to pay it when this is over."

"How long will I lose you for?"

Jacob glanced at me then jerked his attention back to Gideon, the movement so fast I would have missed it if his claim hadn't attuned me to him. "Just one full twenty-four-hour period."

"I see." Gideon gave a tight nod. "I'll make sure the kitchen is stocked up so you can recover quickly."

That meant Jacob was going to get hurt. I jerked forward, and the throbbing in my head swelled, over-coming Kol's enthrallment, making me wince. "We're not letting her torture you. We'll find another way to protect you from Logan's magic."

"It's not intended as torture," Jacob said.

"Not intended as torture? What's that supposed to mean?" Perhaps I couldn't understand because of the pain in my head.

"Sex, Essie," Kol said, sending a shiver of need through me. "Victoria likes a lot of blood with her sex."

"Jeez, Jacob—"

"The deal's been made. Don't worry about it," he said, emphasizing the command.

The claim twisted, and I fought the compulsion and managed to resist it. I gave him my driest look, letting him know he couldn't command me any more.

"The decisions of my team are no longer your concern, Officer Shaw." Gideon crossed his arms, and a hint of heat whispered around me. "They never were. Do you understand?"

"I—" The agony exploded in my head again, stronger than before, as if avoiding it with Kol's magic only made it more powerful. Whatever I'd been about to say vanished as the pain blazed through my skull and down my neck, searing into my heart. I fought to draw breath, fought to relax my muscles, but I was locked tight, worse than being hit with a Taser, worse than Gideon's brand shooting lightning through me.

Marcus and Kol grabbed my shoulders as I convulsed. Jacob jerked forward and knelt before me, bringing a bracing cold with him, while Gideon looked frozen, trapped, horror in his eyes.

The agony released me and my muscles went limp. Marcus and Kol caught me, and Kol pulled me into his arms, wrapping them around my waist and pushing soothing heat into my freezing body.

The frost was back on my cheeks, and Marcus scraped it away with his thumbs, making my pulse pound in fear. They were going to learn the truth. They were going to discover what I was.

I fought to focus on the bone-melting thread of desire curling from Kol's hands. I couldn't let my fear or the pain consume me. *Please, God, let them think the frost is because of the key. Please.*

"Tell me it goes away or eases up or anything," Marcus said to Jacob. "That it won't be like this once the key forms."

"I don't know." Jacob's fear was clear in his eyes. "It was never like this for me."

"We can't let this distract us," Gideon said.

Marcus glared at him and growled.

I grabbed Marcus's hand to keep him by me. "Gideon's right." Jeez, it even hurt to breathe now. "You need to figure out if there's a better way to deal with ferals and zombies, or whatever it was Logan made in that nest, and if there's anything you can learn about Ibizual, the key, and his cage."

"Marcus, get a hold of Bane again and anyone else who might know anything about hellfire princes. Jacob, Kol—"

"I'll stay with Essie," Kol said, his arms tightening around my waist. "I can search the JP's online records and let you know as soon as she can sense the key."

"Fine. Jacob and I will head to the archives and search the books." Gideon shoved away from the chair. "Come on. Maybe we'll get lucky and stumble across something useful."

He marched out of the lounge. Jacob gave my knee a squeeze then followed. Marcus grabbed my hand, his gaze capturing me and stealing my breath, and brushed his lips across my knuckles.

I shivered with desire.

"Hey," Kol groaned. "At least give me time to bleed off the excess first."

Marcus ignored Kol, flashed me a hungry smile, then left.

"I see you've worked things out with Marcus." Kol

pulled his phone from his pocket while keeping one arm around me.

"Until he realizes this is a terrible idea and changes his mind again." I leaned into his side and concentrated on his soft sensual heat pulsing into me. I knew it was a whisper of what his magic was really like. I'd gotten a glimpse of what it would feel like when he'd released it when I'd saved him from the archnephilim, and I struggled not to think about that.

"I don't think he's going to change his mind." Kol's magic seeped deeper and with that, and the heat from his raised body temperature—because of his demonic nature —I was starting to feel like I was drifting.

"I wouldn't put money on that," I said, so relaxed my words slurred. I prayed Marcus had made his final decision, but once this crisis and the glow of sex passed, he was going to realize what a complete and utter mess this was. "It's all so complicated."

I shifted, trying to get more comfortable against Kol's side, our current position straining my neck when I leaned my head back.

Kol sighed, and turned so his back was against the arm of the couch. He slid a leg on the other side of me, boxing me in, and drew me back against his chest.

I leaned in, one hand pressed over his heart, feeling the steady, soothing thump beneath my palm. The pain from the key remained, a far-off stinging in my head, but the overall sensation within me was enveloping warmth and safety. I could do anything in Kol's arms, ask for anything, and he wouldn't judge. His pleasure was my pleasure.

Except it wasn't his pleasure I craved. Well, right now it kind of was, but the need wasn't overwhelming. It was just enough to ease the pain and relax me. Who I really wanted was Marcus. He was all I'd ever wanted. "Why does it have to be so complicated?"

"I hear that's the defining feature of relationships."

"You hear?" I closed my eyes.

"Incubi don't fall in love. We don't have relationships like everyone else because of the nature of our magic." He shrugged, the movement rubbing his body against mine, drawing a curl of desire. "It is what it is."

A hint of mist whispered around me, telling me he wasn't as nonchalant about the situation as he pretended to be.

"Are you really bite-locked with Jacob?" he asked, his tone too bright, forcing the topic change.

Sudden hot need rushed through me at the memory of Jacob's bite and Marcus releasing it.

Kol hissed out a sharp breath, and his pulse picked up. The heat from his magic billowed, swelling from comforting to needy, and made me ache with yearning.

"Shit. Sorry." He wrenched back on his magic, the sudden absence leaving me cold and spiking agony through my head.

I gasped in pain and my muscles contracted, threatening to wrench me into convulsions again.

"Crap." His arm around my waist tightened, and he pressed his lips to the top of my head. A hint of his power returned, steadying me out then dragging me back to the sensual sleepy state. "I've never felt anything like the power of your release before."

"Blame Jacob," I said, my lips heavy. "I've never felt anything like it before, either."

"You know sex magic is dangerous, right?" He tensed beneath me, as if preparing for another surge of my desire, and the heat from his magic grew strained, edging back toward sexual. "You can't do that again."

"There was only Jacob's bite. I swear." Why wouldn't he believe me? Yes, both climaxes with Marcus had been amazing, the second as powerful as the one induced by Jacob's bite, but magic hadn't been involved. It had just been the result of years of pent-up anticipation.

Years of fantasizing, dreaming, aching. Perhaps there was magic involved, because Marcus's wolf had claimed me. I hadn't heard of anything like that in the were community, but maybe it was rare, like a vampire's bite-lock, and shifters didn't talk about it.

I'd have to ask Marcus about that.

I wondered if he knew. He hadn't been a shifter for very long, hadn't been born one. He'd been that one in a million susceptible to the lycanthrope infection.

God, I really didn't know anything about him. Did he belong to a pack? Did his family know? Hell, even before he'd been bitten and we'd been partners, I hadn't known much about him, like how big his family was and if they lived in town.

But did any of that change the way I felt about him?

Not really. It just meant we were going to have to learn about each other, figure out how things were going to work—

If he didn't change his mind.

And if Gideon didn't get in the way. He'd known

Marcus and I had feelings for each other before fate had branded me with his mark, but would knowing we were together change things? Would he free me of the obligation neither of us wanted as mates?

He would free me.

He had to free me.

Free me.

Find it and free me. I can give you power beyond your wildest imagination.

No. But a part of me yearned to say yes. I needed power, needed to protect myself.

I know the darkness within you, the thin thread wrapped around your soul. Ibizual's dark laugher grated against my senses and sliced agony through my head. *You've been touched by my kin. You'll never be able to burn it all away, no matter how hard you try.*

His malevolence swept around me, crushing me just as the archnephilim's had, and I fought to break free, but couldn't move, couldn't breathe, could only think and feel. And I was drowning in fear and helplessness.

Never, I gasped at him.

Lightning exploded through me, and I jerked forward. The silvery remains of the archnephilim's brand burned while Gideon's brand pulsed with snaps of electricity, both grating against the burning crackle of my buzz. My entire body was alight with battling energy.

I'd thought the horror of the archnephilim was behind me, thought I could move on from the darkness that had threatened to consume my soul. I'd thought I was free. But I wasn't. I'd never be free. I had to leave, had to escape before everyone knew the truth, had to—

"Essie, it's okay." Kol sat forward and hugged me, his body and heat wrapping around me. "It's just a dream."

But it wasn't a dream. Once again a demon was in my head and knew exactly what I was.

The pain in my head swept down into my chest, squeezed tight, and yanked me out of Kol's embrace to my feet. I had to go. Now.

Free me.

My body jerked toward the door.

"Essie?" Kol grabbed my wrist, stopping me from leaving.

"I have to go."

"Where?"

Good question. "I don't know."

He frowned, and my gaze jumped past his shoulder and out the patio door. The sky was dark, only a hint of light remaining. It was dusk. The key was calling me.

CHAPTER 19

KOL CALLED GIDEON AND MARCUS, AND WE HURRIED TO the garage to wait for them. Thankfully the pain in my head was mostly gone, and while the pull in my chest was fierce, it wasn't agonizing. Except now that the agony in my head was gone, I was painfully aware of my buzz biting under my skin. If I was smart, I'd run up to my room and change my nicotine patches, but the compulsion to go to the key wouldn't let me head back inside.

Jacob arrived first, in clean clothes and with his bulletproof vest back on, and his matching Berettas and a sword on his belt. He handed Kol a vest, his gaze once again jumping to me, dark, intense, and filled with the need to talk. In private.

Gideon arrived next, decked out like he'd been before to clean out the ferals' nest. He handed me an M4, and I checked the magazine to ensure it was full in hopes that the movement would distract me from the need to move.

Get the key. Now now now.

Marcus rushed out the door last. He also wore the same gear as before, and had brought down my borrowed vest, duty belt, Glock, and extra magazines for both the Glock and the M4. He also handed me a sheathed sword. It wasn't as long as his or Jacob's, but then I doubted I'd be able to handle anything bigger.

"She's not going to need that," Gideon said as Marcus helped me secure it to my duty belt. "She's staying in the SUV."

"I'm not taking any chances," Marcus growled. He finished with the belt and slipped my room keycard into my hand.

Gideon glared at me. "Do you even know how to use that?"

Not really, but I wasn't going to admit that to him. If it came down to me needing the sword, we were in dire straights.

"We need to get going," I said instead, unable to stop myself from shifting from side to side.

Gideon didn't move and his gaze bore into me. "My magic is off limits."

I struggled to hold his gaze, and the electricity from his brand burned up my forearm.

Now. Go now.

"Is that clear?" he said.

"Copy that."

"Let's go." Jacob hurried to the SUV.

Gideon tossed the keys to Marcus, who grabbed them one-handed and ran past Jacob to the driver's door.

We all got in, taking our usual seats. The pull was

yanking me to the back of the garage and, since that direction led out of the Supers' Quarter, I had to assume the key was going to manifest somewhere in town.

"We're going into the city," I said as Marcus pulled out of the garage.

"How's the pain?" he asked.

"Mostly gone." If I didn't take into account my God damn buzz, which, if I leaned against the back of Gideon's seat, was almost at new-patch levels.

"Thank God," he breathed.

"Focus on the job," Gideon said, his voice low as he turned on the SUV's GPS then handed out coms to everyone in the group but me. "Where in town are we going?"

I pointed down the road leading through the park and ringing the Supers' Quarter, squirming in my seat. "That way and a little to the right." It was as specific as I could get.

We left the Quarter, and the pull to the right got stronger. Gideon studied the streets, directing Marcus as I gave vague directions and trying to keep us from getting stopped at a dead end.

The pull kept getting stronger. A part of me feared the agony was going to explode through me again, and I would go back to convulsing and being at best useless and at worst a dangerous distraction. It was getting harder to breathe, and I was getting hot—and I wasn't sure if it was because of the key manifesting or someone's emotions.

We worked our way through town, breaking the

speed limit and running through red lights, until I knew we were almost on top of it.

"Here," I gasped.

Now. Free me now.

Marcus jerked the SUV to the curb, narrowly missing the front of a car already parked there, and swore. We were on a busy street near the heart of downtown. The driver who'd been on the road behind us yelled as he passed us.

"You're sure it's here?" Marcus asked.

Now.

High rises towered to our right, half of the buildings rebuilt from the war, all shiny glass and steel. They sat interspersed among the older, original city buildings, constructed of brick with sculpted concrete ledges—the same turn-of-the-century architecture found in the Supers' Quarter. Most of the main floors were vast lobbies for whatever business resided inside, but a few had cafes or restaurant or stores. Even now, well past regular business hours, there were people on the street. Not nearly as many as there would have been if it hadn't been almost nine at night, but still too many for my liking, given how vicious Logan's ferals had been.

The pressure in my chest was fierce, and I strained to breathe, but the certainty in my soul was also fierce. The key was going to manifest here—

To my left. Across the street. In the park.

Gideon pulled out his phone and hit a pre-programmed number as he climbed out of the SUV. My buzz roared back to life, and I gritted my teeth.

"JP agent o-seven-one-four," he said. "I need a full lockdown on Seventh and Bell by Unity Park and a four-block radius around it. Equip for feral vampires."

"Copy that," a voice said on the other end of the line and hung up.

"The local PD isn't going to deploy in time," Jacob said, getting out of the SUV.

"It's still protocol." Gideon pocketed his phone.

Kol and Marcus got out. I opened my door to get out but Gideon froze me with his icy glare and grabbed the door, blocking my way. "Can you pinpoint where the key will form?"

"In the park. Maybe a hundred feet that way." I pointed directly across from me down a winding gravel path that twisted along the gently sloping lawn, sheltered by tall trees—many magically aged since they'd only been planted in the last twenty-five years. The pressure squeezed with the certainty of my words, and I fought to have enough breath to speak. "Yes, a hundred feet that way."

"Good. Stay here." He moved to close the door but stopped. "Better yet, wait here until Chris can pick you up."

No. I had to go to the key. Now. Everything in my being said I couldn't wait, couldn't leave. I had to go.

Gideon pulled out his phone again as a woman down the street screamed.

We all jerked our attention toward the scream. A woman scrambled into the lobby of an office tower as a pack of ferals barreled down the street toward us. One of them snarled at her but didn't stop to attack, their aim fully on us.

"Essie, get out of here." Marcus tossed me the keys, shoved Gideon out of the way, and slammed my door shut.

The first feral leaped at the guys, and Gideon lunged into its attack, his sword of pure light forming in his hands and plunging into the feral's chest.

Marcus drew his sword and met the next one, while Kol slid over the front of the SUV's hood to meet another.

"Essie, please," Marcus said, frost sweeping over my arms.

I wanted to stay. Fight. But we were already overwhelmed, and I was cop enough to know that even if I could draw a full breath, I was still a liability right now. If I could get some distance, I could use the M4 to slow the ferals down like I'd done in the nest.

Clenching my jaw against the call from the key, I scrambled into the driver's seat and hit the power locks. I fumbled to get the key into the ignition, but a feral shoved past Gideon and Kol and jumped onto the SUV's hood. It slammed its fist into the front windshield, cracking it, then smashed through with the next punch, spraying me with safety glass pebbles.

It shoved its arm up to its shoulder through the hole and clawed for my neck. I grabbed the seat recline and wrenched back out of reach. The feral snarled and smashed its other fist through the windshield. I dropped the keys in my lap, drew my Glock, and shot it point blank in the forehead. Blue lightning crackled around its body and with a howl, it collapsed, dead.

Outside the SUV, the guys were surrounded, at least a dozen ferals clawing and biting and snarling, and more ferals—I wasn't sure if they were ferals or reanimated ferals—rushed down the street toward us. Jacob, the combat too close quarters for his Berettas, was using his sword with deadly efficiency, and Kol's blades were a whirl as he danced and ducked the ferals' attacks.

"We have to get to the key," Gideon said.

Yes. Get the key. It's coming. Now now now.

"Go. I've got Essie," Marcus growled.

Gideon shot a hard glare at me. "Get out of here."

And he was right. They were going to need everyone to fight the ferals and get to the key before Logan. I couldn't let Marcus stay to protect me. But God, I had to get that key. The compulsion was almost as bad as Jacob's claim when it had been new.

I grabbed the keys from my lap to shove them into the ignition, but a feral slammed its shoulder against my door, heaving the SUV off the driver's side wheels.

The wheels crashed back to the asphalt, jarring me, and I missed the ignition. In the rear view mirror, I could see more ferals racing toward us.

Jeez, how many people had Logan turned? There were just so many.

"Officer Shaw, go!" Gideon snapped. He slashed at a feral's neck, but it jerked to the side. The strike didn't decapitate it, only sent a wild spray of blood into his face. He flinched, the action less than a second, but long enough for the feral to grab the front of his vest and wrench him close.

The feral at my door smashed its fist through the

window, sending glass flying toward me, nicking my cheek and neck, and clawed at me as I shoved the key into the ignition. I wrenched to the side, its claws raking over my shoulder with fiery agony, and tried to keep a hand on the key and start the SUV.

For a heartbeat, the idea of glancing into the backseat to grab the M4 flashed through my mind, but I only had time for one thing and getting away would be better for the guys.

Jacob shoved the feral closest to him to the side and rushed to the feral on me. He yanked the feral away from the door, but two more slammed against the driver's side of the SUV before he could stop them.

The vehicle heaved up, and with a roar from the ferals, they tossed it onto its side. My shoulder and head slammed into the passenger side door, and what little breath I had burst from my lungs.

Marcus yelled, his fear frosting over my cheeks, but he was caught five feet from the front of the SUV between two ferals and couldn't get to me.

One of the ferals who'd shoved the SUV over, a guy about Marcus's size and build, dove through the broken driver's side window, showering me with more glass.

He swiped at me, and I yanked my Glock up and fired two shots into his forehead as his claws dug into my forearm. Blood sprayed my face, and he collapsed on top of me, pinning me with his one hundred and fifty plus pounds. I fought to draw breath against his weight and the pressure of the soon-to-be materializing key, and my muscles twitched with the force of my buzz biting under my skin.

Now. Go now.

The other feral leaned into the window, snarling, but someone yanked it away. I gasped in a shallow breath and shoved at the feral's dead weight pinning me, but couldn't move him one-handed. I really didn't want to put my Glock down, but if I was going to get out of the SUV, I had to move the feral.

Out the front windshield, I could only see Marcus and hoped that meant the guys were moving the fight closer to the key. Somehow I knew it hadn't manifested yet, but that didn't mean Logan wasn't already set and waiting, ready to grab it the moment it did while the guys were still fighting his ferals.

Something crashed against the bottom—now side— of the SUV, making it rock. Shit.

Gasping, I set down my Glock, heaved the feral's head and shoulder into the space between the seats, and retrieved my sidearm. I shot at the windshield six times, trying to make enough of a hole to get me started, since windshield safety glass was hard to kick through and even harder if it hadn't already been broken.

I kicked again and again as fast as I could, fighting to get the glass to peel away and create an opening large enough to crawl through.

A feral rushed toward the front of the SUV, its gaze locked on me. Marcus grabbed it by the back of its torn and filthy shirt and yanked it off its feet. Again I consider the M4 in the back seat. I didn't want to leave it behind, but there was no way I'd have time to search for it.

Still fighting for breath, I half crawled, half squirmed

out the windshield, the hole barely big enough for my body, the glass pebbles biting into my palms.

Marcus had decapitated the feral who'd been about to attack me, but another one had tackled him to the road.

"You were supposed to leave," Gideon yelled at me. He stood in the middle of the road, light blazing from his eyes, a match to the light making up his sword. None of the guys had gotten far from the SUV, with Kol the farthest, at the mouth of the path leading into the park.

"Don't think I didn't try. I know I'm best suited to fight this fight from a distance." I drew in a strained breath and fired at a feral lunging for Jacob's back. The buzz made me twitch, and I hit the feral's shoulder and not its chest. Thankfully it still stumbled long enough for Jacob to wrench around and decapitate it.

"So you were going to disobey an order and not leave?" Gideon impaled a feral and grabbed the arm of another about to slash at Marcus.

"Are you really having this fight now?" Kol asked, dodging the claws of one, then another.

Free me. Now.

The pressure of the key billowed, and I gasped, clutching my chest. It still wasn't the agony of before, but it wasn't much of an improvement. "We have to get to the key."

"Officer Shaw, take cover in one of the buildings." Gideon jerked his chin toward the closest high rise lobby door. "The rest of us, in the park."

I bolted toward the lobby door, my chest burning

from the pressure and lack of air, but half a dozen ferals broke away from the guys and chased after me.

Crap. I was as much of a target as the guys.

Marcus swore and ran toward the group going after me. Gideon barreled toward me as well, shooting a light strike at the feral closest to me as he ran. It wasn't enough to kill it, but the blast made it stagger long enough for me to jerk close enough to guarantee my aim and shoot it in the heart. And I had no choice but to stand and fight. All the ferals were faster than me, and with almost no distance between us, there was no point in running away.

The feral I'd shot dropped with a flash of blue lightning, but now I was surrounded by the remaining four.

One slashed at me. I jerked away from it into the claws of another, who sliced rents into the back of my vest.

Marcus yanked that feral out of reach and killed it.

Almost time. Find me. Free me.

"New plan." Gideon reached the pack and impaled another feral. "Officer Shaw in the center." His tone was all business, but I could tell by the waves of searing heat sweeping through the air that he was pissed.

Yeah, well, this wasn't how I'd planned for my evening to go, either. My shoulder and forearm burned from the wounds I'd already received, and blood once again oozed from shallow cuts on my cheek and neck. And God damn it, I could barely breathe.

I shot another feral in the chest to slow it down and bolted toward the park as Marcus and Gideon finished off the other two who'd attacked me. Jacob and Kol fought to clear a path for me, but there were still too many. Jeez, how the hell were there so many?

I jumped over the body of a dead feral, lying in a pool of blood on the asphalt, and its hand jerked out and seized my ankle.

Ah, shit. The damned thing wasn't dead.

CHAPTER 20

I CRASHED TO THE ROAD, THE FERAL'S GRIP A VISE AROUND my ankle, and somehow managed to not smash my face against the asphalt or lose my Glock with the impact. I wrenched around and the feral snarled at me. It grabbed my leg with its other hand and sank its teeth into my calf.

Pain screamed through my leg. I kicked it in the head, and its teeth ripped from my flesh and shredded my jeans.

Shit shit shit.

I shot the feral in the head before it could bite me again. Blue lightning exploded around it, but I scrambled to my feet, not waiting to see if the enspelled ammunition had actually killed it.

Around us, all the ferals who hadn't been decapitated or shot in the head groaned and hissed and climbed to their feet.

"I'm beginning to really hate this guy," Marcus snarled.

Gideon decapitated the feral closest to him, but

another at his feet dug its claws into his thigh. "Just get to the key." He shoved the feral off him, the creature's claws ripping his fatigues and drawing blood.

Now. Now.

I fought to run down the path. The pressure in my chest was so heavy I couldn't catch my breath, barely managing shallow gasps.

Trees crowded close, casting heavy shadows, and even if there had been more than a barely seen sliver of moon in the sky, the path still would have been dark.

A few feet down the path a streetlight, made to look like an early 19th century wrought-iron street lamp, flickered on then went out.

The pressure squeezed tighter, and the whole row of streetlights flickered on and went out.

Now. Free me. Join me. Kin.

"I'm not your kin," I hissed at Ibizual. "Your kin tried to claim me, and I killed him."

Ahead, the path ended in a T-intersection, and the trees opened up to a grassy embankment with a steep incline down to Unity Lake—a crater formed from an eruption of powerful nephilim and angelic magic during the war that had been turned into the lake.

Light shimmered at the top of the embankment, red and pulsing and radiating evil, dispelling any doubt I might have had that the archnephilim and Ibizual were kin. The power felt the same, an inky, consuming darkness that made the remnants of the archnephilim's brand pulse on my biceps.

More ferals crashed through the bushes, the stream

of monsters never ending. They all rushed toward the shimmering light, a pinprick at chest height.

Jacob grabbed two and yanked them into a fight. Kol tackled another, and Gideon cut down two more. Marcus barreled into the bushes, blocking the way for four more.

I scanned the area for Logan. He had to be close by, waiting for the last minute to rush out with his enhanced vampiric speed and grab the key.

A feral broke free from Jacob. I shot at it, missed, and the Glock's slide clicked back. Out of ammo. My thoughts whirled, taking a split second to figure the possibilities. All the guys were caught in fights with multiple ferals, and I wasn't going to have enough time to eject the Glock's magazine and replace it.

I dropped my Glock and drew my sword, sweeping it at the feral at the last minute. The blade dug into the creature's shoulder, drawing a howl, and it batted the weapon aside and dug its claws into the front of my vest.

The pressure in my chest exploded with ferocious power, stealing my breath. My knees buckled, dropping me to the ground. The movement ripped off my vest, still caught in the feral's claws, but saved my neck from a slash by the feral's other hand.

My attention jerked toward the manifesting key of its own volition, and my pulse sped up.

The key had fully formed, now a small red jewel, pulsing with so much power it made my buzz scream in defiance.

"Shaw. Get the key," Gideon yelled. He blasted a light strike at the feral attacking me, the force of the blast tossing it back into a tree trunk.

I scrambled to my feet. Another feral rushed toward me. I was going to get there first, but just barely, and I had no weapon to defend myself with once I had the key—

No, not true. I had a light strike that might be powerful enough—if, God, it was working again—to slow it down long enough for the guys to help me.

I thought the words of the combat spell, unable to draw enough breath to even hiss them as I dashed out of the trees onto the embankment. The power and evil from the key churned my stomach. I didn't want to grab it, didn't want Ibizual's power touching my skin. But I couldn't let the feral get it.

And where the hell was Logan?

With gritted teeth, I seized the key. Its magic burned into my palm, drawing a scream and making my stomach churn. I wrenched up my other hand to shoot the light strike at the feral leaping toward me, but blinding agony exploded in my chest, and the key tumbled from my hand, my fingers suddenly numb.

Gideon screamed, and a blaze of white light flashed through the park.

The muscles in my legs gave out, and my momentum from running heaved me forward. I tumbled down the embankment and crashed into the gravel path skirting the edge of the lake.

Now I really couldn't catch my breath. The pressure was replaced with an agony that leached the strength from every cell in my body.

I strained to get up, to move, to, hell, look at the top of the embankment to see if one of the guys had gotten the key. But I could barely move, barely breathe.

Somewhere in the back of my mind a voice screamed that I'd been shot, that I needed to apply pressure, get help, but I couldn't get my thoughts to focus enough to take action.

Gideon scrambled down the embankment and frost instantly formed on all my exposed skin. His expression was filled with horror and panic, illuminated by the glow from his eyes.

"No. God, no." He slammed his hands against my chest and pressed down hard, shooting white lightning through me. "Jacob! Marcus!" His voice cracked with desperation. "Kol!"

"The key," I gasped. *Did you get the key? I lost the key.*

"Jacob!" Gideon's body shook, and he panted with frantic gasps as a hint of heat whispered through his brand.

"Essie, no." That was Jacob, but I couldn't turn my head to see him.

Marcus tumbled down the embankment. "We have to get her to Amiah." But his gaze jumped to the ground around me, and he collapsed to his knees beside me.

Every breath was agony, gurgling in my lungs.

"No time, there's no time." Gideon yanked me into his lap, clutching me to his chest. "I can't lose her, please, God, not her, too."

"Fly. Now," Kol said from somewhere above me.

"She's bleeding too fast," Jacob growled.

A chill shuddered through me, making me colder even with Gideon's fear already frosting my skin. It sliced agony through my chest, and danced darkness at the edge of my vision.

"The key—" I couldn't get my mind past losing the key. I coughed, and the metallic tang of blood filled my mouth.

Gideon's gaze jumped to Jacob. "Turn her into a vampire. You have to turn her."

"I'm not a master." Jacob grabbed my hand, his expression just as desperate as Gideon's. "Can the brand sustain her?"

"No, not enough. It won't be enough to get her to Amiah. Marcus, please," Gideon begged. His grip on me tightened, and the pain started to bleed into a frozen numbness, the darkness creeping further across my vision. "I can't lose her. I can't."

"Even if she's that one in a million susceptible to lycanthropy, she'll die before the change hits her."

"No," Gideon gasped, a sound too quiet, too broken. "Please, no."

I coughed, more blood slicing agony through the numbness. The darkness filled most of my vision, and all I could see was Gideon, panting, desperate, tears streaming down his cheeks. He clung to me and crumpled forward, his forehead pressing to mine and enveloping me in the brilliant white blaze from his eyes. His scent of springtime, fresh and green and warm, swept around me and entwined with the darkness, dragging me toward it.

"Essie, please. Don't die. Please."

"I can heal her enough to get her to Amiah." Kol shoved Marcus aside and dropped to the gravel beside me.

"Incubi don't have healing magic," Marcus growled.

"Not that we like to tell anyone, but just like I can take energy, I can give it." Kol reached for me, but his gaze was locked with Gideon's, asking permission. "I'm willing to pay the cost."

"Whatever it takes," Gideon said.

I coughed again, slicing more pain through me, and more blood filled my mouth. The darkness swelled over my vision, and I was floating in a heavy, black, numb nothingness.

Kol's warm hands captured my face. The frost instantly melted at his heightened body temperature and my eyes jerked open. Suddenly I was drowning not in black nothingness, but black warmth with a flicker of hellfire.

His lips brushed mine, and a whisper of heat slid into my mouth, cutting through the heavy numbness. Agony roared through my chest, and my muscles convulsed. Kol's grip on my face tightened, forcing me still, and his kiss grew fierce, crushing against my lips.

The whisper of heat flared into a thick thread. He shoved his tongue into my mouth, forcing it open, and dug his fingers into the hinge of my jaw to keep it open. His heat turned into a flood, and I thrashed against the agony, desperate to escape the pain. But it kept growing until my entire body was on fire, burning and wailing.

"You're killing her," Marcus growled.

"He's not," Gideon said, his voice tight. Light snapped from his eyes and lightning from his magic cut through his brand.

The flood turned into an ocean, and I was choking, drowning on Kol's power just like I'd been drowning on the archnephilim's power when it had tried to possess me. Fear clenched tight around my heart. This was too much like the attack from the archnephilim. I had to get away. Had to stop this. I couldn't breathe, couldn't let him take me, couldn't let him possess me—

"Don't fight me, Essie," Kol gasped against my lips.

I fought my panic to accept his magic, but I couldn't concentrate past the pain to do anything other than try to breathe.

He groaned, the sound tight and pained, and his fingers dug into my cheeks. The heat snapped from drowning to sensual and the agony swept into bone-melting desire. I gasped, and his magic poured down my throat without resistance. My muscles went limp and my head spun. I ached with need, with the promise of Kol's magic, knowing that this was just a glimpse of his power, just enough to get me to relax.

It lit up every nerve, and I was suddenly hyper aware of his lips, firm and demanding on mine, his tongue fueling a need within me, and the heat from his hands on my cheeks, seeping into my skin. I also thrummed with awareness of Gideon, every frantic breath that shook his body against mine, and his strong arms clinging to me, desperate to protect me. I ached with a yearning for Gideon that I'd been trying to ignore since his brand had formed on my arm. I had to know him, to be with him. I knew in my soul I belonged with him.

The brand said so.

Fate had decided and permanently bound us together.

Of course my body right now also said I belonged

with Kol. God. I needed him, needed his hands on more than just my face, needed his lips on more than just my lips. My pulse raced with desire and anticipation, and his heat swelled low within me.

I opened my eyes, not realizing I'd closed them, and stared into a hungry darkness filled with hellfire. His gaze captured me completely and held me hostage, promising me satisfaction. Then his eyes rolled back, the power of his magic vanished with a gasp, and he collapsed onto the gravel path beside me.

"Kol—" I tried to reach for him, but my body wouldn't obey my commands and my head was spinning too fast. The darkness now threatening my vision was warm and heavy and comforting, and the agony in my chest was still there, but half of what it had been... maybe. I couldn't tell, because my body was so focused on the aching need brought to life by Kol's magic.

Marcus grabbed him and rolled him over. He was pale and sweat slicked his face and neck, but he was still breathing. Thank God.

Gideon tightened his grip on me and stood, cradling me against his chest. His wings swept out with a flash of white light and he leaped up, caught the air, and pulled us into the sky. Kol's soft sensual darkness blanketed me, and I drifted, only half aware of the wind in my face, Gideon's strong arms around me, and his soothing scent.

My thoughts slid from flying to the archnephilim trying to pull wings I didn't have from my body. A part of me, I guess the angelic part, ached knowing I didn't have wings and I'd never be able to fly like this, while the human part was relieved. It would kill me to know I had the ability to fly but couldn't without endangering my life.

Between one blink and the next we landed in front of the garage, and Gideon ran inside screaming for Amiah, his fear and heartache making me cold and fogging my vision.

I knew it had taken longer than a few seconds to cross town, that I'd passed out, but even just coming to that conclusion was like thinking through water.

Amiah and her assistant met us in triage. Gideon set me on the closest bed, his clothes soaked with my blood, and Amiah shoved him out of the way. The assistant—Cassey?—inserted an IV into my arm, while Amiah cut open my shirt and grabbed something from the tray beside me. Her mouth moved, but I couldn't understand her words. Her tone was sharp, and I couldn't figure out if she was angry with me or not.

Gideon was still hyperventilating, and the chill deepened, thickening the fog. I wanted to tell him it was all right, that it didn't hurt any more, or at least not that much. But I couldn't get my mouth to move, and then I was floating, half hearing, half feeling, riding the heat of Kol's magic.

I blinked, my lids moving in slow motion, the darkness clinging to me, and when I opened my eyes, Gideon, Amiah, and Cassey were gone. So, too, was triage. I lay in one of Operations' hospital rooms, hooked up to a softly beeping monitor and an IV, dressed in a hospital gown. My chest throbbed, with the promise of searing pain tickling at the edge of what I could only assume were drug-muted senses.

The lights in the room were low, which meant the lights in the hall were low, too. Unless I wasn't in a room with an observation window. I turned my head just enough to see. Yep, a window, with the blinds up. Did the low lights mean it was still night and I hadn't been out for that long?

I had no idea.

"I can't do this, Amiah," Gideon said, his voice low and still breaking with pain and fear. "I can't. How the hell do I do this?"

I searched the hall—since his voice was too far away to be in the room—and caught a glimpse of him almost out of sight of the window. He stood shaking, his forehead against the wall opposite the window, and everything within me said I had to go to him, comfort him, tell him I was alive and okay.

"I don't even know her. I don't even want to know her, and yet when I knew she was dying—" He drew in a choked breath and looked at someone out of sight. "It was worse than watching Zella die. I couldn't think of anything else and my soul—" He shuddered. "If she dies, I'm going to lose my mind."

"No," Amiah said, her tone firm. "She's human and you're stronger than her."

He pressed his hand to the wall, and his fear deepened, stinging my cheeks with frost and digging into my chest as a genuine emotion. "She can take my magic and use it."

Amiah gasped, her surprise zinging through me before it twisted into anger. "You can deal with that."

"I don't want to deal with it. I don't want any of this."

And he didn't. I could feel it in my soul. He didn't want me, didn't want our bond, and didn't want a repeat of the terror he'd just experienced.

"Well, you can't fight it," Amiah said, her tone now tender, surprising me. "She has your brand. She's your mate."

Gideon's desperation deepened, and he drew in another ragged breath. "She might have my brand, but she's not my mate. She's Marcus's. And she was his before she was mine." The hand I could see fisted, and he punched the wall, cracking the drywall. "But everything within me says Essie, a complete stranger, is mine. Mine. What am I supposed to do with that? I'm not fighting Marcus for his mate. I'd have to kill him. He'd never submit and give her up."

Amiah huffed and a flicker of something dark and hard, I wasn't sure what, whispered through all the other emotions. "Marcus's wolf will just have to pick someone else."

My thoughts stuttered, stuck on Amiah's strange emotion, then jerked to her words. Marcus would pick someone else? But I didn't want Marcus to pick someone else.

"Easier said than done," Gideon said.

"He at least can do it. You can't." She sounded so certain, so determined.

Except didn't I have a say in this? It was my life, too. Marcus and I had been destined long before Gideon and me. I knew that in the core of my soul.

Amiah's hand slipped into view, rubbing slow circles

over Gideon's back, and her emotions turned to pity. "Fate says she belongs to you and you to her."

"Fate also said this is supposed to be beautiful, magical, perfect destiny," he said, his tone and emotions turning bitter and squeezing in my chest. "Nothing about this is beautiful or magical. It's a nightmare."

"Gideon—"

"I can't love her. I never want to." He spat out the words, his fear and grief and frustration battering me and stealing my breath.

My throat tightened and my eyes burned. I wrenched my face away from the window and pressed my mouth into the pillow to hide my sobs.

His words shouldn't have hurt. God, why did they hurt so much? I didn't want this, either. I wasn't in love with him. I was in love with Marcus. And Gideon was an angel who despised nephilim. I should be terrified of him. Which I was, both because of what he'd do if he found out the truth and of how much his words hurt me. God, those word and the dark storm of his emotions—

They sliced into my soul and shattered me.

CHAPTER 21

I MUST HAVE FALLEN ASLEEP, BECAUSE WHEN I OPENED MY eyes again they were raw, my enspelled contacts scratchy and irritated. Technically I was supposed to be able to have a full night's sleep with them in, but I hadn't taken them out and cleaned them in over twenty-four hours, and I was paying the price. My buzz now screamed at me, grating on my nerves even though I still floated on a hazy cloud of painkillers, and the room's temperature flashed from hot to cold. Agony still throbbed, far away, still at the edge of my senses, and I couldn't focus long enough on that to figure out if that was because Amiah hadn't fully healed me, or if it was some kind of side effect of the massive amount of magic Amiah would have needed to use to save me.

"—need to see her," Marcus said from somewhere in the hall outside my door.

Ah, the source of the temperature fluctuations.

"Let her sleep," Gideon said, his tone flat. But his

emotions, real, inside me and not just the air temperature, twisted, a nauseating whirl in my chest.

"You can't stop me." Marcus's tone darkened and the air grew hotter.

"I'm not, just give her time to rest," Gideon snapped, his anger growing. "Amiah didn't want to risk killing her or giving her brain damage by flooding her with the magic necessary to completely heal her."

"She isn't fully healed?" Jacob asked, his voice a low rumble, drawing a small twist in my chest from his claim.

Well, that explained why my chest still hurt and why I was still doped up on painkillers.

"We can't take her in the field if she's still hurt," Marcus said.

"We're not taking her in the field." Fear from Gideon flashed through me, and my buzz spiked.

"We may not have a choice," Jacob said. "If I couldn't feel the key manifesting, I might not be able to feel where the seal is manifesting."

"I'm not putting her in Logan's sights again," Gideon said. "She's human. She doesn't belong on a JP team."

"That shot would have killed any of us," Marcus growled, "except for maybe Kol, but only if he was at full power."

"That doesn't make it any better." Guilt twisted into Gideon's fear.

"You can't blame yourself." Jacob's back and shoulder shifted into sight at the edge of the window. "She was the best one to grab the key."

"I don't blame myself," Gideon said, but his guilt twisted

tighter. "She's a liability. We lost the key, the remaining ferals, and Logan because she was shot. That wouldn't have happened if it had been anyone else on the team."

"You can't just kick her off," Marcus said, heat flashing through the air.

"How are you not on board with this?" Gideon asked. "I know your wolf has claimed her. Stop pretending you don't care."

"I'm not going to let you destroy her life," Marcus growled. "She's always wanted to be a cop, and she's a damn good one, too. You kick her off the team, and she's lost her job, her identity."

"At least she'd be alive." A hint of fear swept through Gideon's guilt.

"If you actually cared for her, you'd know she wouldn't be, not really," Marcus said, the air jumping and staying at sweltering. "And then what? She's fucking stuck with you. Would your brand let her leave town?"

Gideon's fear exploded within me, and the buzz went crazy. I gritted my teeth against the pain and tried to concentrate on their conversation.

"Of course I would," Gideon said.

But I could tell that was a lie even without his emotions raging through me. My throat tightened with tears again. He didn't want me, but he'd never let me go. And why did that hurt? It should make me furious.

"You could try," Jacob said, "but an angelic mating brand is powerful."

"She's a danger to the team," Gideon said.

"She killed the archnephilim, and saved me in the ferals' nest by nearly killing Logan." Jacob crossed his arms, making his T-shirt strain against his broad, muscular back. "We have to have a human on the team. She's a good candidate. Imagine the kind of asset she'd be if she was properly trained."

"You, too?" White light flickering in the hall had to be the magic in Gideon's eyes flaring.

Jacob's support surprised me, too, since if I died, he would starve to death.

But then if I was kicked off the team and off the police force, what would I do? Gideon wouldn't let me leave town. Would I be happy holding down some office job? The thought made my stomach churn. I didn't want to even think about that. I supposed I could get my P.I.'s license, or do private security or something.

"I've tried letting her go, sending her back to her normal human life," Marcus said, his tone sharp and dark, as if his wolf was fighting to break free. "She keeps ending up in our world. If we push her away, she's going to end up caught in some kind of mess she can't get out of without us. Do you want to freeze up like that for no apparent reason in the middle of a fight? Do you want Essie to? You were shot and a feral almost killed her. At least if you're together, you'll be able to see it coming."

"We're not going to be together. Ever," Gideon said, his tone dark, his fear and guilt and anger choking me as my buzz sliced under my skin.

"Good," Marcus snarled, "because she's fucking mine, and I'm not letting her out of my sight again."

"So if I send her packing—?" Gideon asked.

"I go with her." Marcus shoved past Jacob and

stormed down the hall, his footsteps getting farther and farther away, taking his heat with him.

My heart soared at his words, but also cried at Gideon's. I wanted to scream and sob with frustration but didn't want to face Gideon or Jacob right now, and strained to keep quiet.

"You've had a scare," Jacob said, his voice a low rumble, barely audible even with my enhanced hearing.

"Don't talk to me like I'm a soldier after my first fight."

Jacob shifted back, coming into full view, and now I could see half of Gideon's profile. His expression was hard, with more ice in his eyes than before. His gaze leaped to mine and captured me, stealing my breath.

His anger swelled, and tears filled my eyes and tightened my throat.

God damn, I didn't want to be upset that he hated me.

"I'm going to check on Kol, see if he's awake." He too shoved past Jacob and stormed down the hall, taking his gut-churning emotions and the rest of the flickering heat.

Jacob turned to watch him go, noticed I was awake, and opened my room's door instead of leaving.

"Hey," he said, soft, low, and making my essence vibrate in perfect resonance with the part of his essence entwined with mine. "How are you doing?"

"My chest hurts." And my heart. And my soul.

And my skin. Jeez, my God damn buzz felt like fire ants were chewing me up, one tiny painful bite at a time.

His expression grew grim, and a hint of misty grief whispered around me. "Yeah."

"How badly were you hurt?" I forced out. "Do you need to feed?"

"The extra power Victoria gave me is dealing with my injuries." The mist thickened. "About that—"

"I'm not going to let you starve," I blurted out before he could say anything. I wasn't going to let him argue with me about that. He was in this mess because of me, because I couldn't tell him I was part super and hadn't known the consequences when I'd tried to protect him from Victoria's temper.

He sat on the edge of the chair beside the bed, the strain around his eyes not as tight as it had been before he'd fed on me, but not completely gone, either. He reached to grab my hand but thought better of it and drew back instead, making his claim ache within me. "I'll find a way to fix this. I promise."

A part of me didn't want him to fix this. Which was ridiculous. I didn't want to be Jacob's only means of survival. That was dangerous for the both of us. But that part of me, the part that could only be because of his claim, wanted him near. Just like I wanted Gideon and Marcus near.

"I didn't even know I was old enough to make a claim so strong." He rubbed his face and the mist swelled, obscuring my view of him. "We need to figure out what to do about the bite-lock. I can feed without using my magic, but it'll hurt, and I'd rather not do that to you."

"I'd rather not, either." I'd had a glimpse of what a vampire feeding felt like without the erotic magic seeping into me, and I didn't want to repeat that.

A shiver swept over me, and the buzz bit deeper. "Does the bite-lock cause problems for you, too? Do we need to... you know?" I asked, uncertain how I felt about that. I didn't love him like I loved Marcus, but I was still drawn to him, and I wasn't entirely sure that came only from his claim.

"No," he said, but the mist turned cold and I got the sense he didn't really know. "The best way to manage this is to make sure Marcus is around when I need to feed."

"So you bite me and Marcus releases it?" Poor Kol was going to be high all the time if we kept getting into fights and Jacob kept getting hurt. Except I was off the team, which meant all of it would have to happen someplace else, probably my apartment, and not at Operations.

"It's better than me releasing my bite-lock." Jacob's dark gaze captured mine and filled with a hungry intensity. The room's temperature rose, but I couldn't tell if he was hungry for my blood or my blood *and* my body. "I'm surprised Marcus hasn't lost it on Gideon. Wolves are ferociously territorial, and it's clear now he's claimed you as his mate."

"Marcus recognizes this is a complicated situation." Which was the understatement of the century.

"I'll talk to Marcus about our... necessary arrangement." He looked like he was going to hold my hand again, but rose instead. "You should sleep. If you're still connected to the key and the seal, you're going to need your energy this evening."

"Is Kol okay?" I asked as he headed to the door. While I knew he was alive, I didn't know anything else and my gut twisted with guilt that he might have seriously hurt himself to save me.

"Amiah can't sense anything wrong with him, but we won't know until he wakes up."

God, I hoped that meant he was all right. He'd said there was a cost. Please let that cost only be falling unconscious in the middle of a potentially dangerous situation.

Jacob left, and I stared at the ceiling, trying to think past my buzz. How did everything get so complicated so quickly? And why couldn't I just thrill at the knowledge that Marcus and I were finally figuring out the searing attraction between us? God, and why did Gideon's words have to hurt so much?

My eyelids grew heavy, and I rolled to my side to get more comfortable.

I also needed to figure out if I wanted to stay on the team when Gideon clearly didn't want me around. It would be best if I got as far away from him as possible, except—

Jeez. My mother would be so upset with me. She'd worked so hard, sacrificed so much to protect me from the angels and the Joined Parliament, and here I was, my heart aching because an angel hated me and because I was hoping to become part of a JP team.

Nothing good could come of it, even if I had figured out an explanation for my eyes and next-to-useless empathy. Why couldn't I remember that? I was playing with fire, and it wasn't just Gideon and the Joined Parliament I should be afraid of. I'd been shot and nearly killed. While I suspected this wasn't a typical JP case, I didn't doubt any others would be less dangerous for a powerless human.

But I also knew in my soul that this was where I belonged. God, it was crazy. But I was more certain that I was supposed to be a JP agent helping humans caught up in the world of supers, with these men, than I was of anything else in my completely messed-up life.

My mind drifted, and I yearned for Marcus and the others and the sense of belonging that I'd never had on the force with the other cops. I wanted to be part of a team, respected, not despised. I wanted to have a family, a group of people who cared about me, something I'd gotten a small glimpse of when it had just been me and my mom. But then I'd lost it all when she'd died. I hadn't realized how alone I was, how much of an outsider I was — how much of an outsider I'd made myself to be.

The door opened with a soft *shush* of movement, and Marcus's emotional heat seeped over my skin. At least I thought it was Marcus, but I was still half asleep, floating on fear and warmth and heartache.

"Marcus?" I breathed, needing to know if he was real or just a dream.

"Go back to sleep." His weight settled on the bed behind me and his arms wrapped around me. He drew me close, my back to his chest, his lips pressed to the back of my neck. His perpetual five o'clock shadow tickled my skin while his breath heated it. A hint of desire unfurled low within me, but more of me was warm and secure than turned on.

"I've got you," he said. "Go back to sleep."

Yes, this was definitely where I belonged. Everything else was complicated, but I knew with certainty I belonged with Marcus.

CHAPTER 22

AT some point Marcus left the bed. I didn't feel him go, but when I woke next, I was alone and the spot where he'd been wasn't warm, so he'd been gone long enough for it to cool down.

A hint of an ache squeezed my chest, one part missing Marcus, another part gunshot wound, and the rest Ibizual's seal. Thankfully the seal wasn't calling to me like the key had, not yet at least, but the pressure *was* starting and I knew something would happen soon. Whether I was fully healed or not, I was going to have to get ready, and that started with getting out of the hospital gown and eating something, since I couldn't remember the last time I'd actually had a meal. Oh, and nicotine. I needed to replace my patches before I started scratching my skin off and sobbing.

My clothes weren't in the hospital room, neither were my shoes, and most definitely not the keycard for the room upstairs. I turned off the vitals monitor, peeled away the leads taped to my chest, and carefully pulled out the IV so I could look in the attached bathroom.

No clothes there, either.

Well, shit. I didn't particularly want to be wandering around Operations barefoot in a hospital gown, but I also wasn't going to wait around for someone to check on me since I had no idea when the seal would start calling me. At least the gown wasn't backless, it was the kind with three arm holes that wrap around one and a bit times.

Unfortunately, I had no idea where anyone would be. I was sure Amiah didn't usually hang out in triage and while I'd been to her office once, I'd been doped up on painkillers and Kol's enthrallment at the time and wasn't sure I'd be able to find it again. As for the guys, they could also be anywhere, but I doubted, given the severity of the situation, that they'd be in their rooms waiting for something to happen. They were probably planning or scouting or researching.

Food, however, was something I could immediately fix. Perhaps once I'd had something to eat, my head would clear enough so I could think past the buzz and figure out what to do next.

Like dealing with Gideon.

How the hell was I going to convince him I wasn't a liability to the team? Especially since I was pretty sure I was, no matter what Marcus and Jacob said. But I also had no idea how to make myself accept that I shouldn't be part of the team, not with the certainty that I belonged growing stronger within me.

Jeez. What a mess.

I took the smaller hall away from triage to the hall

that exited by the elevator and the cafeteria. I could hear the guys talking before I reached the end of the hall, and hesitated long enough to consider returning to the hospital room, then to dismiss that idea as stupid. I was going to have to face Gideon eventually and, God damn it, I was hungry.

"—can't afford another mess like downtown," Gideon said. "Both the mayor and the chief of police called head office to complain."

"As if we had any control over where the key manifested," Kol said, his voice lifting a weight from my chest that I hadn't realized was there. He was okay. Thank God he was okay— or at least okay enough to be up and talking.

"We— *I*—" Gideon said. "*I* left a street and park full of bodies."

"I would have loved to have seen that," a smooth tenor said with a laugh, someone I didn't recognize. "You—"

I reached the cafeteria stairs and all eyes turned on me. The guys sat in the middle of the otherwise empty room at their usual six-seater table, all of them strikingly handsome, each in their own way. Even Gideon with his stiff, hard, expression. That merely accentuated his sculpted cheeks and jaw.

Jacob, as always, drew me with his intensity—and the more I thought about it, the more I was certain it wasn't just his claim. With his broad shoulders and massive arms straining his T-shirt, he dwarfed lean-muscled Kol sitting beside him even though Kol wasn't that small. Stunningly handsome Kol always stole my breath and made my thoughts stall, just for a second. God, he was so beautiful. And thank God, he didn't look as if anything had happened to him, not a fight with dozens of ferals or pouring his life force into me. The thought of that sent heat swelling within me and even from the cafeteria steps I could see hellfire flickering in his eyes.

Then Marcus shifted, and my attention jumped to him, my pulse picking up with need and certainty. He did look like he'd had a bad night, but it wasn't anything to do with his physical appearance. His clothes were fresh and there wasn't a hint of a scratch on any visible skin— he must have shifted and healed—but he looked exhausted, with his hair mussed and dark circles under his eyes. He'd said he wanted me on the team, wanted me close, but I had a feeling he was going to regret that decision and change his mind. How many times could I end up in danger just doing my job before he'd had enough?

I pulled my gaze away from him and the panic those thoughts were stirring to look at the new guy. He was also shockingly handsome, almost on the same level as Kol, but where Kol exuded a sense of darkness and fire, this guy was light and cold. His skin was so pale it seemed translucent, which I knew wasn't true because I couldn't see his bones or veins. A hint of a glow, as cold as the glow in Gideon's eyes but barely there, only really noticeable from the corner of my eye, radiated from all skin not covered by his clothes with a hint of icy blue. His eyes were so pale blue they were almost clear, and his hair was a mix of white and silver cut short and spiked.

But what really stole my breath about him were his pointed ears. He was faekin, half human and half fae. I'd never seen one before. Hell, I'd never seen a fae before. They'd stayed in their realm during the war, only sending a few sorcerers to help, and those sorcerers had remained hidden the entire time then returned to the fairy realm once the war was done. Some humans still didn't believe fae existed.

"You're the human," he said, crossing his arms, drawing my attention to the swirl of black tattoo curling out of the V of his blue button-down, over his collarbone, and up his neck. His gaze raked over my body with a slow, sensual perusal, adding fuel to the heat within me that had come from seeing Marcus and thinking about Kol's magic.

His lips curled up just enough for a wicked, inviting smile, which surprised the hell out of me because I was sure I looked like a hot mess in only a hospital gown. I hadn't even thought to pull my—without a doubt wild—locks into a ponytail.

Gideon stood, his expression frigid. "You should be in bed."

"Don't start." I was tired and achy and my skin was on fire with my buzz. "The seal is starting to form, and I'm having a meal before it compels me to wherever the hell it's going to manifest." I headed to the fridge with the pre-made sandwiches and salads. Out the back windows, the sky was starting to darken, and the one cloud I could see was pink. It was nearly dusk, and round two would be beginning any time now.

Gideon's attention jumped to Jacob. "Can *you* sense it?"

Jacob shook his head. "No."

"Shit." Gideon sank back into the chair.

I grabbed a turkey club and a bottle of water and took the last chair at the table between Kol and the new guy.

"Sebastian Bane." He held out his hand. I half expected cold to radiate from him, but I didn't feel anything. Of course, that could be because of my damned distracting buzz.

"Officer Esther Shaw," Gideon said before I could reply.

I sighed and reached to shake Sebastian's hand, but a snap of frozen magic sliced up my arm before we even touched.

Gasping, I jerked back, and Marcus shot up from his seat and growled low in his throat.

Sebastian's wicked smile deepened for just a second before he shoved away from me. His chair screeched against the floor, and he raised his hands palms out, but I didn't buy his no-harm, just-innocent posture. He'd meant to do that.

"Switch seats," Marcus said. "Now."

"Sure," Sebastian said with a laugh as he rose and traded seats with Marcus, who pulled his chair close to me. His hand found my knee under the table and settled there, the action neither sexual nor possessive— well, maybe a little possessive, but also comforting and protective. I'd have loved this new Marcus, if I wasn't certain he was going to have a complete change of mind after we'd dealt with the seal.

"So you can sense the key and seal," Sebastian said, his gaze locking on me. "Fascinating."

The muscles in Gideon's jaw twitched. "And not what we were talking about."

"No, we were talking about messes." Sebastian continued to stare, his gaze boring into me as if he could see something, or was looking for something, hidden within me, which made my pulse pound. *Please, God, don't let it be my angelic nature.*

His eyes narrowed. "Unless the seal manifests in the Supers' Quarter, I have no doubt the mayor will be complaining about another dangerous mess."

"So there's no spell that will stop this?" Jacob asked. Now that I was sitting across from him, his posture was almost as rigid as Gideon's. I couldn't begin to imagine how difficult this whole situation was for him, needing to stop, most likely kill, his blood brother all over again.

"There's nothing you can do at a distance," Sebastian said, still not looking away from me.

Marcus's hand on my knee tightened. "She's taken."

Sebastian's gaze dipped to Gideon's brand on my forearm. "I can see that. Can you feel the key right now, Esther?"

I opened my mouth to say no, that the ache in my chest was definitely the seal, but—

I closed my eyes and concentrated on everything churning and biting and throbbing in my body. The buzz stung and urged me to get closer to Gideon even though we only sat across the table from each other. I slid the foot of my Marcus-free leg as close to Gideon's as I could without touching him, and the buzz softened enough for me to really feel the ache of the seal. But it also made me aware of the wildly fluctuating emotional temperatures.

Which was just something I was going to have to learn to deal with if I could convince Gideon to keep me on the team.

I shoved that thought aside and concentrated on the key, searching for any kind of pain or pressure that would tell me I could still feel it.

"Nothing."

Sebastian pursed his lips. And God damn it, he still stared at me— No, actually his eyes were unfocused, but without a doubt all his senses were focused on me, still searching for something. I shivered at the intensity of his scrutiny. It wasn't like the soul-capturing look I got from Jacob and pretty much every other vampire I'd encountered. My soul wasn't being held. It was being dissected.

"She's telling the truth," he said.

Marcus's eyes darkened, his wolf barely contained, and Jacob sat forward and squared his shoulders.

"She has no reason to lie," Jacob said, his voice soft and low but edged with warning.

Sebastian shrugged and finally turned his attention away from me. Thank God! Now his unnerving gaze was on Gideon, and I dug into my sandwich to hide my relief. Somehow he'd known I wasn't lying about the key—and none of the guys called him out on that, so he must have that magical ability—but did he know I was lying about other things? Would he reveal my secret to Gideon? I didn't get the sense he'd care if I was a nephilim or not, more that he'd do it just to see what would happen, see if Gideon would turn on his mate. Which he would, because while I might have his brand, I wasn't really his mate.

"The only way to stop the spell is to destroy the key," Sebastian said. "How strong is your divine light?"

The muscles in Gideon's jaw flexed. "How powerful does the blast need to be?"

"At the level of divine light ring or stronger."

"That strong?" Kol asked.

"There aren't a lot of angels who can summon a blast that strong," Jacob said.

"You could try less, but I suspect you'll only get one chance on this." Sebastian leaned back in his chair. "Probably not worth the risk."

Gideon's gaze flickered to mine then back.

Sebastian's eyes flashed wide, and his wicked smile returned. "And she can summon divine light, too?" he asked, his unnerving attention back on me. "Gideon, where have you been hiding her?"

Gideon's posture tightened even more. Now the muscles down his neck and across his shoulders joined his jaw. "Her services are not for sale."

Marcus shifted closer to me, heated emotion radiating from his body, and glared at Sebastian.

"I think that's for the lovely Esther to decide." Sebastian leaned toward me. "I know some witches who'd love to buy light magic from you. The salary for one year would make your head spin."

"Yeah, but what would it cost me?" Even if I hadn't known that the team bought information and hard-to-get items from Sebastian, I'd know he was the kind of guy who exacted a price for everything.

Mock surprise filled his expression. "Would I make an offer with a catch to it?"

"Yes," Marcus growled.

"There's a reason angels with light magic don't sell their light to witches," Jacob said.

"Because they're all control freaks with sticks up their asses." Sebastian's smile deepened. "If you ever get tired of Mister Always-in-Control—" He jerked his thumb toward Gideon, his tone filled with sexual invitation.

"I've got better offers on the table," I said before Marcus leaped over the table and ripped out Sebastian's throat.

"Honey, there are no better offers than me."

Kol huffed a soft breath and rolled his eyes.

"The incubus's company excluded, of course," Sebastian said, "but I'd bet that year's wage of light magic *his* offer isn't on *your* table."

A hint of a blush crept across my cheeks at the thought of Kol's magic—

Yep, not going there.

"So we think Gideon's magic might not be enough to destroy the key?" I forced out.

Delight flared in Sebastian's eyes at my obvious change of topic.

"And we won't know where the key is until the seal manifests and Logan arrives to break it." I opened my bottle of water and took a long sip, struggling to keep my hand steady with my buzz making me twitch.

"So other than we need to find enough light magic to end this, this is a repeat of the key," Kol said.

Marcus's grip on my knee relaxed a bit—thank God, because it was starting to get painful. "Hopefully not a repeat."

Hellfire danced in Kol's eyes. "Well, yes."

"Any other information our money purchased?" Gideon asked.

Sebastian huffed. "You have no idea how hard it was to find that, let alone anything else on short notice."

"Then thank you for your time," Jacob said, standing and gesturing to the stairs for Sebastian to leave.

Sebastian stood. "You really should make an effort to stop this. Ibizual is the prince of death."

"We already know that," Gideon said.

"So imagine the kind of terror he'd wreak in this realm if he got loose." A shudder swept over Sebastian and cold rushed around me, revealing a deeper fear than his nonchalant posture and tone implied. "I don't know about you, but there are corpses out there I'd rather stayed in the ground."

Gideon and Jacob shared at glance that then moved to Kol. The incubus's eyes had gone hard, and I could only imagine who they were thinking of. A lot of people, humans and supers, had been killed during the war, but I doubted, considering the nauseating sense of evil that had come from Ibizual, that he would raise any of the good ones from the dead.

Sebastian strode around the table toward me. "It was a pleasure meeting you, Officer Esther Shaw." *And be mindful. Whatever you're hiding under those contact lenses, it's burning up the spell a lot faster than it should. You've got a week left, at best.*

I frowned, fighting to hide my surprise, both at his voice in my head and his warning.

He flashed his wicked smile. "It's been... intriguing."

"It's—" A blast of agony exploded through my chest, then snapped into a crushing pressure that stole my breath and set my buzz screaming under my skin. The mostly full water bottle tumbled from my hand and hit the floor, spraying water up mine, Marcus's, and Sebastian's legs.

Gideon, Jacob, and Kol jerked to their feet.

Marcus grabbed my shoulders and met my gaze, panic in his eyes. "Bane?" he growled. "What did you do?"

Sebastian's eyes were wide with surprise. "Not me."

Find me. Free me. Kin.

"The seal," I gasped.

Deny me and die.

CHAPTER 23

IBIZUAL'S VOICE ROARED IN MY HEAD WITH A FORCE stronger than when the key had manifested. It came with a pressure that threatened to tear me apart from the inside out and stole my breath. His inky darkness swelled within me, too much like the archnephilim's darkness, and my pulse raced, my panic a biting thread slicing into the pressure.

I will be free.

I will stop you, I thought back at him, shoving all of my will and determination into my words.

He laughed at me, a dark grating sound that billowed the pressure in my body. *With what power?*

The force of his magic crashed into me, drowning me, more powerful than the archnephilim's. I gasped, my terror making me shake and my buzz searing through my skin in defiance.

"Essie." Marcus's grip on my shoulders tightened, his gaze filled with concern.

Beside him, Sebastian stared at me, the fear deepening in his gaze and—along with everyone else's fear—dropping the room temperature.

"The payment will be in your account," Gideon said then turned to Marcus, clearly dismissing Sebastian. "Clothes and gear for Officer Shaw."

"What about the light blast?" Jacob asked.

Gideon's expression hardened and frustration swept through me. "Officer Shaw has already demonstrated our powers together can be as strong as a blast from a divine light ring. We don't have time to call in anyone from another JP team or get a loaded ring."

"Absolutely fascinating," Sebastian said to me, his tone edged with awe that only added to my terror.

"What are you still doing here, Bane?" Marcus growled.

"Just leaving." He headed to the stairs. "Don't get killed, Gideon. You're not by far my best customer, but you're the most entertaining."

"Why do I always want to strangle him every time I see him?" Jacob asked.

Another explosion tore through me, and the pressure contracted even more, making my buzz blaze stronger. I wasn't sure I'd be able to rise let alone walk, but as much as I wanted Marcus's arms around me, I also wanted to stand on my own two feet. I needed to prove as much to myself as to Gideon that I could handle this job.

Free me and you'll have more power than all of them combined.

I don't want your power. I shoved up to my feet, using

the table to keep my balance. "We need to get moving. We can plan in the SUV. Hell, I should probably change in it, too, and not waste time going to wherever my clothes are." I turned to Jacob. "You can grab my clothes and gear faster than I can."

Gideon gave a tight nod to Jacob. "Go."

Jacob ran out of the cafeteria. While he wasn't nearly as fast as a master vampire, he was still faster than a human.

But you do want power. Ibizual laughed again, and I gritted my teeth against the pain. *You've accepted you can't be human, but you're too weak to be anything else.*

"I restocked the locker in the garage and added enough swords for the team," Marcus said, picking me up while I was distracted by Ibizual and couldn't argue with him.

"Good." Gideon pulled his phone from his pocket, dialed a number, and headed toward the steps. "Meet us in the garage."

You're weak, Esther.

I'm strong enough. I had to be strong enough. I couldn't go back to life as normal. Whether I wanted to be or not, I was a super and couldn't avoid the world of the supernatural any more.

We hurried out of the cafeteria and down the hall to the garage. Amiah rushed out triage's frosted-glass door and met us just before we left the building. Her attention jumped to me in Marcus's arms and her expression darkened, then she turned to Gideon.

"She has to go?" she asked.

"Yes." Gideon's tone was flat. Whatever emotion he might have been feeling was locked down tight. I couldn't feel anything from him inside me, and the temperature right now was hot, most likely from Marcus, whose fear seemed to manifest more like hot rage.

"Fine." She pressed her hand over my heart, and a searing blast of magic sliced through me.

All my muscles contracted, and Marcus's grip on me tightened. Then it was over in a flash, and I was left trying to pant past the pressure in my chest and think past the buzz.

"Hunh," she said. "You're farther along than I would have thought, even with Jacob's claim."

Jeez, I just couldn't catch a break. Yet another thing I was going to have to come up with an explanation for. My eyes, my weird empathy, and now my faster-than-average healing.

They'll learn the truth, and you'll be powerless to defend yourself, Ibizual said in my head.

Still not freeing you. The archnephilim had told me that as well, threatened me with my greatest fear. I hadn't listened then and I wasn't going to listen now.

"Jacob's claim is a little stronger than expected," I said.

Kol rolled his eyes. "You could say that."

Marcus shot a quick glare at him, the look clear—*shut up.* And I could fully understand why. The situation was complicated and without a doubt others—chiefly among them Amiah, with her feelings for Marcus—wouldn't understand or approve of my arrangement with Jacob and Marcus, even if it was the best solution for this mess.

The less attention that was brought to our situation, the better.

They won't understand.

Just shut the fuck up.

"Is she good to go?" Gideon asked.

Amiah shrugged. "Yes." She didn't sound happy about that at all.

"Good." Gideon strode out the door to the garage and we followed.

He headed around the corner to the black metal locker recessed into the wall, and unlocked it with his thumbprint.

Another blast of agony swept through me, drawing a gasp, and Gideon's eyes narrowed, while Marcus's grip on me tightened.

Only a matter of time before I'm free.

"Get Officer Shaw in the SUV," Gideon said, handing me the keys.

I hit the unlock button on the key fob, and Marcus set me in the SUV then returned to the locker to get his gear. The guys loaded up with sidearms, vests, and swords, while I fought to breathe. The pain wasn't as bad as when the key had formed, but the pressure was worse and filled with Ibizual's malicious darkness. That and my buzz was going wild, the bites so forceful they now felt more like miniature explosions under my skin, and I couldn't hide my twitching.

Jacob rushed through the glass door as the guys were closing up the locker. Marcus tossed a vest and sword into the back for Jacob and handed me a Glock, M4, and vest.

"Keep that on this time," he said as he climbed into the driver's seat.

"We both know Logan's shot would have gone right through the vest." I checked the magazine in the M4, fighting to keep my hands steady and failing. Full, but no spare. It was just going to have to be enough.

Kol climbed onto the bench beside me, setting his gear on the floor, and took my clothes and duty belt from Jacob, who then climbed into the back.

"Where to this time, Officer Shaw?" Gideon asked, his tone still flat and hard, breaking my heart, as he settled into the front passenger seat, turned on the GPS, and put his com in his ear.

I drew in a steadying breath and tried to concentrate past my emotional hurt and physical agony. This time the pull wasn't as obvious, and I wasn't sure if that was because the seal wasn't fully calling me yet or because of something else. I did, however, sense a slight pull to the back of the garage.

Join me, and I'll tell you where the seal is manifesting.

Sure, I lied.

Ibizual's pressure snapped, jerking every muscle taut for an agonizing second. *Try again.*

Yeah, I hadn't thought it would work, but I didn't want to actually commit to my lie for fear he'd be able to control me like the archnephilim had. Sure, the arch-nephilim had needed a false angelic mating brand on my arm to possess me, but Ibizual, even trapped in a cage, was more powerful.

"Head out of the Quarter," I told Marcus.

"Swell." Marcus inserted his com and pulled the SUV out of its parking space.

Kol handed me my jeans, his expression worried, and I leaned back on the seat and pulled them on.

"So you think if we combine our magic, we'll have enough power to destroy the key?" I asked Gideon.

No, Ibizual hissed. *You're weak.*

But just like he could sense I was lying, I could sense he was, too.

"Marcus?" Gideon asked, his attention locked on the road out the front windshield. "You said her blast on Logan was as strong as a blast from a divine light ring."

"It was," Marcus said, swerving around a vehicle pulling out of a driveway.

Gideon gave a tight nod. "Then that's the plan."

"So we what? Fight who knows how many ferals so you and Essie can get the key away from Logan?" Marcus asked. "That's a terrible plan."

Gideon shot him a frozen glare. "If you can think of something better, I'm all ears."

"I agree it's a terrible plan," I gasped, fighting the pressure and pain drowning me.

It'll never work. My servant will kill you unless you join me.

I ignored Ibizual and shrugged out of the first of the three sleeve holes in the hospital gown, trying to figure out how to pull on my T-shirt without flashing the guys and everyone on the street since I wasn't wearing a bra. We were nearing the center of town again and on this warm early summer evening, people were on the streets shopping and dining, while the roads had a steady stream of traffic. "But there isn't any other option."

And crap. There was no good way to remove the hospital gown without baring my breasts. Well, at this point the only one in the SUV who hadn't seen them was Gideon, and his attention was rigidly focused on the road as if he were making a point of offering me privacy. As for the street and other motorists... well, maybe if I did it fast enough, not too many would notice.

The pressure jerked me to the left. "Turn left."

Are you sure? Ibizual asked. *Maybe I'm sending you in the wrong direction.*

Try again, I said back to him.

Marcus wrenched the wheel to take the next left, throwing me into the door and squealing the tires. Then he gunned it through a just-turned-red light, and swerved around a slower-moving cargo van.

You'll die this time.

My buzz burned hotter. *So be it.*

I slipped my arm out of the next armhole and moved to take off the gown completely, when Kol leaned forward. He grabbed the gown by the shoulders and held it up to offer me privacy.

"Any idea how we're going to deal with Logan?" he asked.

"If you and Marcus can hold off the ferals, I can deal with Logan," Jacob said.

They will all die.

The pressure tugged forward and to the right. "We need to head more right."

I pulled on my T-shirt and Kol shoved the hospital gown under the seat to get it out of the way.

"Did Victoria give you enough power for that?" Gideon asked.

She didn't. Not to defeat my servant. I'm going to keep you alive long enough to watch them all die.

"Not to kill him," Jacob said. "With Ibizual's magic empowering him, I'm not sure even Victoria could kill him. But I have enough to hold out until you destroy the key."

Ibizual roared with laughter, making the pressure surge, and I fought to gasp in any small amount of air. Kol pressed his hand to my knee. A whisper of sensual heat swept through me, muting some of the pain, pressure, and buzz.

Oh, thank God. I drew in an almost full breath. "Thank you."

He handed me an earpiece and gave a half shrug, a hint of hellfire dancing in his eyes before he looked away.

I'll make the demon suffer the most. Slowly rip the life from him, Ibizual snarled.

"Do we know what will happen with Logan once we destroy the key?" I asked through gritted teeth as I shrugged into my vest and buckled on my duty belt. "Stopping him from breaking the seal might not be the end of it."

There will never be an end for me.

I secured my seatbelt and pulled on my runners.

We sped past Unity Park, and a flash of hot and cold swept through the air with a churning mix of the guys' emotions.

This time my servant will kill you. Your demon won't be around to save you.

Promises, promises, I thought at him, feigning bravado more for myself than him since he knew it was an act.

"I hope to God it's the end of it," Marcus said.

"We can't count on that," Kol said.

You won't stop me.

The pressure squeezed tighter, drawing a groan. I clutched my chest, not that it would ease anything, and curled forward, unable to help myself. Kol's magic swelled, turning my pain into sensual, dreamy need, and making Ibizual howl with laughter.

So weak. Powerless.

Gideon twisted in his seat, capturing me with his icy gaze. God, I ached for it to return to its warm summer sky, like it had been when I'd first met him, but that yearning had to be Kol's magic and the brand influencing me. That, and no matter what I wanted, it was clear that he was going to be forever angry that I was his destined mate.

"If destroying Ibizual's connection with this realm doesn't end the unnatural magic that brought Logan back, you get to the SUV and get out of there," he said to me.

I glared back at him, still bent forward, clutching my chest. "If I still have the M4, I'm staying at a distance and supporting the team."

"You're not part of this team."

"Right now I am. You can't do this job without me." The pressure erupted into a blazing, consuming fire. Holy fuck.

I bit back a scream. "Straight ahead," I gasped. "We're close. Directly ahead of us."

Marcus slammed on the brakes, jerking us forward and making the seatbelt dig into my gut. "Are you shitting me?"

I looked out the front windshield. We were at a T-intersection and straight ahead lay a winding road into Union City's largest cemetery.

The road curved around a small fountain then disappeared over a gentle, grassy rise. Rows upon rows of headstones stretched ahead of us, intermixed with mausoleums and towering trees. Statues of weeping and guardian angels stood sentinel, and off to the left sat the massive memorials for those from Union City and the surrounding area who'd served and died in the war, as well as those who Michael and his nephilim had slaughtered. The two-story twin walls of white marble, facing each other, curved in a symbolic embrace to those who visited.

Come find me, Ibizual taunted with another roaring laugh.

"Stay here. I'll scout for Logan." Gideon jumped out of the SUV, his wings sweeping from his back with a blaze of white light. He was the epitome of the perfect, gorgeous angel, fully illuminated with blond hair, blue eyes, and a face and body sculpted by a master. Just looking at him stole my breath and made my heart ache. Then with a sweep of his wings, he took off into the air.

"Be careful," I said before I could stop myself.

"I'm not going to get shot," he said, his voice coming through the coms, his tone exasperated.

"You better not," I said, trying to hide my genuine worry and hurt at his tone, "because I've got enough going on without also needing to keep you alive through the brand."

He huffed and soared up into the darkening sky until I could only see him because I was watching him go.

"Gideon is right," Marcus said. "If destroying the key doesn't end Logan, you get out of here. Completely. No hanging back." He pulled out his com, muffling it in his fist, and looked past me to Jacob. "We're agreed?"

"Agreed," Jacob said, his voice low.

So much for being competent enough to be on the team. But I couldn't voice that thought out loud without alerting Gideon that the guys were having a conversation without him.

Kol gave a tight nod.

Jeez, you, too?

They know you're weak. Ibizual laughed, and I shook with the swelling pressure. *They think they can protect you, but they can't. And when they learn what you really are, they'll turn on you, kill you like they killed our kin.*

I'm not your kin.

Marcus slid the earpiece back into his ear. "What's the word, Gideon?"

Accept the truth, Esther. Ibizual's darkness surged inside me.

My buzz flared, burning some of it away, but not all.

"There's a flicker of magic forming in the center of the large fountain on the other side of the hill," Gideon said. "I don't see any ferals, but there's a significant area with trees beyond the rise. They could be hiding there."

Accept it, Ibizual snarled. *Accept the truth that you're kin.*

I'm a nephilim. That's the truth. I gritted my teeth against the pain. *A naturally born nephilim.*

"Do you see Logan?" Jacob scanned the surrounding buildings. We were in a mostly residential area with single detached homes and a few three-story low-rises, which thankfully meant there weren't a lot of good perches for a sniper to lie in wait for someone to approach the seal manifesting beyond the rise. In fact, the best shots from the surrounding buildings were for right there, and I had no doubt Logan would have tried to pick at least one of us off while we'd been sitting there if he'd been lying in wait.

"I don't— No, he's— Marcus, go. Straight ahead," Gideon said. "Logan is making a beeline for the fountain."

"Hang on," Marcus said and gunned the SUV into the cemetery, throwing us back into our seats.

Last chance to join me, Ibizual said.

"Never," I hissed.

"Essie?" Kol asked.

Shit. I'd said that out loud.

Join me.

The SUV screeched around the small fountain just inside the gates. The passenger-side wheels hit grass, jerking and bumping us, then hit asphalt again.

White light shot from the sky ahead of us down to the ground somewhere beyond the rise, and I caught a glimpse of Gideon, pulling his wings back and diving down after it.

"Gideon, we need you alive to end this," Jacob said. "Don't fight Logan."

"We won't be able to do anything if he breaks the seal," Gideon said. Another blast of light exploded behind the rise.

We careened up the road, hit the top of the rise, and I gasped in horror.

Sickly red magic seeped from the ground in pulsing thick strands. "Holy shit."

"Jesus," Kol said beside me.

"What?" Marcus asked.

"What do you mean what? The ground— The magic —" Perhaps this was just something that happened all the time on this job and Marcus was used to seeing massive amounts of magic, but Kol had sounded as surprised as I had.

"It's demonic," Kol said. "He can't see it yet, not until it gets more powerful."

"More powerful?" I could already feel the massive power pulsing from it.

"Can I avoid it?" Marcus asked as we hurtled down the road.

"No," I said. "It's everywhere." The whole ground all the way into the group of trees on the left and where the rise dropped away to the right was filled with magic. And it grew brighter and thicker the closer it got to the fountain straight ahead of us.

Agony and seething darkness exploded inside me as we drove into it. Red tendrils rushed into the SUV right through the floor, twisting around my legs and burning my skin. Kol groaned, the magic flooding into his body and not just wrapping around him, while Jacob hissed and clenched his jaw.

My buzz blazed through me, devouring the darkness, burning so hot it radiated from my skin and consumed the magic around me.

Ahead, Gideon jerked into the air to avoid Logan's grasp and shot another light strike at him. They'd drawn even closer to the fountain and the blazing sphere of the seal's manifesting magic.

The demonic magic grew stronger, and more strands, thick as rope, shot up from the ground.

"Shit." Marcus swerved, avoiding a red pillar of power shooting out from the middle of the road.

I slammed into the door and Kol slid into me, the touch of his skin against mine burning, all that demonic magic raising his body temperature.

My buzz blazed hotter, suddenly turning his body heat from searing to freezing. He gasped, his wide eyes, filled with hellfire, locking with mine, and my buzz started to consume the magic within him.

Marcus swerved again. The sudden movement jerked Kol off me, and I grabbed the door handle to stay in my seat. My buzz released him, but I couldn't help fearing that it would have consumed all of his magic, not just Ibizual's excess.

And from the look in Kol's eyes, he feared that, too.

The SUV fishtailed off the road, rattled over the uneven grass, and scraped against a squat tombstone. Marcus growled, yanked us back on the road, and floored it. Ahead, the magic of the manifesting seal blazed like a miniature sun.

We were almost there. Gideon just had to hold on a little longer.

More pillars of magic exploded from the road, and a massive one slammed into the bottom front of the SUV instead of passing through.

The impact tossed us into the air. My head hit the side airbag, and Kol crashed into me. Then he smashed into the ceiling, and I was jerked hard against the seatbelt before being wrenched around and around and around.

CHAPTER 24

THE WORLD WHIRLED AND JERKED, BLURRY, DARK, AND edged with burning red magic. The windows shattered and showered us with glass. Agony screamed through my neck, chest, and gut, and I couldn't catch my breath. We smashed through tombstones, careened off a statue, and crashed to a jarring halt.

Everything was muffled and spinning, and my buzz was burning me up.

"Guys," Gideon said through the earpiece. "Status."

I tried to respond but couldn't make my thoughts turn into action.

Someone groaned, and I struggled to focus my eyes to see who it was— Hell, just to see anything clearly.

The SUV lay upside down on an angle, with the driver's side edge of the roof dug into the ground. My head pressed against an airbag, and red magic pooled around me, the source of my burning and the reason I couldn't tell if I had any serious injuries, since its fire was all I could feel.

Kol was gone and panic clenched around my heart. *Please, God, be alive.* The idiot hadn't put on his seatbelt after helping me dress. Ahead of me, Marcus hissed, and I dragged my attention to him, struggling to make my sluggish thoughts speed up.

"Sit. rep. Now," Gideon said with a gasp, and blinding white light flared somewhere ahead of us, his fight obscured by the spiderweb of cracks in the front windshield, the airbags, and a toppled-over angel statue.

"Here," Jacob said. "Essie? Marcus? Kol?"

"Here," Marcus groaned.

"Kol got ejected." I fumbled with the seatbelt release.

"I'm here," Kol gasped through the earpiece.

Jacob shifted in the seat behind me, and the SUV shuddered, showering gravel—? No, stone and concrete from the crumbling mausoleum wall we were wedged against.

"Essie, you're bleeding," he said.

"I am?" I couldn't feel anything but my buzz, the fire as powerful as when the archnephilim had been trying to pull wings I didn't have from my body.

"How bad?" Marcus asked. He fought with his seatbelt then gave up and sliced through the belt with a claw. "I can't smell anything other than the reek of the demonic magic."

My seatbelt catch released, and I slid, head and shoulder, into a chunk of broken tombstone.

"The brand isn't draining me," Gideon said. "She'll live. Now get out. All of you out. Now."

Ibizual's magic surged, and the ground shuddered. Someone moaned, but it didn't come through the coms.

"Get out!" Kol cried.

The SUV crashed back into its wheels, jerking me onto the bench, and a skeletal hand clawed through the broken window.

"Oh, shit." Marcus kicked open the driver's side door, snapping it off its hinges and sending it flying to the crumbling mausoleum wall.

I scrambled back and wrenched on my door but couldn't get it to open. The skeletal hand ripped out the airbag blocking most of the window across from me, and my pulse stuttered. There were dozens of animated skeletons—? Zombies—? They moved too fast to be real zombies— God, I had no idea what they were! They pressed against the SUV, their claws screeching against the metal and tearing into the airbags. While hundreds more rushed toward us and more climbed out of their graves. Ibizual's magic bathed them in a sickly red aura and glowed from their eyes. They moaned and screamed and hissed, in varying stages of decay, some only skeletons, some skeletons with filthy tattered clothes, and some with rotting flesh.

Kol stood about thirty yards away surrounded by them. He sliced and jabbed, but his movement was stiff and slower than usual, and his expression was strained. Without a doubt he'd broken something, probably many somethings, when he'd been ejected from the SUV, and all his magic was focused on healing him.

You really think you can stop me? Ibizual asked in my head, and he howled with laughter. *I'm a prince of celestial darkness.*

The zombie-skeleton across from me lunged through

the window, clawing at me. I wrenched back but its claws sliced into my thigh. I drew my Glock, and fired into its head. It howled and blue lightning swept around its body.

With a growl Marcus ripped off my door, and I tumbled out of the SUV.

How much ammunition do you have? Ibizual taunted. *You should have accepted my offer.*

Marcus grabbed my arm and jerked me to my feet, and I pressed my back to the mausoleum wall to get my bearings. My body burned, my buzz slicing out of my back, enveloping me and still devouring Ibizual's demonic magic. The inferno threatened to consume me, and no matter how hard I concentrated, it was still the only thing I could feel. Blood stained my jeans where the creature had clawed me, but I couldn't feel the wound and I couldn't feel the other injury Jacob had mentioned.

Jacob kicked open the rear door and dove into the closest group of zombies, punching one into another behind it while drawing his sword with his other hand.

"Go," he said. "Get her to the seal. I've got your back."

I fired at a zombie lunging for Jacob, making it stagger long enough for Jacob to decapitate it. He wrenched back to face me, his vampiric intensity capturing me and making time stutter in my head.

"Go," he snarled, and the claim seized my muscles and jerked me toward the manifesting seal despite the press of creatures between me and it.

"Shit, Essie." Marcus shoved ahead of me and drew his sword. He barreled into the closest zombie, ramming it into the two behind it, and gutted the one beside him.

But more pressed in, replacing the ones he'd knocked over.

A zombie leaped onto Marcus's back, more skeleton than zombie. I grabbed it around the neck, wrenching its head back before it sank a mouthful of sharp teeth into his neck. It snarled and dug its claws into Marcus's shoulders.

My buzz surged and the magic around the creature swept into my hands. The creature thrashed and screamed, then Jacob jerked close, grabbed the creature's head, and ripped it from its body. It went limp, and I yanked it off Marcus's back.

How much more of my magic can you consume before you burn up? Ibizual laughed. *And you can't control it, can you? Your very nature will destroy you.*

I twisted out of the way of a zombie's claws and aimed for the head of another one, but the bullet grazed its skull. Jacob decapitated one beside me, then wrenched around to face the horde surging in behind us.

"Kol, we need you," Marcus said, shouldering a zombie back and impaling another.

"Trying," Kol gasped. He rose above the group surrounding him—he must have jumped onto a tomb-stone or something—and somersaulted over the zombies' heads onto the back of a weeping angel statue. The zombies closest to the statue wrenched around and clawed at him and he was back again trying to slice his way through the group.

Marcus snarled and hacked another two in front of us. "This isn't working."

Blood seeped from a deep gash on his biceps and

another on his thigh. His chest heaved from the exertion of fighting so many zombies. The fountain stood less than a hundred yards away, but it could have been miles for all the progress we were making. We were barely holding our own, let alone moving forward.

Then the pressure within me pulsed with such force it made me gasp. I stumbled over a toppled tombstone and fell to my hands and knees.

The seal had formed.

Red magic undulated around me and surged under my skin. I fought to stand, to stop my buzz from consuming Ibizual's magic, but the fire within me just burned hotter. I had to get to the key, get it out of Logan's possession, and join my magic with Gideon's. It was the only way to stop this.

You can't stop this, Ibizual hissed. *You won't even live long enough to see me free.*

Jacob grabbed the back of my vest and wrenched me to my feet. "Gideon, fly in. We have to get Essie to join you."

"No." I shot a zombie in the chest as another one tore its claws through the back of my vest. "Protect the seal."

"Fuck," Marcus growled. "Jacob, you have to grab her and run. We have no choice."

Jacob flipped the grip on his sword so the flat rested against the underside of his arm then grabbed me and threw me against his shoulder with an arm under my butt. "Grab my neck and protect your face."

Marcus roared and dove into the group ahead of us, crashing through the press of zombies. I holstered my Glock and grabbed Jacob's neck as he barreled after

Marcus. The zombies howled and clawed and threw themselves at us. A set of wickedly sharp claws swiped at my head, too close for comfort, and I buried my face into Jacob's neck to protect my eyes.

Pinpricks of pain bit through the fire consuming me, and the zombies' howling grew stronger. Jacob's muscles bunched and released beneath me as he ran and dodged and heaved them out of the way.

He grunted, his muscles contracting, then he stumbled. His grip on me tightened and he wrenched to the side. My foot bashed against something solid—likely a statue or a tombstone—and Jacob heaved to the side again, loosening my hold around his neck.

Claws dug into my vest and yanked me out of Jacob's grip. My shoulder crashed against something hard and I tumbled to the ground. A zombie lunged on top of me and sank its teeth into my neck with a pain that sliced through the fire and the pressure. But that fire, my buzz, raced through the magic animating the corpse, consuming it, and the zombie collapsed on top of me.

Jacob yanked it off me—hopefully not realizing I'd already killed it with magic I shouldn't possess—and killed another zombie as it swiped at my legs. He grabbed the neck of my vest and wrenched me up to my feet and shoved me behind him in the direction of the fountain.

I stumbled but managed to catch my balance. We stood at the edge of the fountain's wide concrete deck, beside one of the many stone benches placed around its perimeter—what my shoulder had struck when I'd fallen. The whole thing was enormous, with a vast space to stroll around, a large bottom basin, and a smaller second one above it. Water sprayed from the center in gentle arcs, filling the top basin then pouring over the edges into the shallower bottom bowl.

The seal, a complicated glyph of pulsing magic, floated in the air at waist height, almost hidden by the edge of the fountain from where I stood. It sat a few inches from the lip of the upper basin and blazed blood red, a deadly star in the dimming light reflected in the fountain's undulating water. And between me and it were Gideon and Logan, which didn't really matter since it wasn't the seal I needed to get to, but the key in Logan's possession.

Blood splattered the white concrete around their feet and an automatic pistol lay a few feet away under one of the benches. With a roar, Logan smashed his fist into Gideon's gut, grabbed his arm, and flung him, one handed, at the fountain. His wing and shoulder smashed against the lip of the upper basin, and spinning, he crashed into the water and lay still.

My pulse stuttered. Gideon wasn't getting up. He had to get up. But I wasn't frozen in agony and his brand wasn't draining me, so he had to be all right... unless of course I couldn't feel the drain through my burning buzz.

Which didn't matter.

No matter how much everything within me screamed that it did.

Ibizual had to be stopped at all costs, even if that cost were the lives of me and all my guys.

I'll still be free, and you'll still pay that price, Ibizual said. *Come. Now.* And I knew the command wasn't for me.

"Yes," Logan hissed. He yanked the key, a small red pulsing jewel, from his pocket and ran toward the seal.

I drew my gun and prayed I could make a good enough shot to seriously slow him down. I was too far away to catch him before he reached the seal, and I couldn't afford to cast the light strike spell to slow him down and risk not having enough juice to destroy the key.

Gideon staggered to his feet, and my heart soared. Water dripped from his wings and clothes, and his face was battered, one eye almost completely swollen shut. I couldn't sense his exhaustion through the brand or with my empathy because of the fire burning me up, but I could see it in the tight line of his jaw and the heave of his chest with each heavy breath. With a guttural yell, he dove at Logan, but the vampire was still going to get to the seal first.

I fired—*please let it be enough for Gideon to reach him first*—and hit Logan in the center of his back. Blue lightning swept around him, and he staggered.

Gideon crashed into him, tackling him to the ground, and the key flew from his hand and tumbled over the concrete.

Ibizual roared with fury, and the agony threatened to bring me to my knees, but I screamed back at him, a sound of desperate, primal rage, and ran toward the key. No way in hell would I let him win.

The key hit the edge of the bottom basin, stopping in a thick pool of red magic, and began to pulse with rapid, fluttering beats like an unsteady heart.

Logan rammed an elbow into Gideon's face. He

lurched back, then rammed a spear of light into the vampire's chest, drawing a howl of pain.

A zombie dashed past Marcus and dove for me. I twisted out of the way, fired at it, but kept running. My shot missed the creature, and it seized my ankle. I slammed to the ground, catching myself on my left arm —the one with the already injured shoulder so I wouldn't drop my Glock. Agony tore through me, screaming up my neck and across my chest. My arm gave out, the entire limb numb, and I knew I'd broken something, probably my collarbone.

"Essie," Gideon gasped, and Logan shoved Gideon off him, sending the angel crashing into a bench in the opposite direction of the key.

The zombie sank its claws into my thigh, and my buzz devoured more of Ibizual's magic, the fire blazing through the pain. With a screech the zombie convulsed and collapsed, and I kicked it off me and scrambled to my feet.

A little more and you'll burn up, Ibizual said, and a rope of magic swept around my legs and sank into my skin, fueling the inferno.

Another rope disappeared into me. I screamed and pushed forward. Get the key. Only a few feet more. Stop this.

More zombies rushed for me, and Jacob ran into their midst to hold them off, while another group boxed Gideon in.

Logan jumped to his feet and bolted to the key. I dove to grab it before he could. But he didn't lunge for it and kicked at my head instead.

I twisted, slamming my broken shoulder against the ground, sending more agony screaming through me.

Shit. I dropped my Glock and grabbed the key with my good hand.

Logan seized my arm and wrenched me up, but Gideon barreled into him, and we crashed into the bottom basin. My head hit the wall of the second basin and darkness fluttered across my vision. Logan shoved my head under the water. It was only a foot deep, but that was more than enough to drown me.

I thrashed against his grip and clutched the key underneath me, desperate to keep it out of reach. He snarled, his face distorted by the churning water, and his fingers tightened around my skull. My lungs screamed for air, and the fire within me shuddered with a heavy pulse, a precursor to its final eruption.

A light strike flared and slammed into his back. His grip on my head loosened, and Gideon appeared behind his shoulder, his eyes blazing white, his face battered, ferocious, and terrifying. He wrenched Logan off me and I jerked up, gasping for breath.

"Essie, end this." Gideon heaved Logan out of the fountain and slammed him to the ground, as zombies surged around him and slashed at his arms and face. "Take my magic and end this."

My thoughts stuttered over the command. He'd been so adamant about me never using his magic again.

"Essie. Take it!" His magic exploded through the brand, crackling lightning that entwined with the fire of my buzz.

Logan kicked Gideon off him, and the zombies piled

on top of him as Logan leaped for me. I scrambled out of the way, but all the power rushing through me made my muscles seize, and I couldn't get up to my feet.

"Essie." Jacob dove onto Logan, capturing him in a headlock, and wrenched him back.

The spell to cast the light strike leaped into my mind, and the combined magic within me roared into a hurricane, threatening to tear me to pieces and turn me to ash.

You should have joined me, Ibizual said. *I could have saved you, made you powerful, made you a god.*

I clenched my teeth and pressed the key between my palms. Gideon yelled something, so did Jacob, but all my concentration was on the spell, on blasting all the magic within me into the key and ending this.

You'll burn up. There won't be anything left, Ibizual sneered. *Not even your soul.*

"So be it," I said to him, then yelled the combat spell and released all the magic within me out through my palms and into the key.

The fire and lightning scorched every nerve in my body, just like the blast from the light ring when I'd released its power into the archnephilim's brand on my arm. Except this time, the agony was worse, edged with all the bloody dark magic my buzz had consumed. It rushed from my back and my heart and my soul, taking all of me with it.

Ibizual screeched. His magic surged, flooding me, burning me up, and with a scream, I forced all of it back out my hands and into the key.

The key exploded with a blaze of light that left darkness clouding my vision and my head spinning.

Logan howled behind me, and I jerked around as he dove for me. Time stuttered. I wasn't going to be fast enough to stop him, hell, even if I was, I wasn't powerful enough. Gideon and Jacob were too far away to reach me in time. Logan was going to kill me.

Time lurched back to regular speed, and I wrenched my good hand up on instinct, knowing it was futile but unable to stop myself. Fire and lightning—God, I hadn't thought I had any more magic in me—screamed down my arm and a sword of light surged into my hand. Logan was too close to pull back before the blade plunged into his chest.

His eyes flashed wide with surprise then darkened. With a snarl, he shoved his body down the blade and slashed his short, deadly vampire claws at my face.

I jerked back and down, and Jacob rushed into sight and slashed his sword through Logan's neck, decapitating him.

CHAPTER 25

Logan's blood sprayed me in the face, mixing with the fountain's water and oozing down my cheeks and neck. Then his body burst into a thick dust that filled the air and coated me in grime—and I wasn't going to think too hard about the fact that I was covered in corpse dust.

All the zombies lay on the ground not moving, and Ibizual's magic sparked and fluttered around them like embers caught in a breeze. The seal flared with a blinding burst of light and then vanished, and Ibizual's screams in my head stopped, the sudden silence making my ears ring.

I sagged onto my butt, not caring that I was still in the fountain. It was over.

Jacob dropped to his knees in the fountain beside me, but Gideon stayed lying on the ground, gasping for breath. Marcus and Kol, looking like they'd tumbled through a mess of whirling knives—which they pretty much had—staggered toward us. The guys were all bleeding, their clothes torn and filthy, but they were all alive.

Relief flooded me, and the tears of pain and terror that I'd been holding back leaked from my eyes. *They're alive. I haven't lost one of them. Thank God. Oh, thank God.*

I didn't even try to stop crying. I was too numb and raw to fight myself. The pressure from the manifesting seal was gone. So too was the snap of Gideon's magic and the burn of Ibizual's, but that had left an achy void within me.

My buzz, however, still remained, although it was now back to just painful bites under my skin and not a blazing inferno. Except those bites accentuated the fact that every nerve within me had been burned raw. I was still alight with pain, just not the kind that threatened to erupt and turn me into a human bonfire.

"Essie," Marcus said as he sagged into the edge of the basin, his expression a mix of emotions like mine: relief, pain, exhaustion. "Your hands."

I dropped my gaze, my body and thoughts sluggish. My hands were raw, bleeding, and charred. "At least I'm still conscious this time."

Kol snorted and wrapped his arms across his chest, as if his ribs were broken, his face twisting in agony. "I'm not sure this counts as an improvement from the fight with the archnephilim."

"Baby steps," Marcus said. "Next time we'll get her through without the serious burns."

If there was a next time.

Which, even exhausted and in pain, my soul prayed there would be. This was where I belonged, where I made the biggest difference in peoples' lives. I didn't know how I was going to convince Gideon that I belonged on the team, but everything within me said I had to.

Gideon made a call, and Chris and a JP clean-up team arrived at the cemetery. We returned to Operations, where Amiah greeted us in the garage with a gurney which Jacob insisted I take, while Gideon leaned heavily against it to keep standing.

The healing angel gave Marcus a quick blast of magic, enough so that when he shifted he'd be able to finish the job himself, then she turned to Gideon, gently angling his head to get a better look at the mess Logan had made of his face.

"Essie," Marcus said, his voice soft.

I dragged my attention to him. I hadn't even realized I'd zoned out. He jerked his gaze to Jacob then back to me, and even with my sluggish thoughts the message was clear. Jacob needed to feed, his injuries were as severe or worse than the fight with Logan in the tunnels, so blood from a bunny wasn't going to heal him fast enough. It was time to test our new arrangement.

"Yeah." I tried to nod, but moving even just a little bit made my head hurt.

"Amiah first, Essie," Jacob said.

"Yes." Marcus glanced at Gideon, who thankfully looked as stunned as I felt and was focusing on Amiah and not our conversation. "Give me five."

Jacob nodded.

Kol frowned, his gaze darting between the three of us.

"Consider this your phone call," Marcus said to him, and he strode to the back of the garage to shift in private.

"My what—?" Realization flashed through Kol's eyes. He'd asked for a call the next time Marcus and I had sex so he could prepare himself. At least this way he wouldn't need to leave Operations to replenish his magic. In a way it was perfect. I could be with Marcus and help heal both Jacob and Kol at the same time.

The guys helped push the gurney to triage than slipped away, Jacob mumbling something about having bagged blood in his suite, and Kol not saying anything at all.

Amiah, with her usual scowl, gave me a blast of healing magic that hurt. It healed all my physical injuries, but not my magical ones. Whatever veins or passages or whatever they were called that were inside me channeling all that magic had been burned raw, and still hurt. Not as much as before, but I sensed that Amiah's magic couldn't fully heal them.

Still exhausted, I pushed any fear about that aside. I'd worry about what all of it meant later, after I'd had time to clear my head.

I left her with Gideon, took the elevator to the fifth floor, and met Jacob outside Marcus's door. A few minutes later, Marcus joined us, dressed once again in a pair of baggy workout shorts and carrying his gear.

He let us in and there was an awkward moment with us just standing at the doorway, that would have been more awkward if we all hadn't been so tired. As instructed, I cleaned off a wrist, so Jacob could feed at a modest location on my body. Then Marcus and I—

starting in the shower and cleaning off the rest of the blood and grime before moving to the bedroom—both rode the powerful pleasure of Jacob's magic to a screaming, satisfying climax.

I fell asleep in Marcus's arms, snuggled in his bed, warm and content—if still a little internally sore—and woke a few hours later still in his arms. Warmth seeped from his body into mine, and his breath, steady with sleep, caressed the back of my neck. He was so still, so peaceful, all his ferocious energy, an energy that made my pulse race and my heart thrill, hidden within him. I could sense his contentment, not as a temperature but as an honest to goodness emotion, and it mirrored a contentment within me. This was exactly where I belonged, and who I belonged with.

But a sliver of doubt seeped in, and I slipped out of his bed before I became too restless and woke him.

Everything would become more difficult if I couldn't stay on the team, and yet everything would be difficult if I stayed.

I left my shredded and bloody clothes on the bathroom floor and dressed in Marcus's workout shorts—tying the drawstrings as tight as I could to keep them up—and pulled on one of his T-shirts. Once I left his suite, I wouldn't be able to get back in, so I wrote him a note saying I'd be in the lounge then slipped out into the hall. I needed air. I needed to think.

I didn't believe that our arrangement with Jacob would change if I wasn't on the team. The guys would just find me at my apartment whenever Jacob needed me. But it still was more complicated than if I stayed. And I still didn't know, if Gideon did send me packing, what I'd do if I couldn't be a cop any more.

God, I didn't know what I'd do if Marcus changed his mind about us. He didn't seem freaked out about the aftermath of the battle with Logan, but that could have been shock and then the glow of amazing sex. Once he'd had time to really think about it, there was a good chance he'd lock me in his suite and never let me out, or worse, he'd push me away again.

I wandered down the hall to the elevator and hit the call button. The door slid open, but instead of pushing the button for the main floor, I decided to hit the top unlabeled button. The elevator took me up one floor and the door opened, revealing a helicopter pad and a small rooftop patio.

Before me stretched the Supers' Quarter, the thick canopy of the ring park to my left and the UV-filtering glass canopy protecting the vampire part of the Quarter to my right. Streetlights illuminated the roads and buildings, and lights glimmered in a few windows, while a hint of light glowed on the eastern horizon. Dawn wasn't far off.

I wandered to a wrought-iron patio chair—secured to the roof with a length of chain so it wouldn't fly away in a strong wind but could also be moved around a bit—drew it out from the matching patio table, and sat. A cool breeze swept through my loose locks, and I shifted so it blew the strands away from my face. I should have put on a jacket, but I didn't have one. In fact I didn't have any clean or unshredded clothes at Operations, and didn't want to go back downstairs to search for something heavier—even if I could figure out where to look. That, and now that I'd shaken the lull of sleep and sex, I was too aware that the magical channels in my body still hurt and my buzz still wasn't back down to its new—after battling the archnephilim—normal, and I didn't want to move too much.

A crackle of electricity, nothing strong, just enough for me to notice, danced through Gideon's brand, and a flicker of shadow against the low-hanging clouds caught my attention. It drew closer and fear squeezed my chest. The archnephilim had flown through the air, a dense, deadly shadow.

I pushed my fear away. The archnephilim was dead. I'd killed him. I had nothing to fear from him any more.

Gideon's magic danced up my arm again, and I caught a flash of white with my Jacob-enhanced vision. Gideon's wings catching the streetlight.

My fear shifted from the terror of the archnephilim to the fear of facing Gideon and losing my job. But that fear was soon also edged with awe as he soared closer. He was majestic. He made my chest ache with yearning for him, for the wings I didn't have, for the freedom I couldn't allow myself to have to just be myself.

He landed on the roof on the other side of the table from me, his attention on something behind and to my right, and he drew his wings back into his body with a flare of the magic that made an angel an angel and allowed him to release his wings from his body and return them back again without destroying his clothes. He was back to being his handsome self, not a hint of a scratch or bruise on his face, and that only made my ache stronger.

I didn't understand how he could have such an effect on me. He didn't want me as his mate— *I* didn't want me to be his mate, and yet just thinking about overhearing his rejection hurt something deep within me.

Then he turned his glowing gaze on me, and I was falling into a summer sky. All the things that hurt within me stilled and everything else fell away. There was only him and the angel brand that bound our souls together.

His gaze travelled over me and my borrowed clothes, and a hint of ice chilled his summer sky. Wonderful. Just by being me, I'd reminded him that Marcus and I were a thing and Marcus would leave the team if Gideon fired me. Staying on the team because Gideon didn't want to lose Marcus was not the way I wanted it. I wanted him to realize I wasn't a liability, that even if I was a powerless human I could offer something to them.

Another crackle of his electricity snapped through the brand, making me wince.

His eyes narrowed, and he pulled his phone from his pocket. "You're still hurt. I'll wake Amiah."

"It's okay," I said before he could call, surprised he cared that I was still sore. Even if I was in agony right now, I still wouldn't want to piss off Amiah any more than I already had. "I don't think this is something she can heal. I've channeled massive amounts of power twice now in as many weeks. There's got to be a cost to that."

"You shouldn't have had to pay it."

A hint of heat whispered around me, and my stomach

bottomed out with fear. Here it came, the moment where he said I didn't belong and I lost my job.

"Essie—" Pain flashed through the ice in his eyes, making my pulse stall. But he jerked his gaze away from me before I could figure out what that pain meant.

The temperature around me warmed a bit more, giving me even less of a clue about his emotions. Was he angry? The pain in his eyes should have turned the air humid or misty, but there was nothing.

"Just say it." I couldn't fight my worry, heartache, and buzz all at the same time right now. I was just too tired.

He ran a hand through his hair. "Officer Shaw."

"Joined Parliament Senior Agent Gideon." I stood and squared my shoulders. If he was going to ruin my career, end the only job I'd ever wanted, I was damn well going to make him say it to my face.

"I don't like the emotional complications you bring to the team." Ice flickered through the heat. "But we couldn't have stopped Logan without you."

So was this thank you and goodbye?

The muscles in his jaw flexed. "Do I need to arrange for a suite, or will you be sharing with Marcus?"

"Arrange for a suite?" For a second his words didn't make sense, then realization caught up to me. I was moving into Operations. I was on the team.

Oh, God. I was *moving* into Operations, angel central, living with all the angels in Union City. Working with Gideon was one thing, but living and eating and socializing with *all* the angels multiplied the risk of someone noticing something different about me.

"I, ah..."

"You're wearing his clothes. I've figured it out already," he said.

"That's because I don't have any more clothes fit to wear here."

"Then you should fix that, *Agent* Shaw." He strode past me toward the elevator, his hand pressing at the brand on his forearm that matched the one on mine before jerking away, as if the touch had been unconscious and undesired. "Report with the rest of the team in my office at o'eight hundred with your answer."

With the *rest* of the team. A whirl of emotions churned through me. This was what I wanted and where I belonged. I knew it in my soul. I couldn't resist it. But a part of me, a small voice whispering against all that certainty, said it would also be my doom.

Don't miss the next book in the series!

DESTINED FIRE
Nephilim's Destiny: Book Three

One reckless move could cost her everything...

It used to be easy to pass as human beat cop Essie Shaw. Lay low, don't draw too much attention. Now I'm hiding in plain sight, working for the JP, praying my teammates won't notice my non-human magical quirks and figure out I'm a nephilim.

As the magic clawing within me threatens to reveal me, my complicated emotional bond with the team grows: Gideon, whose cold, professional distance cuts me; Jacob, whose mixed messages confuse me; Kol, whose friendship warms me; and Marcus, whose wolf could turn on me.

Thanks to the messy public disasters we've barely survived, the Head Office sends in the big guns: Cassius, who'd love nothing more than to rip his brother Gideon's mating brand from my arm and kick me off the team.

So, no pressure in cracking a ring of vicious magical drug smugglers. But when things go sideways, my magic threatens to expose my secret and cost me the only place where I've ever belonged. With the men my very bones tell me are *mine*.

Destined Fire is the third book in the Nephilim's Destiny series, an action-packed full-length paranormal romance with four irresistible guys and a kick-ass heroine who doesn't have to choose.

OTHER BOOKS BY TESSA COLE

THE NEPHILIM'S DESTINY SERIES

Destined Shadows, prequel story

Destined Darkness, book 1

Destined Blood, book 2

Destined Fire, book 3

Destined Storm, book 4

Destined Radiance, book 5